The Red Pagoda is Robert Mendelsohn's third novel, following *Clash of Honour* (1990) and *Footsteps on a Drum* (1991), also published by Prion. Robert Mendelsohn is married, with a son and two daughters, lives in London, England, and divides his time between writing and dealing in the international wine and spirit trade. He is an ardent yachtsman, a student of medieval history, and a collector of Fauve paintings. His extensive travels have given him an intimate knowledge of the Far East. Echoing through his writing is the clash between cultures. He writes of relationships in far away places and the puzzling man-made differences that arise when people meet unusual circumstances.

Other books by Robert Mendelsohn

Footsteps on a Drum
Clash of Honour

THE
RED PAGODA
Robert Mendelsohn

PRION

Published in the United Kingdom by
PRION, an imprint of Multimedia Books Ltd
32–34 Gordon House Road, London NW5 1LP

A catalogue record for this book is available from the
British Library.

ISBN 1-85375-094-8 (paperback)
ISBN 1-85375-069-7 (hardback)

Typeset by Vision Typesetting, Manchester, UK
Printed in the United Kingdom by Clays Ltd, St Ives plc

For Jack

Who never forgot humility, nor the simple pleasures of life. In affectionate gratitude for unfailing friendship and generosity.

CHAPTER ONE

■

MARBELLA, SEPTEMBER 1991

I must set the record straight, before it's too late. Tell the story of Bernadette and Clay the way it was. I have spent much time and have travelled many miles to unearth it. Someone should know.

I have seen him twice, only once to talk to. Her I got close to for a moment, but I still shudder at the memory of it. Yet even now, after all these years, I think of them and talk to them when no one is about, as if they were my friends, not my intended victims. As if I had grown up with them, watched over them, shared their secrets, their moments of solitude and glory and defeat and love. Once I had been their shadow, having chased them across much of Europe like a pair of criminals. And that I did because those were my orders and I had lived with orders and had learned to obey them without question.

The south of Spain is full of people like me. Ex-convicts rub shoulders with ex-policemen. The waterside cafés are crowded with late summer visitors watching each other and the pavement is full of talk. Celebrities pass by pretending not to be noticed. Across the masts and breakers, the afternoon sun is gently lowered into the Mediterranean. Soon, the coloured lights of Port Banus will stretch all the way to the great white yachts and it will be time to go. My man Pepe will ease me into his ingenious metal contraption and wheel me home.

The Orient, from where Bernadette and Clay and I started our journey, might as well be a million miles away. Of course, no one talks of Vietnam or Ho Chi Minh any more. The other day I saw a drink called Saigon in a place that sells pizzas. I am not a religious man, but I could have sworn the Almighty was nudging me.

There were many witnesses to this tale, but some did not notice and others were not interested or did not recognize what they were watching. Others still have since died. Some of old age, some because of these two and some by my own hand.

The frail frame of me betrays a corpulent past. My man Pepe keeps trying to fatten me with all kinds of goodies I would have given plenty for years ago. When a man can no longer indulge in the pleasures of food, it is a signal. It is the sound of that clock on everybody's wall telling us how late it is. Time is the only thing we can never have enough of.

Now it is running out on me and I must tell.

I was a policeman in Hong Kong before I became what I am. Before that I was a sergeant major in the British Army and before that I fought the Japanese in Burma. But I like to think my life really started the day Mr Patel gave me his last orders. He was an Indian gentleman who dared to take me in and employ me after I had fallen from grace. He was a wheeler dealer of sorts and perhaps he did things differently, but then everybody in Hong Kong did. His reputation was not worth a light, but I always think of him with much affection because he trusted me. It was this very affection and loyalty to him that made me go after them in the first place.

Not everything about my years with the police was bad. I do owe much to my training. I would have never been able to find where Bernadette and Clay had gone, much less to follow them across many borders without being noticed by anyone. A large, red-faced Englishman and a wiry Vietnamese at his side were strange bedfellows and raised many an eyebrow in Europe of the sixties. But most of all, my years with the police equipped me to find the truth after the chase was over. To discover where Bernadette and Clay began their separate trails towards each other. It took lots of time and money and I had both. But there was more. I was burning to find out the big bad why of it all. I had been lied to. My orders were false. I should have never stalked her.

She should not have been born at all. She was told that often enough. A sick joke nature played on her mother had introduced Bernadette to life at the hospital for officers in Saigon. Her mother never knew her since she died while the little girl was struggling to leave her young body. Her father, an elderly French tea-planter who remained in Indo-China during the war, considered her advent to be a miracle, hence the child's name.

Her stunning appearance more than compensated for what was lacking in the church's eyes. Bernadette was to grow up slim and tall, with thick coal-black hair that showered down around a beautifully chiselled, haunting face. Her large, round eyes shone with the colour of burnt almond. She was born with an extroverted nature and she loved listening to the chattering gossip of the servants in the yard, but her infectious smile was soon stifled by her over-zealous nanny.

Expecting the Vietnamese to seek independence in the wake of the war, Louis Mourniese de la Courcelle foresaw the hostility his daughter would encounter. He decided to send her to a convent outside Fontainbleu. She was seven years old when she saw France for the first time. First, Jesus and Mary Magdalene, then Baudelaire and Monet welcomed her there. Quiet voices along stony, cold corridors replaced the green, tropical world she knew.

Dressed with an old family name but not its blessing,

Bernadette was set to become a fully-fledged Frenchwoman regardless of her origins. This was not too difficult a task in a society tolerant and well versed in mixing. People from all over the world had been collected by France for centuries and their children were accepted without question.

Bernadette did not look foreign. She resembled, her first lover said, a Michelle Morgan with oriental hair, impossibly beautiful skin and legs that stopped the traffic. He had said that often, proudly, when bragging of his conquest. But he never said that to her.

She was fifteen when her father's death signalled the first shot in the battle for his estate. Louis Mourniese de la Courcelle was a rich man and the last male descendant of his family. It was during that prolonged, silent war of letters and claims and mounting lawyers' bills that Bernadette discovered the ugly face of greed. The rest of the family sought to disown her because her parents never married. They had proof her mother had been an eighteen year old whore. There was a serious doubt, they claimed, of her being Louis's natural daughter.

While cousins, aunts and other, more distant relations argued the toss about who should get what, the growing girl stood aside bewildered. The tenderness, however reserved, she had known whenever she saw her father was now gone. At the school there was tension. Everybody knew Bernadette's bills were late in being settled while the case was contested. She was called in to see the Mother Superior and an agreement was struck whereby she would help look after the smaller girls and move out of her room to another, smaller place to be shared with the school cook. She promised to be a good girl and work hard. Not that Bernadette was anything but that. She so wanted someone to be proud of her. To excel at something, anything, would have been her version of paradise on earth. They tried to make her sign pieces of paper she did not understand in exchange for school fees, but she refused.

And then the family won the case. She was allowed to stay in France, but the proud name of Mourniese de la Courcelle was taken away from her. No one came to visit her after that. It did not take long for her classmates to find out that her rich colonial connections were no longer there. There used to be jealousies for the parcels and presents and day trips she used to be taken on. That accumulated aggression they had felt for her in her days of wealth now found satisfaction in the sight of her drawn face. They had little to say to her then, but now she was treated like a leper.

Her smiles of old disappeared as she withdrew into a world of her own. The only ray of light left for Bernadette was the smaller children she remained in charge of. They warmed to the comfort they found in her soft voice within the stony walls of the convent. She knew they too felt cheated of a family life and, now that she had no one, she gave all her emotional attention to them. Her concentration she dedicated to books and study. If this corner of the world did not want her anymore, she reasoned, she would take all the education she could get before she'd move on.

I am becoming morose. Sadness sails into my old veins when I think of that part. I get angry. What a bunch of selfish dwarfs we Europeans can be. I have managed to talk to some of Bernadette's so-called school friends. Mostly middle-aged matrons by the time I found them. I went to see three of them. Only one expressed regret at the harsh treatment they had dished out to Bernadette.

She received me at her spacious flat in Paris. She sounded lonely and bored. I am sure she dressed herself up for the occasion.

'I don't know why it happened,' she said with an apologetic smile. 'Once the family got rid of her, there was nothing to be envious of any more. But,' she added, 'Bernadette was, you know, foreign. Perhaps the girls hated her for her beauty. She was an oriental madonna, you see. And we did our best to crucify her. We told her she was ugly and we made her unhappy, but I never saw her cry. No one did. That must have upset us even more. Children are cruel.'

'I suppose they are,' I said.

'They threw her mother's shame at her face. It must have been frightful for her.'

'Worse. Some things stay in a child's head. Refuse to leave. Cause much damage later.'

'I never said a thing to her myself. I was far too shy,' she said and I knew she would say no more. I felt I brought embarrassment into the ornate living room. I said I was grateful and she excused herself. I think she felt ashamed or was busy or whatever. She walked me to the door. She may have waved, but I did not look back.

I can feel my pulse racing. I must not dwell too much on that. In any case, the sun has almost reached the sea wall. My man Pepe does not like me to sit here by myself in the dark. He's always afraid I'll catch a cold.

Bernadette seemed to have accepted rejection in her stride. That must have been the oriental in her. I suppose her disenchantment with Europe and Europeans and all things white started then, but she wasn't aware of that. She wasn't bitter, of that I am sure. Just a little lost. But she didn't waste too much time on that. She worked hard. I know. I have seen her grades. Disillusion aside, Bernadette came top of the school when the final exam papers came back. Years later I looked through those papers myself. Yes. At the convent near Fontainbleu in France. I was proud of her when I saw how well she did. I did not tell her I was. I do now though, whenever I imagine talking to Clay and her I sneak a private little word about that to her. Nonetheless, I like to think that Bernadette, the way she was five years later, would have fought back.

At eighteen, Bernadette was recommended by the convent for a position of librarian in Paris, where she enrolled at the university for evening classes in history. At about that time, she had reached her physical maturity which by all accounts was striking. Her haunting eyes looked at the bustle and the lights of the great city as if she was seeing the world for the first time. She had a deep, husky voice which matched her full lips and sad smile. Her walk, gentle and sensual as it was, had a distinct rhythm. It was steady and full of purpose. I believe that confidence was mostly pretence, but as she strode to work each morning passers-by stopped to look. Some whistled. She did not notice any of it. The owner of a newspaper kiosk where she stopped to cross the road each morning remembered her vividly years later. He said he'd never seen someone like that before. Nor after. He remembered a hesitant undertone to her voice one morning when she bought *Le Figaro* from him. There was a marked change to her posture six months after that, when she stopped to buy a paper again. It was a foreign paper. The *Tribune* perhaps. He wasn't sure. But he remembered her perfectly.

The man who put an end to her hesitation was a lecturer on the Middle Ages. He had noticed her at the back of the class. Saw her embarrassed shyness at the heated argument that flared up one evening during a discussion about the plague. The disease they called the Black Death. I don't know much about history. I wish I did. I would have gone to university to learn all about it had I had my time again. As it is I am better at watching or describing people and facts. Things I can see or hear or touch. Anyway, the Black

Death killed off entire streets as it raged across the narrow passages of Europe's cities. You had to get out of town quickly and that was only possible if you had several fast horses. So I've heard anyway. The trouble was if you were poor, you were stuck, and you died and they burned you and your house. The rich went off into the safety of the countryside.

The argument they had after the lecture was really to do with injustice. The poor discovered they were expendable. Something like that. It was all explained to me years later by that professor himself, but I have since forgotten. Funny how some things stick in your mind and others do not. What I do remember was the way he talked about Bernadette. He was the one I have mentioned before. Her first lover who said she looked like Michelle Morgan. He told me that himself, the bastard. He used her and his attention and left wing views had a tremendous effect on her.

The professor was one of the first people I had gone to see. I got a half-hour appointment with him between lectures and he received me in his study at the university. He was in his mid-sixties then, a tall, large man with a mop of silvery hair. His face was lined, but his grey eyes still burned with curiosity.

'Thank you for your time,' I said.

'You wanted to see me about Bernadette. It is for me to thank you.'

He had a disarming smile and I could not help falling for it. He started asking me about her and what had happened, but I did not tell him anything.

'How did you notice her?' I asked. 'There were many students in your class.'

'Yes. My lectures are popular. But you couldn't help noticing her,' he said. 'She sat at the back of the room. She radiated a mysterious sort of beauty. Heavenly, I would say.

She lifted her hand to speak, but she was shy and as soon as someone else butted in she dropped her hand and just sat there. She definitely wanted to say something, but with the heat of the occasion she did not get a chance. Everybody talked. All at the same time. It was a noisy session.'

'What happened?'

'Well,' he said, 'I called her over. I did that at the end of the lesson. I called her over to my desk. I asked her what it was she had wanted to talk about. Then one thing led to another, you know how these things are,' he said and he winked.

Yes. I know how these things are, I thought and said nothing. I hated what he said and the way he had said it. I felt then and still do now that the seduction of Bernadette was like snatching a sweet out of an infant's mouth. However, I wanted to hear what he had to say, so I said nothing and listened.

'You see,' he continued, 'she was fascinated by the Black Death. It is an interesting subject. One of the first communes in Europe was born as a result of it. The death of the poor induced people to denounce the class system. Bernadette homed in on that as if it had answered all her problems.'

'Problems,' I ventured, 'what problems?'

'She was a strange girl, you know. She did have problems. Sometimes she would slip into deep, dark moods of desolation. I don't know what was tormenting her. She didn't talk about herself at all.'

He walked about the room as he spoke and waved his arms expansively while he lectured. He did not hide his pride when he told me what happened next. He went on and on in his eloquent way. He loved the sound of his voice.

A couple of days later, he took her to some sleazy hotel you rent by the hour. Her fascination with his mind and his theories made her forget the cheap, squeaky bed they shared. At the end of the term, when his wife and children were shipped off to the south for the summer, he had her move in with him. The apartment, paid for by his capitalist father-in-law, was in a fashionable part of Paris.

'I suppose,' he said, 'I vented my confusion and guilt-ridden soul by talking non-stop about the ugly face of big business and money and she listened. I was young and red then and she drank in every word. I wonder whatever happened to her after that summer,' he said sadly. 'I never saw her again.'

I knew the answer to that, but did not tell him.

'I promise you,' he whispered with a lecherous smile, 'she knew she was beautiful and desirable by the time our thing was over.'

He made me sick, but I faked admiration and smiled. He must have forgotten what happened. How he introduced her to his other followers. How proud she must have been when they all sat in those romantic cafés. Him, never shy of parading his pride of possessing her, talking of a better world and her exaltation of belonging to him. All through that summer they went to meetings. His followers were looking for reasons to rebel against the middle class who were paying their tuition fees. She was soon with him in the streets shouting slogans and setting police cars on fire. The shy young woman was released by a new sense of freedom and the ardent sexual attention of a man she could listen to forever. It was all exciting and her world was young and naïve and people read books, not battle manuals and threw stones, not grenades.

But at the end of the summer, the professor's family came back to town and he dropped her to go back to his cosy middle class dining room. I didn't remind him of that. It's funny how people like to forget the dark part of their adventures. It will, however, catch up with the bastard one day if it hasn't already. When he lies in his bed dying of something. He dropped her like a sack of rotten potatoes, but she survived.

The bell rang for his class and he got up. 'Come see me any time,' he said and handed me his arm, like a royal. I thanked him and left. I did not see him again.

That summer she met Ming Ho, a young Vietnamese poetry student who ran an underground newspaper which had a small but faithful circle of readers. It talked of rights and national aspirations and the downfall of colonialism and of changing the world. It sent stirring calls for independence. Some copies found their way back to Vietnam. Ming Ho was a gentle intellectual. A soft-spoken man who was sent to France by his merchant father to make sure the young man's revolutionary ideas couldn't hurt the family's interests. He eked out a living sitting in lectures for other students, making notes and sometimes tutoring. There was another side to him too. A dark, hateful side.

Ming Ho admired Bernadette's professor. I suppose with the Frenchman's political opinions matching his it's understandable. They went to the same lectures and organized meetings and demonstrations with other Vietnamese students in the city. She threw herself into helping him with his work. She distributed his paper. She cooked meals for him and his friends. She drank his theories up like nectar. Keeping busy helped her overcome the pain her all too short affair had dealt her. When the war intensified, Ming Ho returned to his country and Bernadette followed him to Saigon.

Eight years later, the bustle of Paris and the whistle of the law were far from Bernadette, now in her twenty-sixth year and in the bush. Curiously, she was not too far that day from where her father grew his tea before the war. She looked up and she saw an American warplane catch fire in the sky. She saw the shape of a man and his parachute jump out of the falling machine then float, suspended under the great white canopy, down into the rice fields in the valley below her.

CHAPTER TWO

He uttered an unrehearsed curse as he thumped into the soggy soil. There, with the silk spread over the young rice, Clay saw at close quarters what he recognized to be the battlefield. He was shown aerial pictures of it often enough, but the scenery did not look hostile. He assembled his chute and stuffed it easily into the soft earth. This was Vietcong territory. Someone must have seen where he had landed and they would soon come looking for him. It would be best if they just shot him on sight. Things would get too complicated otherwise.

He lay on his back and pulled a card out of his pocket. Colonel Clayton Wayne-Turner, USAF. There was a photograph of his boat, bare masted and at anchor. He had no business being here, playing hide-and-seek with a bunch of reds. But for that heat seeking missile he would have been far away from this. Lost amongst the crowded pavements of Bangkok where all foreigners look alike. Or on his way to one of the luxury hotels at Pattaya beach, that spicy stretch of sand in Thailand some six hundred miles south-west of here. The whole idea was crazy. He must have been crazy. A whining mosquito flew past and he felt his forehead itch. It was a humid, earthy afternoon. He must smell like hell. Christ, why didn't they just get here and finish him off?

His fate would soon be known. No one would expect him to survive this. He'd seen the plane crash into the ground and explode a few minutes before he'd landed. There would be a memorial service for him in a few days. The thought brought a rare smile to Clay's face. He might now become a real hero after having looked the part for years. Being who he was, he was sure to be talked of. The name Wayne-Turner still made interesting reading back home. He found himself wishing they'd notice his absence sooner rather than later. Inform his wife. With his rank and background it would mean a personal visit. Marge would like that. She would enjoy the top billing his presence used to deny her. Maybe not. She would be in Paris at this time of the year.

Clay followed the mosquito with his eyes, lining his hand up for the kill. The buzzing sound of the hovering insect stopped as it flew past his ear, landing below his cheek—bone. The flat smack of his hand sounded louder than gunfire, but the buzz continued. Failed again, he concluded and then a new itch came where he'd been bitten. He felt the gooks all around and he looked up at the hills, but saw no one.

He thought he had fallen asleep when he heard the voices. He was almost relieved to hear them. He pulled his pistol out of the holster and lifted his head out of the soft greenery. He'd shoot a few before they took him. This had to be the end of it. The air was still and he held his breath and then he saw the enemy. He did not pull the trigger. Everything appeared to be in slow-motion in the valley that afternoon. It seemed to him the sun had not moved at all and then he realized he was aiming at a woman.

It couldn't be, he thought as the unmistakable shape of her showed through the fatigues. Her hair was long and still as the day. Mustn't waver now, he thought and shut his right eye to aim. Then a dull thump on the back of his head told him he had not watched the rear. In bright sunshine, Clay's valley went dark.

That was how they met. They were much more than mere enemies, but they did not know it. I suppose they viewed each other with curiosity and suspicion and a sort of hate. I had been familiar with that sensation myself, when interviewing a freshly caught thief or a murderer. There is an element of surprise, perhaps even suppressed fear, when you first glimpse your opponent face to face. You've imagined him in all sorts of ways, you've planned your actions. And then the shooting is over and he stands before you. You forget what you thought and what you were going to say. You are in a state of shock. You take a deep breath and start all over again. These two knew nothing about each other beyond the moment. He was an intruder who was about to become a prisoner. She was what his people called a gook. He was a man; she was a woman. They could not have been more different.

I am not a psychologist. I have only seen him twice. We spoke just once, that's all. But I know all there is to know about him. I was to hear about him day and night within months of his unintended jump into the valley. On that day he was some thirty-six years old, a colonel in the United States Air Force and more than a little confused.

Some are born of love, others of frustration or despair, but he was born of necessity and into hate. It may sound pompous, but it's true. I have heard it said that his parents tolerated their marriage and even each other until he arrived. When that happened, all hell broke loose. For the rest of his childhood his affection was to be a first prize in a life or death contest between them.

Clayton Wayne-Turner was blessed with two family trees whose branches covered the south from Newport News to Augusta. In their time, the Waynes and the Turners had been cotton farmers, bankers, stock brokers and naval officers. By the late 1920s, a cloud of stagnation had settled over both famous names. They had been everywhere and had done everything. Since the heirs apparent of that generation belonged to opposite sexes, and had no evident attachment elsewhere, a matrimonial union of the two families became inevitable. Money sticks to money, an old man who was a boy at the time had told me. Them big names keep it all, he said. Until I started tracking Clay's origins down, I had always thought we English were the only nation besotted by class.

No one bothered to ask the individuals concerned about their own feelings. A treaty in the tradition of 19th century Europe was sought, negotiated and agreed upon. Champagne glasses were raised to celebrate the occasion. Overheated telegraph wires buzzed above the countryside with the news. The young couple had met socially before the engagement, and I understand the sky was not set alight by that event. They might even have been hostile to each other, but big money coupled with a medieval set of rules forced them into it. World War One had left plenty of elderly scions behind with little prospect of carrying their proud names into the future. Without a protest, therefore, and after a sumptuous society wedding attended by four senators and two state governors, Emma Kate Wayne and Keith Clayton Turner were pronounced man and wife. The year was 1934, the year I joined the British Army to learn discipline and see the world.

The wedding night was never consummated. I have it on a very reliable house source that they did not sleep in the same bed. The next morning, the newlyweds set out on their European honeymoon. It was to be an extended trip. The Wayne-Turners only returned to their nest at the end of the Berlin Olympics, having announced the arrival of little Clayton by cable from the SS *Deutschland*. The story appeared in all the glossy magazines. There were no details, and no place of birth was mentioned. I was told it was the sole secret his parents shared. Clay himself only discovered the circumstances of his birth many years later and only by chance.

Both families began out-spending each other to win his affections. Elderly relatives visited every day. Clay was never left alone. They talked about him among themselves and had little to say to him. He was made to thank everybody for every gift they produced. He was made to grace them with his angelic smile when they came to the house. He was made to stand quietly, stiff and head bowed at their funerals. By the time Clay reached the age of six, he had mastered the art of pretence.

Having been tutored at home, he never got the chance to vent his frustrations with his teachers. He was tall for his years and his army of nannies, his impeccable manners and the name he carried intimidated others. Even on those rare occasions when he did meet people of his own age, Clay didn't talk much. His every whim was granted him. Wooden horses, live ones and toy racing cars were put at his feet. No efforts were required of him. His future, he was told by everyone, was assured and had been mapped out for him on a scale that would take three lifetimes to consume. Clay never argued. He was polite and obedient; he did not raise his voice. He was never beaten. He began to think he could never be wrong.

Knowing his story as I do, I could never blame him for that. Clay had no one to guide him, as his parents drifted apart and their opposing influences were nullified and added to his isolation. He was not encouraged by anyone to take his teachers seriously. There were no examples to follow, no idols to imitate. Tolerance, preached by his paternal grandfather, was seen by his mother as weakness.

When the Japanese attacked Pearl Harbor, Keith Turner went to war. It was during a short shore leave that he noticed seven year old Clay harassing the gardener's son. I believe the whole incident centred around a bicycle the little boy had been given. A carefully assembled affair made of bits and pieces found around the estate. Clay had accused the other boy of stealing the machine. In the argument that ensued, Clay attacked the tubes and wires with a pickaxe. The gardener's boy did not offer a fight before running off crying to his father who was mowing the lawn in the back of the house.

Keith, who was about to be driven to the railroad station for the trip to Newport News, witnessed the episode from his bedroom window. He came running down to face his son. It was the first time someone had told Clay off for bad behaviour, and it was to be the last. Leaving behind an unrepentant son, Keith Turner joined his ship for a journey via the Panama Canal to the bottom of the Pacific. For the rest of his life, Clay would remember that last humiliating monologue and his mother's defence of him. She called her straying, uniformed husband a nigger lover. For a little while then, she'd become an angel in his eyes. She never bid her husband goodbye.

Apparently, Clay's school days did not improve him. At seventeen, his early character was fully formed. He was a young man of independent means and extremist views. People who knew him at college said he was a keen sailor and had won many cups. They said he was quiet and aloof and an arrogant son of a bitch. The memory of his own father had faded, while his mother's indulgence in alcohol had dimmed Clay's respect for her. The playmates she chose were spending her allowance in downtown Atlanta without her consent or presence. No one was left to tame his growing intolerance for all things different. He was clever enough to hide his views behind his charm and humour while the air force taught him to fly. But his wife knew. He had married at the age of twenty-four. Twelve years before the afternoon that saw him jump out of his burning plane.

I have read the Bible and when I heard what happened that day I couldn't help thinking how Joshua's halting mid-sky sun had come to southeast Asia. Darkness took forever arriving in the valley that afternoon. That was the time and place when Clay and Bernadette saw each other first. I know about that from one of the other Vietcong who was there. Ming Ho, the one time poet. That man played a big part in my own life later on. He became my tormentor, but I prefer not to think of him for now. Ming Ho. How I hate that name. The thought of him still brings shivers up my spine. Anyway, this is their story.

CHAPTER THREE

He woke with the pressure of rough ropes that curled around his arms and his ankles. Someone poured water on his face. He licked his lips and he looked up. There were more of them now. They had come from nowhere. As if the sea of rice had opened and spat them out of the earth. He stared them all in the face. The woman was gone. Must have been a dream. He felt strangely rested and calm. The urge to die was suddenly gone from his mind. He wanted to talk.

'You can take these ropes off,' he said. His voice was stiff. 'I am in no hurry to go anywhere.'

The young faces looked at him through many pairs of slanted dark eyes. He smiled. So this was the enemy, he thought with amusement. They looked young enough to be school children, but their expressions were serious. Their skin was dirty with soot. They were all talking at him and they seemed to smile. One touched his shoulder and he recoiled. They laughed. He looked behind him and then he saw her.

She was taller than the rest. Her eyes were round and they shot piercing gazes of cold hate in his direction. The gentle breeze brushed her hair across her elongated face like a curtain. Her mouth hardened and her long fingers closed around the gun that had been his. From behind, a sandalled foot kicked his shoulder.

Clay turned back to look. The man was short and wiry, the oversized khaki hung on him like on a skeleton. His bloodshot eyes burned behind a pair of black rimmed glasses. There was a fresh scar along his hairless cheek. His uniform seemed new and he was unarmed. The others looked at him in awe.

'Your name,' he said in a surprisingly soft, French voice.

'Clayton Wayne-Turner,' Clay answered. 'What's yours?'

'You pigs think you own the world,' the woman shouted.

The thin man looked at him and smiled and said, 'My name is Ming Ho.'

Machine-gun fire pushed them all closer to the earth. A helicopter was circling overhead, spraying the ground with bullets. One of his captors lay at Clay's side, his chest slashed open, his dead eyes looking straight at his own. Ming Ho's knee was bleeding. The woman sat where she had stood, her face ashen. All the others had disappeared as if swallowed by the rice. More helicopters appeared, carefully approaching the valley. Then someone opened fire from the hillside just above them. One machine exploded and the rest roared off.

'They won't be back today,' Clay said, looking at the darkening horizon. The woman crawled over to Ming Ho. She ripped his trousers open with a knife. The little man did not speak, but his strained eyes begged for her help. She looked at the wound. The heavy bullet had torn the flesh open, revealing a mass of tissue that barely covered the bone above his knee. She pushed Clay over.

'You have a gauze?' she barked with a harsh, accented voice.

'Cut me loose,' he said. 'I'll have a look.'

'Don't you try anything, you pig,' she screamed. She pointed his gun at him. The barrel looked large and menacing.

'You'd better look for it yourself, you red whore.'

She hit him across the face with the butt. He felt his body expand into the rope. 'Don't you do that,' he said quietly. 'While you're wasting time on me, your friend's running out of blood here.'

'Move closer,' she said. She motioned to Ming Ho who took the pistol from her and pointed it at Clay. She stretched her hand and felt his pockets and then she pulled the zipper open to check inside. There was nothing there but his clean shirt. She took her knife out of her belt again.

'Don't cut me up, lady. Just shoot.'

'We don't kill unarmed people, mister. I want a little of that shirt.'

He thought that was funny and he laughed and moved closer. This wasn't real. More like children playing doctor and nurse. He'd seen his daughter do that.

'Be my guest,' Clay said. Ming Ho fainted, dropping the gun into the grass. 'You'd better watch me.'

'I am not afraid. You can do nothing when you are down here. You are a coward when you are helpless. All you are good at is bomb and maim and kill from up there.'

She cut a slice of cotton away, rolling it expertly round her fingers. She then pulled a handful of green leaves out of somewhere and chewed them before pressing the mash onto Ming Ho's leg. The pain shook him and he woke with a jerk. She wound the cloth around his thin leg and rolled it tight with a stick of wood that appeared from nowhere. Clay watched her with amazement.

'There's a safety pin stuck on my sleeve, lady.'

She pulled it out and with a quick 'thank you' she fastened the bandage. Ming Ho fainted again. His breathing was slow and silent. The woman looked at him with deep concern.

The air force was a cleaner place to die, Clay thought. You can shower between missions and smell of aftershave lotion while you drop the bombs.

'Got something to eat lady?'

She didn't hear him. She just looked at the sky.

'I told you. They won't be back today,' he said. 'Got any food?'

She handed him a green bundle. He had seen that stuff sold in the streets of Saigon and Bangkok. He knew what was in it.

'Thank you', he said. They could have been sitting on some far away verandah, enjoying the ancient hills as they turned mauve with the evening. He'd gone bananas. She was his captor and armed and an enemy and a gook. Nor did she linger much with her sightseeing. She bent over Ming Ho and wiped his brow and took his glasses off and cleaned them. His face contorted with an intensity that came from the world he was in. He was clearly someone she cared about. Perhaps even her husband. The gooks were known

21

to marry each other in the field.

He ate. The rice was cold and sticky, but the bitter sting of the banana leaf wrapper gave it some zing. She was feeding him to keep him alive. He wished they'd make their minds up soon. The wounded man came to, and the woman handed him the pistol. She mumbled to him and he whispered something back. He pointed the weapon at Clay and looked him straight in the eye. His glasses and his voice seemed out of place here.

The woman pulled an antenna out of what looked like a jute-wrapped bundle of junk. The bundle crackled and she spoke into it. She listened and spoke again and she repeated things. Clay tried to decipher his fate from her face, but her expression did not change. She was concentrating and every time she opened her mouth to say something she looked like she was smiling, but her eyes remained cold. He thought he detected a hint of sadness in them as darkness began to engulf the valley. She then said something final into the instrument and clicked it off. Ming Ho spoke and she took her knife out and cut Clay's arms loose.

'Dig a hole and bury our comrade,' she ordered.

'You're out of your mind. No spade?'

'Bravo, you pig. You're a hero. Now dig. You have hands, no?' The dead man looked darker and so did her eyes. Clay got up on his knees and started clearing the mud. It was easy and the dead man was unceremoniously rolled into his resting place. They covered the body with earth. As the dead face disappeared under the soil, total darkness fell. He could smell her sweat and his own and then he lay down. The grass felt soft. He knew she was somewhere near or above him, but he was tired. The last thing he thought of was how angry her face became every time she looked at him. He did not feel the rope being tied around his wrists as he slept.

CHAPTER FOUR

—■—

Ming Ho was wide awake now. They lifted him carefully and carried him away. Behind him, like a procession, they dragged the heavy American along the flattening rice and lowered him into the tunnel. He slept as if he had been drugged. Bernadette watched in silence. He was the first white man she had seen at close quarters for many months. The sight of him troubled her. Back came the memories of white bodies she was forced to caress in the beginning. When her devotion to the cause was in doubt. Those trying days were long gone, but the nightmare of them was as terrifying as ever. Why did she have to think of that now? She followed them all down the tunnel. There were candles and a kerosene lamp down there, and along the walls hung water cans and ammunition belts and baskets of food and medicine.

The Chinese herbalist waited for her where she had last seen him that morning. He'd always brought a smile to her face.

'You look tired,' he said.

'Is there much to do tonight?'

'No. One wounded. The dead have been buried. You go to sleep.'

'What about Ming Ho?'

'They are wheeling him down the line. He'll be in a hospital in a few hours. He needs to be operated on. There will be a truck at the end of the tunnel, close to the town. I keep forgetting the name. Are you hungry?'

'No thank you, comrade.'

'Spare me your titles, Bernadette. I am not here for the politics.'

'Independence is politics.'

'No it isn't. It's a right.'

'We have to fight for our rights.'

'You go ahead and do that, Bernadette. I'm only here to stuff my leaves and grasses up bullet holes your politics leave behind. I wish all this didn't happen. I'd be helping old farmers to have a proper piss again instead of patching up young ones.'

'Here you go again. . . .'

'Yes. Here I go again. I have been on this earth nearly seventy years. I have still to discover all the plants God put on it and work out how to use them. My father tried as did his father before him. I have vowed I'd write it all down one day. Draw the flowers and the leaves and name them and where to find them and how to brew them. Instead of risking their lives to rob pharmacies for pills and injections, more people should learn about the wild fields. This is a dying art, Bernadette. There are life saving properties in many wild plants.'

'But if the pigs don't stop bombing our fields and poisoning them, there won't be any plants left for you to put down for posterity. That's what we're fighting for.'

'Let men do the fighting, Bernadette. You were a good nurse, you know. You could learn a lot more about the wild fields. It's a pity they are sending you up north.'

'What are you saying?'

'Don't you know? You've caught an important fish this afternoon. He is being taken up north for interrogation. You are escorting him there. Ming Ho's last orders before they took him away.'

She sat down. The Chinese herbalist poured her a cup of tea.

'Why me?'

'I don't know. I suppose it's because you speak English.'

'I'm not the only one.'

'You'll soon be back.'

She was wide awake now. Was this another test? Didn't they know she was one of them? How much proof did they want? She had been so happy working with the eccentric old man who was sitting up, his back against the wall opposite, making one of his brews.

How can a man change so much? Her best friend, her only friend at a time when she was lovesick and lonely and lost. Ming Ho had been so trusting, so gentle and compassionate and he understood the hell she had gone through. He had brought her here. He had shown her the way to a new life. A life with a purpose. A life where you depended on people, not on the fickle love of a man. Perhaps it was his position that had changed him. But then she had always sensed something immensely powerful behind the soft whispers of support that had once saved her sanity.

It's for the cause, he'd always assured her. Everything. Even that dreadful time when she worked in the brothel in Saigon. The others don't know you, he'd said. They must be sure of your loyalty before you can become a part of it. You are almost a foreigner here. You hardly speak the language. She knew he had been right. She understood he had put himself on the line for her. She had to learn to hate the white bodies before being allowed to kill them. I told you it won't be easy, he'd said. Our people have been colonized by the Chinese for a thousand years, by the French for a hundred and by the Japanese for five. They are suspicious. They were promised independence by the Americans in exchange for fighting Japan. And now the Americans are here in their place. You've got to understand, he'd said.

Yes, yes, yes. She understood. He was right, of course he was right. They were all right. She was bad. And ungrateful. Just as she'd been told by her father's family and the girls at school. She was no good. Nothing good would ever come of her.

But Ming Ho was good. He'd helped her. He had vouched for her. He had risked his life by introducing her to the cause and the people in it. And now she was bitching about him. Why did she always have to blame someone? If only she could sleep. Just for a little.

The day had started so well. A beautiful day with cool temperatures and bright sunshine. Ming Ho had come to see her at the dressing station. He'd risked betrayal and death by coming out from across the border, now he was wounded. He used to write to her. His letters were beautiful. They sang to her like the birds. With Ming Ho away the herbalist had become her father. God how happy she had been selecting herbs with that old fool. The six months she had spent roaming the countryside looking for leaves and roots and cutting special grass had helped her forget the time in Saigon. Those sweaty bodies invading her own like they did her country. And yet Ming Ho's friends did not believe she belonged. She was sinking again. The old black horse of depression was approaching. She must sleep.

The Chinese herbalist was standing above her. His good round face was wrinkled with concern. 'Let me give you something to sleep,' he said. He tried to smile. 'Be a patient for a change.'

'I need to think.'

'Not in your state, Bernadette. Things always look different in the morning.' He had a cup ready for her.

'Let's talk a little,' she ventured.

'We've talked enough these past few months. You'll be back. I'll request it. I'll fight for you. I have contacts too.'

'You're not a fighter,' she said with a smile.

'You are worth it,' he said and handed her the tissane.

She drank it slowly. The bitter taste of it was new. It numbed her lips and then her mouth and tongue. She had forgotten how hungry she was as the heat spread through her body. Her head sank forward.

The old man laid her down and took her sandals off. He washed her feet. Not thirty feet away from the snoring American pilot, Bernadette slept. Her face, the face he had often seen drawn and sad for no apparent reason, had lost the worrying lines.

How different she had been the day she was brought into his little station. Until her arrival, there were only two old ladies and a deaf farmer who made bandages. He was told she had never been in the bush before. Born in the city and educated in France, she was spoilt, they said and he was to discipline her. Teach her, but first make her do the most menial, dirty jobs.

The first time he had tried to talk to her, she could barely answer. She did what she was told. She dug earth and with her bare hands spread excrement on plants that needed fattening. She washed wounds. She seemed to revel in humiliation as if she was repenting. But whenever she had time, and always in the evening, he saw her clean herself and wash her clothes and scrub every inch of her body as if she was trying to skin herself. Once or twice he had seen her under a tree or at the mouth of their tunnel. Her head was down and her shoulders shook and he knew she had been crying, but he never approached her. He concluded that she had not long been back from France and that she had led a despicable life in Paris.

Then they suffered a direct hit and the two old ladies were killed. The deaf farmer ran off in the night and was never seen again and they were left alone. She had started making small talk about the weather and the trees and she opened up to him. She listened to his long discourses the way none of his own children and grandchildren ever did. He spoke of his youth and his father and his father's father and the wild plants and the medicines that hid inside them.

He talked of his family who had ignored him and of how he had found solace among the fighters of the Vietcong. She never spoke of herself at all.

They were becoming famous, he and Bernadette and two other ladies who were sent to replace the others. They were given generous bundles of fruits and vegetables and sometimes rice and even a live chicken. When they passed villages, people asked for his old remedies for colds and pregnancy and impotence. Now and again he even saw her laugh. So pure and beautiful she looked when a smile took her over, that he'd often try to tell her amusing stories about his successes and failures as a man of unconventional medicine. Sometimes he would invent such stories, but she always knew and she'd call him an old liar. And then her face would burst into happiness that would make his lie worthwhile. She could have become the disciple he had long tried to find. She had become indispensable. Once she saved his life by dismantling a field mine that lay on their path. Or maybe it was an unexploded bomb. He did not remember. With her the little field hospital he ran became a legend. The wounded soldiers kept brave faces for her. Now they were sending her away.

The old Chinese herbalist sat by her and looked at her long into the night. He had often thought she was the most beautiful woman he had ever seen. She could have attained fame somewhere. She had what he had wanted and had chased when he was young. She could have been an actress or a rich man's mistress. In his village, when he was a child, people would have given a lot to possess her. Even the local landowner would have taken someone like her into his house.

This woman was a little girl. She needed to be protected. She didn't understand the sinful habits of men. He must have been mistaken about her bad ways in Paris.

She had dreams. He did not agree with her dreams yet he liked her to have them because he knew she needed them to stay alive. He knew that but he did not know why. Now that he was no longer young, he did not need to know. Old age had killed his curiosity.

He knew she had been happy working with him. He showed her which plants to pluck, which to boil or roast. Which to dry and which to use when fresh and green. Most days she looked fulfilled. Even when they were hiding from the bombs, she would smile. Now she felt sad and older than ever. Something told him he wouldn't see her again. He wiped her peaceful face and looked again. Had he not known she was fast asleep, he would have thought she was dead.

In the morning, they woke her up early. They led her down the tunnel where her instructions were spelt out for her carefully. A young fighter was introduced to her. He was not a man of many talents nor did he speak any French or English. He was, they said, light on his feet and could outrun a motorcycle. But he was not to be involved in the interrogation and was to be sent back as soon as they'd reached their destination. He was a simple man of peasant stock, but was disciplined and loyal and his battle experience would come in handy. He was to act as rear guard, no more, in case the American tried to escape. She was not to talk to him at all. Just concentrate on the prisoner and make sure any bits of information given out by him were not lost.

CHAPTER FIVE

The track she was following was hardly visible. No more than a goat path that snaked down the valleys and hugged the hills. The man was walking close behind her, his foul breath floating into her nostrils with the breeze. The other man walked behind, his sub-machine-gun always at the ready.

Don't talk to him, she had been told. Just listen to everything he says. Everything is important. Every word. They must have thought a lot of him. A local interrogation was not enough. She was ordered to take him up north, across the border. From there they were going to take him to Hanoi. She was to forget everything that had happened to her before, all her friends and Saigon. For the duration, she was told, she must concentrate on nothing but getting him safely across the border.

Ming Ho's orders had been passed on to her that morning by his deputy, but she could hear his voice. This is the big one, he would have said. You get this man over there and you'll be accepted. No more proof. They repeatedly warned her not to stop anywhere. Not to talk to anyone. Find their own food once their provisions were gone. His people would try and get him back. Did they think she was a fool?

Once she delivered him, she was to find her way back. They were sure to find a position for her back in Saigon. Do not be afraid, they said. Afraid? She had not been afraid for a very long time now. Long before the prisoner had fallen into her life. Not since that fire that hit the brothel she had been assigned to. Most of the girls there were burned alive along with the white guests they were entertaining. When the fire struck, it spread quickly. There were screams.

The heat began to penetrate her narrow cubicle. The young man who had been with her had fallen asleep. She tried to wake him, not knowing why. Then the door opened and two men burst into her cubicle. Ming Ho was one. She was not surprised to see him. He stuck a knife into the American's throat and the other pulled her out. The scorching air peeled the skin off her face as they ran through the crumbling corridor. Outside, as fire fighting equipment poured water over the wooden building, she was pushed into the front hold of a tricycle. A carpet was thrown over her body and then, to the sound of screaming sirens, she was whisked away. Her career as a listening whore was over.

You have passed the test, Ming Ho had told her after that. You are important. That's why we've pulled you out of there. He had spoken tenderly. Did he not notice how she had hardened? She must stop thinking of that. She must find some water soon. Scrub that offending skin off. The pain of it always made her feel better. And yet the trials were not over. This new task made it clear. She was being ungrateful again. 'No one asked you to come back to Vietnam,' they used to say. And they were right. No one had. She would have been walking the streets of Paris living the lie of being a Frenchwoman. She should be grateful to them for taking her in. They had given her a chance to find herself. Ming Ho had saved her life. She should make him proud of her.

The morning had started badly. The old Chinese herbalist had died in the night. She was called to the mouth of the tunnel where she was given Ming Ho's orders. She wanted to cry then, but had kept a straight face. He was a kind old man. Always hungry and cold, yet he had cared for her. The others said he must have poisoned himself with one of his elixirs.

You are talking nonsense, her insides had cried out. He

was just cold and hungry and full of years. He had nowhere else to go. He simply willed himself to die. I knew him well. But not a word of it came out and all she did was to nod. They gave her the American's pistol and took her back to where he was waiting, hands tied behind his back. The road to the village of Ha Thuong was further away than the stars. And there were no tunnels along the way she could hide in. How many fathers can one woman lose in a lifetime? She would cry for the Chinese herbalist tonight, she thought as she gritted her teeth and walked on. And then the American started to talk.

'The first time I met Marge, I thought she was the most beautiful thing I had ever seen in my life. Boy she was tall and slim and proud. She had a clear, clean voice. Nothing like my mother's smoker's croak. That got worse with all that drink. Yeah, drink. Dammit she was too drunk on my wedding day. Couldn't even turn up for the ceremony. My mother was going to be queen of the show. Lady of the house. Head of the fucking clan. The bitch couldn't wait until it was over. We had to lock her up in her room and do an official photograph the next day. Everybody turned up again for the camera.

'Oh, I think I married Marge because my mother objected. We had this game we played together, mother and I. See who could upset the other more. No, I'd have married her anyway. She's a strong minded girl and she'd made up her mind to get me. My mother said she was only after our money, but I didn't care. I wanted to have her. I craved her like mad and she sure kept me waiting. She thought she'd make me more keen. And me? I was the perfect gentleman. I held her hand and kissed her cheek by her porch every night for two weeks. I was frustrated as hell, but I had these two hookers in the town near the base. Went there every night and screwed the shit out of both.

Yes, while Marge and I were courting. I had her on my mind all the time, but she didn't put out. She was the lady. Belle of the south. Good family, but no cash. And she made me wait because her head was full of all that stuff about virginity and hell and that. But those hookers made me feel good all right. The way only hookers know how.

'We met at a party on the base and from that evening on we were together. We went to the movies and parties and on long walks and she did all the talking. You wouldn't believe it was me. Silent Clay they used to call me. Marge wanted to be a society journalist. Anyway, things could have turned out better. She should have let me ... when ... well, yeah, the wedding. I wanted to go sailing. She wanted to go to France. So we went on this honeymoon to Florida and even then I had to wait a week before she'd let me. She had the curse on our wedding night, and I'll tell you a secret. When we finally made it I was so frustrated and wanted her so bad the whole thing was over in two seconds. And this is how it's been ever since. Isn't it a scream? She excited me too much or something and she was afraid of it and when she wanted me for real, later on, I got used to the others. You know, women I paid for who told me how great I was. Shit. It always did work with the others. Maybe I'm only good with a whore. . . .'

She stopped, turned around and looked at him. His eyes were bright with excitement.

'Be quiet,' she shouted. 'Can't you be quiet?'

'What's the matter with you?'

'Just be quiet.'

'Why don't you shoot me, lady? I'll be quiet then.'

She shrugged her shoulders and walked on. She walked faster. She was quite right, Clay thought. He was talking too much. But then he was entitled. Madness changes a man. Brings out stuff that wasn't there before. It was fun, being someone else.

'Hey, wait for me,' he said. She heard his steps. They sounded clumsy as he tried to hurry. 'I don't care if you like what I say or hate it or if you don't understand it. You ... you ... who asked you to listen? This talk is doing me a hell of a lot of good. I've never talked that much in all my life. The whole stinking mess I'm in is coming out here, see? Coming out with words. Marge said I should see a shrink. They get paid to listen. Here it's all for free. All I need is to get it all out and I'll be fine. Anyway, we're separated now. You know, married but not living together. She's found things to do with all the time she's got. My daughter's at school and Marge's too mean to spend my money so she's a student again. You know, history of art, something like that. Hell, I'm having a good time here. I talk and no one talks back. She should see me now and hear me talking like this. She wouldn't believe it. She said I never talk. I don't care how dumb you are or how little you know about marriage. You people don't bother with that, eh? You just lie down in the bush and fuck. That's why there's so many of you, right? I can see a face dancing in front of me. Right where your ass is. That face belongs to me. Clayton Wayne-Turner in person is painted on your ass. Marge wanted to be a journalist, but settled for being Mama first. She was a good mama. Must give her that. Better than the drunken bitch who was supposed to mama me, I'll tell you.

'I can say that about my mother because she wasn't my mother at all and nothing I ever did was right. It would have been okay if it had always been like that, but no. I was king of the castle for years. I couldn't put a foot wrong. I even shit gold bricks. Then, suddenly her way of life caught up with her and that was that. Everything changed. She'd had a drinking problem all her life and then she got fat and

34

boring and ugly and could only scream. She couldn't find anyone to play with anymore. Had to buy sex, like me, but she didn't like it. You see, my mother was an American aristocrat. The kind of people you guys hate. . . .

'Anyway, she died a couple of months ago. I was busy fighting this war, but I went back. I didn't want to, but I did. Marge went, too. You should have seen the pictures in the papers. Half the bigshots in the city and the church and the senate came to see her off. I guess they put a whole crate of booze in the box with her. Oh listen, Marge isn't like that. She's every bit as blueblooded as my mother was. Her people didn't marry as well as ours, that's all. They didn't move on when king cotton died. Marge was born well, but being born well without money is a prison. I was her ticket to freedom, see?'

'Hell, we have nothing in common. She doesn't like sailing and I don't care much for those lines and colour spots she calls modern art. She hates the uniform and hates making love with me. You'd think my mother would have known all this. Would have tried to help me. Protect me. She didn't protect me from anything. Only tolerated me because I had the money. My old man and her old man and their clan knew how to look after it. Make sure it goes on forever. Once you guys rub me out, Marge will carry it on until my daughter produces a child with our blood in his veins. Marge will keep it because she's mean. Well, she doesn't spend my money and my name isn't really mine anyhow. So why didn't she get rid of me? That's why I like whores. Use them, pay them, drop them. Right?'

God she hated him now. More than ever. His sick mind and his convoluted monologue were intruding on her world. She had been listening to every word. He made her shudder. What an arrogant insensitive selfish *salaud* he was. His lean face hidden behind an ugly growth of dirty blond hair. She hated the way he walked. The way he talked of that class his mother and his wife had come from. His money. He didn't like anything. Maybe he hated himself, too. Why was she being so bitter about the man? True, he was an American pig who bombed her people and from the way he spoke he had no respect for anyone, but what was all that to her? She was ordered to listen and learn and report. No one had told her to get angry.

She stopped to take a look at him, but he didn't notice. He kept right on walking and his body crashed into hers.

'I'm sorry,' he said. 'Didn't notice.'

'Do not apologize.'

He smelled foul. She had to do something about his stench. His face was sweaty. Large wet spots stained his clothes.

'I am not apologizing. I'm just filthy. I haven't had a wash for two days. Even the flies avoid me like the plague.'

A shadow of a smile passed his lips. 'Can't you do something for me?'

'Keep going.' The other man sat on a rock behind Clay, gun at the ready. His face betrayed nothing. He looked like a machine.

'If you want to get me wherever we're heading, you'd better find me a bath pretty damn quick. God knows what diseases I could catch in this crappy country of yours. I'd rather die clean, lady.'

'I have a name.'

'No kidding, so have I. I'm Clay.' He smiled. 'And I don't always smell like this. What do people call you?' He looked like a child.

'Bernadette,' she said simply. 'My name is Bernadette.'

'That's a French name, right?'

'It is.'

'How come you have a French name?'

'My father was French.'

He took a step forward to look at her face. His gaze startled her. She pulled the gun out and held it ready.

'What's your problem, Bernadette? I'm only trying to get a better look at you.' She smiled. Or so it seemed to him. She really was quite pretty for a gook. And suddenly he felt a strange need for her. Perhaps because she had listened.

'I'll find somewhere for you to clean up,' she said. 'Now let's go.'

CHAPTER SIX

He heard the thunder of engines above them and he pushed her to the ground. She was too shocked to pull the gun at him. Behind them, the other man found cover under a bush. Clay looked up. There were two of them up there and they banked, then dived, came rocketing up again and disappeared.

'Bombers,' he said. 'Something deadly is going to hit the ground there any minute now.'

The horizon beyond the hill they were scaling roared. Smoke gushed at the sky and he got up. She pointed the gun at him. He almost wished she'd pull the trigger. He'd opened himself up too much and what he saw he didn't like.

'It's over now, Bernadette,' he said. 'Short and sweet. They have got no business being here I reckon. Must have dropped their last bit somewhere or made a mistake. Let's go take a look.'

He started for the peak and she ran behind. He was quick. He soon got to the top and slowed down, then dropped to the ground and crawled. He motioned to her to do the same and looked at her to make sure. She was no longer behind him. They lay side by side among the tea bushes, looking at the scene like curious children. Their faces were close, nearly touching. She could hear the young guard's breath panting close by. The countryside below them was on fire. Between the black and grey and white columns of rising smoke they saw the shape of a sprawling village. Explosions burst out of the earth and fire grabbed the roof of a hut that stood close to the village pond. The orange flames reflected in the water. There were fallen palm trees strewn everywhere. A vehicle of sorts, a truck or a tractor, was being eaten by fire, black smoke rising from its carcass. She surveyed the scene sadly and then they heard screams.

'I hate fires,' she said. Her voice sounded fragile.

'Let's go down,' he said.

'No we won't. We cannot. We mustn't.'

'Why not?'

'They've just been bombed by your people. They'll kill you on sight.'

'That's good,' he said and got up. 'That's great.' Before she could react, he was running down the hill. She started after him, but he was faster. She shouted at him to stop. The young man got up and followed them. She must make the American stop. That would be the greatest failure of her life. She was told to avoid all villages. If they killed him, her life was over. As she ran down, the thought came to her that he wanted to die. There was something desperate about the way he had talked before. The story of his life and marriage had exploded out of him as if it had been buried there by years of repression.

And now he was racing down the tea covered slope as if driven by madness. She tried to make out the shapes and movements of the people below. They were busy pouring water over fires and clearing away the debris. The young guard flew down the hill. He overtook the American. He was waving his weapon as if he intended to hit the pilot. Two men by the pond looked up in their direction and pointed. One lifted his rifle. A burst of fire shot up their way and it caught the young guard in the neck. He fell to the ground without a word like a rag doll.

'Comrades,' she heard herself scream, 'comrades don't shoot.'

The two looked at them and within seconds they were joined by others. The American reached the little group and was swallowed by a human circle. She could not see him.

'Don't shoot,' she panted. They turned to look at her. Some had glaring eyes, others seemed shocked and frightened. A short, powerfully built man came up to her. He looked like a bull.

'You mustn't hurt him,' she said. He motioned towards something, but she did not understand. He walked closer to her, gun in hand, and his face was serious. She saw her dead comrade being dragged down the hill by two villagers. The American was nowhere to be seen. Another man came towards her. Then someone hit her face. For a moment she was blinded, then she looked at the squat man and clearly saw him smile. A second blow fell on the back of her head and she fell to the ground.

'Red bitch,' the man said and spat on her. 'The Americans would have never ruined our village if it hadn't been for your lot. If you like Ho Chi Minh, go north and whore the streets of Hanoi. Your syphilis might do their balls some good up there.'

She couldn't believe her ears. She sank into a dreamlike listlessness. Someone was stripping her of her gun and her rucksack. She saw Clay's shape close above her. From the corner of her eye, she saw the villagers kicking the young guard's lifeless body. Then, before the next blow fell on her head, she saw the squat man smile at the American and then the pain came and she fainted.

Clay looked at her, then at the squat man. He wore army fatigues and his powerful torso was naked. His surprise was complete. This didn't make sense at all. He thought they would have shot him on sight. The gooks had killed the wrong man. He wanted to speak, but no words came. Confusion engulfed him. The man put his hand on his shoulder while another cut the rope around his hands with a knife. He was free, but the shock of it all numbed him.

'Come and get to eat,' the squat man said in English. 'I am Captain Nguyen Nang Ding. Army of the Republic of Vietnam. Your side. I am monthly leave visit my village. Arrive this morning. You call me New, sir. Name give to me by American boys. Easy can say Captain New, right?'

Clay didn't answer. A hideous pair of gold front teeth shone out of Captain New's mouth. 'We get you food now, sir. We had VCs in village for one week. They run when I arrive. They take nothing. Only eat and talk to villagers, but no one believe. By secret, village inform army by radio so bombers come, but come one day late. Our mistake. Anyway we get this VC woman who catch you. Good enemy is dead enemy, right? You want bath and shave, sir? Maybe food first? We check woman after eat.'

'Where is she, Captain New?' Clay asked. His voice was deep and steady.

'We lock her up in hut back there. Wood thick and plenty strong. She get no food no fear, sir.'

'Show me where she is.'

The Captain pointed his finger at a hut further up the road, beyond the village pond. It stood alone, close to the hill they had come from. It had a red door. A flag hung down above it.

'Strong wood, I promise sure. She never get out of there.'

'What will you do with her?'

'You no worry. First we interrogate good. Then we kill her.'

They walked through the remains of the village. Burned palm treetops pointed at the sky like masts. In the little square, a full sized feast was being prepared. Mountains of steamed rice. Suckling pigs and fruits and vegetables and river shrimps and American cookies and Hershey's chocolate bars.

'Village celebrate my visit, sir. Make food before planes come. No damage here. Sign from God my coming good. Want bourbon?'

'Not now, thanks.'

'We got everything here, sir. With no VC we live well. Never starve in my village. This province rich, and people learn to hide food from VC when come here. Ho Chi Minh tell them they save us all, but no one in here wants words, right? Want smoke?'

'No thanks, Captain. You spent time in the States?'

'I speak good English, no?'

'Oh sure.'

Captain New's eyes were glowing with pride. 'I been California only six months. Best place. Best place. God bless America. Tomorrow my jeep come back. If I know you come I never let go. I give it to Sergeant to go visit his village. Not far, but marry short time, only one month, so he go see his woman. He need it, she need it. We no big hurry, right?'

They sat down and Captain New kept talking. He tried to ask questions. Beyond telling him his first name, Clay revealed nothing. The man looked at him with great intensity. In spite of his never ending small talk, he was memorizing Clay's voice, his face, the way he walked and sat. His flying suit. His watch. Here was a man he could emulate if he watched him carefully. A man who belonged to a race of giants. People who came here to save his village from the northern reds.

Captain New made sure Clay got the best cut of meat and the choicest unmarked fruits. 'I protect you, sir. You no fear,' Captain New said with admiration.

With the food and the iced water, comforts of the moment were taking him over. He felt tired but aware. There was no salvation for him now. He was getting deeper into a mess. He could never go back. There would be too much to explain. He settled down, resigned to his fate. He was further than ever from his goal. No one would understand him. Not one soul in the whole wide world. He had planned this so well and yet nothing had come of it. He would never get the answer to those desperate questions that had troubled him. That monkey of a Captain New blabbered on. He must have drunk two whole bottles of bourbon with his food. The world was full of Captain News. Millions of them everywhere. No one he could talk to. No one to listen to him and understand. Like she had. As the evening came and went and turned into a starry night, he began to wonder about his erstwhile captor.

On the other side of the village, the cold air entered the hut where Bernadette lay in darkness. She shivered, and convulsions shook her into consciousness. She was hungry and the tingling of dried mud in her mouth made her feel dirty. She had disobeyed her orders. She had strayed and had caused the death of a fellow fighter. She didn't know who he was or what his mother had called him. And all for nothing. Not even in the line of duty because she had failed her duty. No one would believe her that the American just started running into the village. She could have shot him in the leg. She was a failure again. She had failed Ming Ho. She could not be trusted. She never did deserve to last as long as she had.

She had no illusions about her own fate. A southern army uniform hung menacingly above her, nailed to the bolted door. The face of the squat officer came into her mind. They way he looked at her left her in no doubt. All she could hope for was a quick death. She did not want a priest, but she wished to die clean.

CHAPTER SEVEN

The way they sometimes greeted her was embarrassing. She had stayed there every time she came to Paris and they knew her by name. The uniformed porter opened the taxi door and his stern face broke into a respectful smile. She knew it was the fat tip they were after, but that was what they lived on. In any case, they deserved it because they were always extremely courteous to her at the hotel.

'Welcome, Madame Wayne-Turner,' he said. He looked at the sky to make sure he wouldn't need the large umbrella to shield his guest. She emerged from the taxi. At the sign of his eye, two red-coated baggage boys raced for the parcels. He escorted her to the main door which opened as if by magic as soon as her shape appeared.

There were a few boutiques in the arcade and the buildings adjoining the Intercontinental Hotel, but Marge had been looking at shops all day. Paris was as ravishing as ever and she'd planned to take her daughter to the Faubourg Saint Honoré as soon as she came back from the Eiffel Tower. The reception chief came out with her key. He had an envelope in his hand.

'A gentleman has been trying to call you all day, Madame,' he said. 'A Colonel Carter of the US Embassy. I hope it's good news.'

'I'm on my way up,' she said. 'Would you ask the operator to get them for me?'

'With pleasure,' he said. He waited with her until the lift arrived, then she saw him bow as the doors closed.

The phone was ringing as she walked into the room. She kicked her shoes off with a sigh of relief and sat on the bed. The voice on the other end sounded friendly enough, even concerned. Colonel Mike Carter was out, but his secretary knew he'd wanted to arrange an early meeting with her. That very afternoon if possible. No, she didn't know what it was about. She was sorry. Three o'clock? Would that be okay? Marge said it would. Where did they want her to go? Nowhere, the girl said. Colonel Carter would be pleased to come to her hotel. He'd been in all day. Just went out to grab a quick lunch.

Marge peeled off her blouse and lay on the wide bed. The clouds outside must have dispersed. The sun was now streaming into the room, lighting the large painting that hung above the brassy fireplace. She looked about her. The room seemed pink. She'd never noticed that before. The old wooden clock said it was two. She'd have no time for a nap. What did they want with her? How did they know where she'd be? Possibly it was Clay. Perhaps he wanted to contact her. That was strange enough in he circumstances. Now that all was cut and dried between them, what would he want her for? If he did, he'd have called her himself. He'd done that before, regardless of the time of day or night or where she'd been. Calling her via the embassy was a new tack. Very unlike him. He didn't like diplomats.

It was a weird sensation, lying there on that strange

bed with Clay's presence running up and down her mind. They'd been married for fourteen years, but he had never been so remote. Not even six months ago, when she finally accepted that he was lost to her. He had asked her not to bother coming to Bangkok for the little holiday they had planned. Not to take the girl out of school. Not to say anything to anyone. Live her life the way she wanted to. Study whatever and wherever she wanted. See what happens.

At the time, she thought he'd gone crazy, but with his silence the estrangement grew and she'd heard nothing more. She knew he'd written to their daughter at school. Two postcards. One from Hong Kong and another from Bangkok.

The last time they had been together was strange. He had come out for his mother's funeral and they took a few days off to go sailing in Florida. To start with, she had thought it was a success. He'd tried to get close to her. He'd been affectionate. Had it gone on, it could have become a sort of second honeymoon. But on the second day, he changed. He talked more than ever. Talked of nothing in particular, but he did not give her a chance to answer. As if he was bouncing half-witted theories off her. There was something erratic about him. It could have been a delayed reaction to his mother's death. Often he passed the wheel to her and went forward. He pulled a piece of paper out of his pocket and read it. She did not ask him what it was. But she noticed every time he looked at it his demeanour changed. There was no sex. She had not expected any. That part of their life had started badly. First it was the clumsy, fumbling affair her mother had warned her it would be. Sometimes it was painful. Other times she lay there on the brink of excitement, only for him to roll off and mumble an apology. Then it became nothing. But on that last boating trip he had been considerate. He didn't once put her down and sometimes he'd tried to say something funny. The old anger had gone. She really thought they had at last reached that peace she'd been hoping for.

But then he changed again abruptly. They had been sailing off Fort Lauderdale when he came out with it. He said he was going back to Vietnam in the morning. Two weeks before his leave was over.

'What does that mean?' she had asked.

'Whatever you want it to mean.'

'Weren't we going to spend a week in Atlanta?'

'We were. We aren't now.'

He changed the subject then, and as he guided the boat into the port he suggested a teriyaki dinner. He told her how he saw things. How they'd live their own lives. How there was no need for a divorce. She could continue to live the way she had lived before. Stay at the beach house in Lauderdale and the ski lodge at Aspen. He hoped she'd start spending some of that money. Go back to school. Do anything. You like being busy, he'd said. Doing something is a way of life for you. You've always done it, but without me. The marriage had been over for years, he'd said. He suddenly turned arrogant. He didn't let her answer. Said he'd leave that very night if she persisted. He wasn't going to talk about the separation any more.

He had talked a lot that last time. More than he had ever done before. She got drunk that night and he was gone before she woke. He'd never called her nor sent any messages with anyone.

She lay there and thought of what had been and then the telephone rang. The man's voice introduced himself as Colonel Mike Carter, US Air Force.

'Thank you for waiting,' the voice said. 'I make it three o'clock. I believe we have an appointment.'

She said she was coming down and hung up. Suddenly she was glad to leave the room. It looked smaller than it had before. The sun had gone from the window.

Mike Carter was waiting for her by the lift. He was a short man, that was all she noticed.

'Shall we go to the coffee shop, Colonel Carter?'

'Perhaps you'd like to go for a drive?'

'I've been out on the town all day. Why don't we just....'

'It might be better if we went somewhere ... er ... private....'

'Very well then.'

They walked towards the door. The whole hotel staff seemed to be there. A black limousine stretched by the kerb. The porter opened the door and they got in. Carter pressed a button and the glass partition rose, separating them from the uniformed driver.

'What's the mystery, Colonel Carter?'

'It's about your husband....'

'Yes. I figured it was. What about my husband?'

'He's missing in action.'

'Missing?'

'Yes. He was brought down by a missile. The plane exploded on contact.'

'Did he....'

'No parachute was sighted.'

'I want the truth. You can be open with me.'

'He's MIA, Mrs Wayne-Turner.'

'You must have more.'

'We have no more information.'

'You said no one saw his parachute, right?'

'That's correct.'

'Come on, what do you think happened? I won't quote you. There's no need to prolong this.'

'It's difficult to imagine he'd have survived that.'

'He's dead, then. Is that what you are saying?'

'He is missing. Presumed dead. Yes, that is what I'm saying.'

Marge had nothing more to say. The quick questions she had fired at him had drained her. She didn't expect that. Anything but that. Did he say he was sorry? He might have done. Don't they usually say something like that? Isn't there a cable from the president? Did she hear right? Yes she did. He did not say it officially, but he believed this was it. The man had said Clay was presumed dead. Death is more than a word. It's a new situation. A state that changes everything. And yet in the silence that spread through the limousine, it seemed to her nothing was going to be any different. In all her thoughts about the future there was their daughter, her mother, the places they'd lived in. Never Clay. It was a strange time for him to die. She'd always thought of him as someone who was going to live forever, like the moon and just as remote.

The traffic outside was heavy and the car moved slowly. The windscreen wipers fought heavy raindrops. They crawled towards the Place de la Concorde. The Colonel was talking about the hows and wheres and whens of Clay's last flight. Marge heard nothing.

'Did he . . .?'

The man looked at her face. His eyes tried to anticipate the second part of the question, but her face was blank. He thought she simply forgot what she was going to say. Carter had been on this sort of mission before. People's reactions were never the same. Some screamed, others sobbed quietly or tried to keep a brave silent posture. There was always some reaction, but the woman beside him did not react at all. The madonna-like expression on her attractive open face was unchanged. She was looking straight through him. As if he wasn't there. As if he hadn't told her a thing.

What a strange little man this officer was, she thought. His contorted face showed concern while his eyes remained nonchalant. He didn't look particularly striking in any way. Must have come up through the ranks. Perhaps his rank was temporary. A rank required for an attaché. This was no leader of men. But then he wasn't there in the car with her for that. He could be as dull as he wished. He was a mouthpiece for Clay's destiny, that was all.

'Is there anything I can do for you?' he asked.

'I don't think. . . .' There was no need to offend him. 'I don't know, Colonel Carter. . . .'

'Call me Mike,' he said and regretted it.

'Thank you,' she said, not aware of her words. 'I'm Marge.'

It was a strange occasion for that familiarity, Mike thought. He should have stuck to his official voice. But nothing seemed to bother her. There were no tears in her green eyes. Her high cheeks were dry. Something unreal was happening to him. He felt no commiseration or sympathy for her. Only lust. Crazy. He must have been going out of his mind. Her shape, clearly floating through and out of her elegant dress was doing things to him. An eerie sensation came upon him as he looked at her. Her long legs stretched forward. She did not look lost or lonely, but he wanted to put his arms around her. He must have been mad. He was a selfish, insensitive bastard. How dare he? But all he could think of was how he would carry this woman off somewhere. Like a caveman. He was having a nightmare. Drops of sweat appeared on his brow below his hairline. He turned away and looked out of the window. Her vibes harassed him still. He fought to regulate his erratic breath. Outside, the rain hit the car with a harsh, deafening clang.

CHAPTER EIGHT

'Why you no drink?' Captain New slobbered. 'You no drink all night. This here genuine stuff. No imitation. Bourbon. Best drink in the world. I love bourbon after America visit.'

'No thanks, Captain.'

'You no mind I do, right?'

'You go ahead. You live pretty good here.'

'Sure we do. We have all whisky and cigarettes we want. Village people hide everything when VC come. Pretend to be poor. Here, have more food. Fruits maybe?' The Captain's voice was as shaky as his hands.

'Thanks. I've had all I can take.'

'I take you back to base personal. After tomorrow. Maybe before end of week. We have jeep back then sure. You relax now. Great honour to have you here our guest. God bless America. America is saving us and we sure appreciate. I never dream I can protect big American brass in my village. Farmers will remember, too. They will make songs about you long long after you go.'

'Are you originally from this village?'

'Sure. Born here. Best boy in village. You ask farmers yourself. Only boy make officer. I get all farmers need here. Put paper money in bank and bring corned beef and cigarettes from canteen. Gold from Chinese dealers in Saigon.'

'They are lucky to have you.'

'Sure. You lucky too. If you come to bad village, they kill you quick sticks no questions. I bring you to base pretty soon, right?'

'We should get some sleep.'

'How's about bourbon nightcap?'

'No thanks.'

The Captain got up. He led Clay to a nearby hut. He didn't stay long beyond showing him the mattress. There was a bucket of water by the door. A heap of cans and boxes were thrown all over the floor. Bowls of fruit and rice. It looked like a store.

'This food if you get more hungry. Good night, sir,' Captain New said.

'Good night.'

Clay lay down and stretched. He looked out at the stars. He was dog tired, but he had to do something now. To sleep and wake and be taken back to where he had started from was impossible. A man cannot come back from the dead. Perhaps they'd had a funeral service for him in his absence. There, at the corrugated steel chapel at the base. They would have informed Marge, too, by now. He had crashed three days ago. Or was it four? It didn't matter anyway. He could not go back. That was clear.

Images of people and places flew through his mind. All the care he had taken to destroy any record of his flight was useless. In his room they would find his clothes and his papers and credit cards. Maybe more. Maybe he had been careless about that too. Maybe they had dug the briefcase out of the wreckage. He had to get out of here this very night. The briefcase in the plane would prove useful to them. It would tell them things. Oh how he'd taken care to collect all the rubies and sapphires and those diamonds. The gold coins and the cash. The little treasure he had assembled could buy him a passage out of Vietnam into anonymity. He remembered every detail. How he bought each bit. How much he'd paid. How each little item brought him closer to his goal. To freedom. But all that was buried somewhere, testifying to his failure.

He smiled to himself. Proceed with the original plan.

Remember the target means everything. Had he been too arrogant to plan an alternative? What was he going to live on? There was that money in Lucerne, Switzerland. At the bank by the lake. The thought of it made him chuckle in the dark.

He could get to the Gulf of Tonkin, but how? Walk, that's how. He was in no hurry. Get there by sea. Pass as someone else. That's it. Buy someone's papers. A dead GI maybe. He should have thought of that when he was with the Vietcong. Steal. Then go. But where was he, anyway? He tried to bring to mind an aerial map of the country. Get Captain New to co-operate. Sell him a story of sorts. The man would do it. He was greedy enough. Still, he was no fool. And he wanted to be a hero. No, no, no. Captain New was hell-bent on taking him back to his base. Captain New did not believe in American desertion. The word shook him, but then he wasn't a deserter. He was dead. He had to think again. He was wasting time lying there like a stuffed animal. The woman. The woman would know where they were. Bernadette.

He got up and walked to the door and stretched. The cool air filled his lungs. It was almost sweet. There was no moon and no human voices. There were crackles of embers and crickets. He'd eaten far too much. The woman. That's where he'd go to first. What exactly he'd do when he got there he wasn't sure of. She was a gook, but she hadn't been that bad to him. She had shared her food with him in the hills. And she had listened. He missed that.

She must be hungry, he thought. And then he remembered the cans and food the Captain had left in the hut for him. He stopped and doubled back to the hut. He looked through what was strewn all over the floor and then searched inside a large tea chest. There were cans of meat and biscuits and bottles and molten Hershey bars. There was a large kitbag by the door and Clay threw all he thought he could carry into it. He lifted the bag over his shoulder. It seemed incredibly heavy, but he did not stop to investigate. He took a deep breath to overcome an impending panic and stepped out into the shadows. He walked fast. He knew where. The Captain had pointed out the place to him earlier.

A sleeping man sprawled outside her door, his gun slumped against the wall. The man did not move as Clay unlocked the heavy wooden bolt. The door creaked open. There was a dark void inside the hut, but he could hear her breathing. The bag was unbearably heavy and he dropped it to the floor as he walked in. He felt sure no one could hear. There was a strange elation within him now. He had managed to get thus far. No one had seen him. Perhaps his luck was turning.

'Bernadette,' he whispered. 'Bernadette.'

She did not answer. The stench inside was sickening.

'Bernadette.' Had he got her name wrong? Shapes began to form in the dark and his eyes found her. She looked like a frightened ghost as she sat up, staring at him from her corner. She did not believe her ears. The American was whispering her name. She had slept for a while, or had fainted, but the hunger kept bringing her to. She had expected someone to come in, but not with a whisper and certainly not him. Her blood froze. There had been fear in her all day and half the evening and now, with his appearance there was shock. What could he possibly want with her now? He had won. He was with his friends. Was he going to rape her? Maybe he knew of her time in the back streets. It must have been written all over her face. She could never have hidden it. She shivered. Into her mind came grey, cold, oppressive walls. She was back in the convent, and alone.

'Bernadette,' she heard him say, 'wake up.' There was urgency in his voice. She nodded, but he did not see her clearly. 'Bernadette!'

'I'm here,' she said quietly. 'I'm awake. What do you want?'

'I've got some food for you.'

'I can't eat now.'

'You've got to eat.'

'I'll be sick if I do. Please don't force me.' Her voice sounded so different now. The hardness had gone from it. She sounded like a little girl.

'What have they done to you?' She detected compassion in his whisper. Perhaps it was a trick, but she was too numb to be suspicious. She could not talk. She broke into a sob. 'Are you okay?'

He leaned forward and touched her shoulder. She didn't answer.

'Let's get out of here, Bernadette. No time to cry now.'

What was he saying? She was so confused. Her will power was dead. What could he possibly want with her here, now?

'Come on, lady, let's go,' he heard his voice command. It was unexpected, but it was the right thing to say. The right thing to do. The clarity of his mind and vision astounded him. Yes. He'd take her with him. Alone he'd have no chance at all. He needed her. She knew the countryside. She knew how to find food. She would guide him to some border. Laos or Cambodia or Thailand. Or the sea. He would then let her go back to her people. Or kill her if need be. Taking her with him would save him time and buy him distance. Then he'd let her go back.

And then it came to him, clear as a bell. She might not know it, but she couldn't go back either. What had happened there had meant failure. Neither of them could go back. They had only each other to rely on. The comfort of mutual failure.

Peace had come to Clayton Wayne-Turner. Right there, with hardly any time on his hands to fathom it. He knew his mind. He tapped her shoulder. 'Come on, Bernadette. Get up. If we don't go now, we'll never make it.'

She felt in a daze, but she obeyed. She got up. He lifted the heavy kitbag up and led her out. By the door, Clay collected the guard's gun. He picked up a spare magazine from the ground and stuffed it into his belt. He would hardly be able to walk with the load he was carrying. He turned and handed the weapon to her.

'Why are you giving this to me?'

'I can't carry it all. Take it. Now let's go.'

'Where are we going?' she asked.

'I don't know. Away from here, that's for sure. We'll work something out once we're back on top of that hill again.' His phosphorus watch told him it was eleven o'clock. The village would sleep for a long time yet. They started for the hill.

The quick, light footsteps in the dry grass behind them made her stop. She saw the shape of a dog that had followed them from the village. She started walking again, then looked back. He seemed a friendly animal who tried to come closer every time she halted, then changed his mind and kept his distance. His quick breath was comforting. As long as she could hear it, she knew there were no people about. They got to the top of the hill and Clay stopped and consulted the stars.

'What now?' she asked.

'You let me do the thinking,' he said and smiled. 'You have the gun, haven't you? You can stop me anytime you want to.'

CHAPTER NINE

— ■ —

She was tired and hungry and what had happened had weakened her spirit. All she could do was walk behind him and keep up and try to listen to what he would say. The absurdity of it was lost to her for now. In a strange way, she felt safe. Her bewilderment had subsided. Perhaps there was reason to be content. More than anything, she needed someone to look up to again. Someone she could trust. Someone who'd tell her what to do.

His face seemed invincible. His tiredness and doubts had vanished. He had never been as sure of his step as he was at that moment. He decided on a south-easterly direction that would lead them to the coast. No one was going to follow them there. Captain New would assume that if she had gained the upper hand, she would make her way to the north. It was a long shot, but the coast held infinite possibilities. He'd heard somewhere that the war had hardly touched the small fishing villages.

Clay had always felt comfortable near the ocean. And they might find a boat going somewhere. If they were seen, he could always say he was a member of a crashed bomber crew. Or something. Near the coast he would encounter only civilians or older people who had little to do with the war. People who were not too conversant with military procedure. They'd believe anything he'd tell them. They were interested only in survival and the black market. They would never be able to tell he was a deserter. They didn't even know what a deserter was. And if they did, it wouldn't mean the same thing to them. To run away from war had been a way of life in this part of the world forever. They were survivors. Not deserters.

Deserter, he murmured to himself. Deserter, he repeated. The sound of the word planted horror in his mind. It refused to leave. It pushed his feet forward and he began to walk at speed. He didn't look in her direction, but he knew she was there. Deserter. Was he a deserter? Of course he was not. He was taking a break from his own life to look into his soul and balance it out. Anyway, a deserter was something other people called you. And according to the Pentagon's list he was a dead man. His file was closed and the dead cannot be deserters. Mostly they are heroes. He was free. He didn't need to explain anything to anyone. Didn't need to fill out reports. Didn't even need to explain the girl's presence. By the time they reached the coast he would either send her back home or think of something. They walked on in silence.

Hours passed. To the east, the night was folding away. The darkness lifted and the hills were graced with a pink halo. They would avoid the roads and find a place to hide once the sun was up. Above them the breeze blew the remaining clouds to the horizon. It was going to be a hot, clear day. Soon he'd need to talk to her. Explain things to her. Tell her why he did what he did. He'd need to pump her for information. Where they were. How far the ocean was. He knew so little about her, he thought. Slowly the hills gave way to level ground and rice fields. There would be people ahead.

She spoke first. 'We should not be walking in daylight.'

The dog came running towards him as soon as it heard her voice. It was a brown Chinese dog with a bear's face. The open maw made him seem to be smiling. Clay couldn't help smiling back at the animal who was sniffing him out as though making sure he could be trusted. He was larger and fluffier than Clay had thought. His vertical tail shook hesitantly. He was a well fed dog, but despite his corpulence he was agile. Clay tried to stroke his thick, friendly head but the dog jumped away playfully at each attempt.

Bernadette was amused. The big man was trying to make a friend. 'You like dogs?'

'Come on, hang that gun over your shoulder and walk with me. Not behind me.'

'Why?' she asked and came towards him. They were facing each other.

She was tall for a gook, he thought. She wasn't ugly at all. 'It might not be clever to look like enemies.'

'Country people do not walk side by side. Especially if one is a man and the other a woman. Not even when they are married. We don't look like we belong together.'

'What do you mean?'

'There is no equality here. You either lead or you are led. Walking together won't change the social order here.'

'Don't preach any of your red crap to me.'

'I was only trying to give you some advice. If we walk together, people will know something is wrong.'

'We could be lovers.'

'Don't be ridiculous.'

Her harsh voice was back. And her suspicion. Enduring his conversation was only a form of payment for saving her last night. He needed her as a guide. He wanted nothing to do with her. No one who knew her would. He was using her. Spoils of war. She had the gun and soon, somewhere, there would be food. She could easily kill him then. The world could do without the likes of him. Not long ago, she remembered, he'd wanted to die. It was no sin to kill a man who wanted to die. True, he did exhibit some humane touch toward the dog, but then she was less than a dog in his eyes. And yet he did save her life. She mustn't allow her spirits to sag again. She'd pull herself together. Play it all by ear.

'All right,' she said, 'I'll walk with you, if that's what

you want.'

Clay looked at her. Her voice sounded totally French. Strange, that accent coming out of that face and in the middle of nowhere. Perhaps she was mocking him. He'd soon put her in her place and yet ... and yet her eyes had a haunting quality that took some of his old poison away. Her high cheek-bones appeared as she shook her hair. She was beautiful, really. Her voice was deep and dreamy. His imagination was taking off. He had to remember who she was. A gook and a commie. Half French or not. She was riding with him for a time, that was all.

'You must be starving,' he said, 'but I figure we'd better put some more mileage in.' She nodded and they walked on.

The sun was up and the heat of the day began to dry the dew off the greenery. It would soon be sweltering. They had to get off the rice before they could stop. They walked side by side and didn't talk. He wanted to say something, but her gaze seemed far away. He thought of what he had told her that first day. The confessions he had made. That had made him feel as if his past life had come out of his system with his own words. His mother's drinking and his perplexity at Marge's rejection of him did not pain him now. If he could only talk to her about his plan. Tell her what made him take off that day. Tell her where he was going. Just explain.

He wasn't explaining anything to her. He needed to hear himself talk about it, that was all. Talk it out of himself like he did the rest. Maybe he was going mad. People would have said that had they known what his intention had been. Perhaps he was, but he had never felt better. He'd have to tell her everything at some stage. Tell her before he was found out. Before she asked. The pressure of his obligation tightened around him as they walked.

Then they reached a big tamarind tree that was in full bloom and spread like a canopy over the grass.

'Let's sit down here in the shade,' Clay said. 'The rice field is far back there. No one will come. We'll eat. I've got stuff in the bag.'

As they sat down, Bernadette held on to the gun. The dog looked at them both as if it understood the suspicion in the air. It hesitated, making sure they were going to stay where they were. Far up above, a formation of bombers flung long white lines along the sky on their way back from the north.

CHAPTER TEN

From his hammock, Captain New saw the planes through a pair of aching eyes. May the Buddah bless America, he thought to himself. The reds must have got another well-deserved pounding. His eyes were heavy and as the bombers disappeared across the tree tops he shut his eyes again. There was no need for him to wake yet. He recalled the reason for his heavy head and he smiled. He stretched his square torso as far as he could. It was surely early still. His American guest would still be asleep. He'd looked so tired. This was Sunday and in America everything stops on Sundays. He'd instil the same custom in the village once the war was won. His head felt like lead and he sighed and thought he'd sleep a little longer. Perhaps his pounding head would go away. Soon, as the remainder of last night's bourbon made him drowsy, he started snoring again.

The villagers were up and busy clearing debris and sorting out usable bits. Their treasure, the gold bars, was safe. Couldn't be safer. They were in the hut with the big

American himself. Their Captain New had told them so last night and he was their hero. He was their main contact with the outside world. It would take time to build the village again, but then all the materials were right there, provided by the Buddah and their forefathers' spirits. There was no hurry. The rice was not ready yet and the pigs, the chicken and the fruit trees could look after themselves in the valley. There was plenty of food. Captain New had seen to that. He'd sent a truckload only days before.

Through a layer of coconut branches, the sun nibbled at the centre of the village. Captain New heard a large fruit hit the ground. The thump sounded near and it woke him. His head was heavy still, but clear. That was another sign from the creator. He craved the cool white liquid of a coconut. He rolled off his hammock and clapped his hand. In a moment, a coconut was handed to him, ready and open, a straw sticking out of its top. He would deal with his guest as soon as he'd had his drink. No sound came from the American's hut. Perhaps he should see the woman first. A little interrogation would be fun, he chuckled. His batman stood to attention while he gulped the liquid down. At length he was finished and the batman handed him a paper tissue.

'Bring the woman,' he barked. His voice sounded clean and crisp and he knew for sure that all the alcohol had gone from his blood. 'Hit her if she gives any trouble. Hit her anyway. But keep her conscious.'

He started for the American's hut, walking slowly. He got to the door and stood back. No sound came from inside. Perhaps the American was still sleeping. He shrugged his shoulder and lifted his fist to tap the door. Then he heard the scream. He turned.

'She's gone, Captain,' the batman shouted. 'She isn't there.'

New pushed the door open. The light streamed in, revealing that the hut was empty.

'What the hell is going on? Are there reds in this village? Someone we don't know about?'

'Maybe they came back in the night.'

'What happened to the watch? Get the people over here. I want an immediate search in every corner. The American was snatched away from under our own roof. You're all crazy. You're all dead. I'm going to shoot every one of you.'

He slammed the door and walked back to his hammock. He had to think. This was impossible. Others raced into the hut. There were gasps. One of the village elders came running to him. He tapped his arm.

'Captain, sir. . . .'

'Leave me now. I'm busy.'

'The gold is gone.'

'What are you talking about?'

The old man's head was shaking. 'The gold bars, Captain. All
four of them...gone.'

'I should have kept myself awake. You people are useless.'

'The American has taken it.'

'Don't be stupid, you old fool. The woman has taken it. She took the American too. She and her accomplice. Someone we all know. We'll have to have a count. See who is missing.'

'Vietcong have no use for gold, Captain. Only food and arms and ammunition.'

'You are mad. Of course they have. They can get any quantity of food and guns and shells in the black market. Gold, you stupid old man, gold buys everything. This is why I've been collecting it all these months.'

The others stood in silence. They had never heard their Captain talk to a village elder that way. The batman motioned to them to go away, but no one moved.

'We have no Vietcong among us. You know that, Captain.'

'They are everywhere,' Captain New screamed. 'Get me the Sergeant right away. Get the jeep. Start counting the people.'

The batman stood to attention. 'We are stuck, sir,' he said. 'We will never catch up with them on foot. The Sergeant has taken the jeep. It won't be back for days.'

Captain New slapped the batman across his face. Something strange had happened here during the night. Why did he have to get drunk? What if some harm had come to the American?

'Who gave the Sergeant permission to leave?'

'You did, sir,' the batman said. 'He's newly married, sir, remember? Don't you worry. He'll be back very soon. Then we'll take the jeep and go after them.'

'What are you talking about? That bastard is always late. I gave him three days. He'll take a week if I know him. God knows who he's showing off to. I'll have him shot for desertion.'

'What about the gold bars?' the village elder asked.

'Don't worry about the gold. Have a count of the people, I said. The woman couldn't have done this by herself. Others were involved. And bring the man who guarded her to me right now. And don't panic.'

His own private American had been kidnapped, he thought sadly. And he was going to make the grade with that man. They would have decorated him. He would have become a major overnight. Or more. His pictures in the papers. Medals. An audience with the president. He was going to show them all. Why did he have to give the

Sergeant three days off?

He was angry and confused and with it he started to feel despondent. There was nothing he could do for now, but he hated waiting.

'Get me a drink,' he hollered at the batman. 'I must think. You get the bottle now and open it and pour it into my throat and keep pouring it until the jeep is back here. Understand?'

CHAPTER ELEVEN

'We should be going,' Bernadette said. 'The Captain will be after us.'

'We've got plenty of time. He won't be leaving yet. He'll need to sober up. He got very drunk last night.'

'He's slept if off by now. It's late.'

'He won't be coming after us on foot. He will have to wait for his jeep. It'll be a few days. He told me he sent it off somewhere.'

They had just finished their lunch. The dog got a share of the corned beef and the crackers, but still kept its distance.

Bernadette got up. 'We should be going.'

'Take it easy, Bernadette. You are nervous and tired. You get some sleep. Regain your strength. We have a long way to go.'

'I am not tired.'

'I am. There's no shame in being tired.'

'We can't both sleep at the same time.'

'We're quite safe where we are. No one is looking for us yet. You aren't planning to leave without me, are you? Come on, lady, we do have a little lead here. Let's get some rest while we can.'

They sat there under the tamarind tree, looking at each other. Why was he so condescending? He looked much younger than she'd remembered. His eyes had a childish sparkle in them, or was it cockiness? Should she try and get word to her people? To Ming Ho? This man was naïve. He was easy prey. What sort of woman would cheat a man out of his freedom when he'd just saved her life?

Things were easier before. Less than twenty-four hours earlier, the borders between them were clearly defined. He was an enemy and an invader and a pig and she could act without any qualms. Now they were together and still she wasn't sure of him. How could she be? He'd let her hold the gun. But that was because he didn't think she had it in her. She would commit a crime against a fellow human being if she betrayed him now. She looked at his eyes again. There was trust in them. She was tired. She must not make any decisions now, yes, of course she must. If he was an enemy, she must shoot him. Or else join forces with him. Stay with him and even protect him against whatever he was running from. He had obviously not been afraid of her or her comrades. Nor had he been afraid of the southern army officer. He might have been an American flyer, but he was brave and vulnerable and kind in his own way.

This field was no whorehouse in Saigon. The man who sat opposite her had given her her life and a gun. He wasn't like those white skinned people in the rented rooms she hated. Yes he was. They were all the same. No, she wasn't going to kill him now, for whatever reason. She was too tired to kill anybody.

She sat down and leaned backwards. Clay pulled the bag along the grass and placed it behind her back. She picked up a dry tamarind pod and opened it. She took out the seed and sucked it. The taste brought her childhood back.

'Would you like a natural sweet?' she asked softly.

'Only if it ain't fattening. I'm on a diet. Sure I'll have one.' They laughed. 'Nice to meet you, Bernadette,' he said and she knew he'd meant it. She handed a few seeds to him and he sucked them. The bitter-sweet taste was pleasant. He lay back and looked at the thick trunk. Then he turned to her.

'We're stuck, aren't we Bernadette?'

'What do you mean?'

'There's no way out.'

'You can go anywhere. The country is full of your people.'

'No I can't.'

'Why not?'

'Because I'm dead. I have been dead for years. I was never even born. You wouldn't understand.'

'You are an officer in the air force. Many of our people think you are their saviour. You saw what happened in the village? That captain would have carried you back to your plane on his back if he had to. He still would, if he catches up with us. It is I who is stuck. It is I who failed in my duty.'

'I told you you wouldn't understand.'

'Try me.'

'It's a long story.'

'You really can't go back to your people?'

'I don't really want to. I have planned this for a long time.'

'Planned what?'

'To get lost somewhere. Be like everybody else. Find out who I am.'

'You're Clayton Wayne-Turner. That's who you said you were.'

'I am not. That is the name they gave me, but I was born with another.'

'What do you mean?'

'I'm not any son of my parents. I was adopted, somewhere in Germany in 1935. I don't know what my real name is or who my real parents were. I intended to find that out before you people shot me down.'

'What difference does it make? You'll only get yourself all confused.'

'You may be right, but I couldn't be more confused than I am. I was brought up with a ready-made future. My career was planned for me. I was told my name would open every door I cared to touch. And boy they were right. It did. I sailed through a predetermined life like a knife through butter. I had justified every hope the family hung on me. Lived up to the great name. But then it ain't my name. It's all been one big fat lie.'

'They should have told you you were adopted when you were a child.'

'Maybe, but they didn't. They didn't care for me. That's why they lied.'

'Of course they cared for you. Maybe they were afraid you'd run away.'

'Perhaps. I don't know. Anyway, if we ever get out of this place, I'm going to Europe and there I'll find out who I am.'

'You are who you are, what your school and education and upbringing and career have made you. You are what your experience has been.'

'I want to know what I am, then. Whose son I am. What name they put on my real birth papers. Was my mother married? Is she alive? Did she ever wonder what became of me?'

'Maybe she needed to give you away.'

'Maybe she did, but I want to know. The Wayne-Turners only understand money. They must have bought me. Like a dog.'

'And you need to know that so badly you've decided to desert?'

'Desert. That bitch of a word again. Can't a man be free? Do you know what it's like to be pushed along a defined route mapped out for you by a committee? Be told where you're going and for how long and where you get off without ever being told why? I was a good little boy. I always tried to please them. And all the time they lied. Sometimes I wake up in the night and I feel I am falling down a void, do you understand? A package of meat dropping into nowhere. Without a sign post anywhere. I began to think crazy. Do crazy things. I should not have been where I was. I could damage others if I went on. Sometimes I want to live and sometimes I want to die. I am not a deserter. I've told you. I'm dead. Dead, you understand?'

His voice was aggressive, but his eyes cried. He was hiding his confusion. He reminded her of herself. She must be mad. She wanted to stroke his hair. All about them the afternoon was peaceful. The Chinese dog found himself a corner in the shade and dozed off.

'When did you find out ... how?'

'Oh some five years ago. First my mother told me. No, she didn't tell me. She cursed me for something and I said I wished she weren't my mother and then she yelled you ain't my son, sonny boy or something. I thought she was drunk then and she was, but that didn't matter. I didn't really believe her then. I was too busy pretending to live happily ever after with my wife and the air force and then, two months ago, my mother died. I flew home for the funeral. A day later the family lawyer came to see me. We locked ourselves up in my grandfather's old office and we talked. He told me my mother had come to see him shortly before she died. She gave him a sealed envelope for me.

Told him not to ask me what it contained. She made him swear he wouldn't. It must have been during one of those rare sober days she sometimes had. The lawyer told me about the shares and the money and the land and everything and then he handed the envelope to me. The back was sealed with wax and a half dozen signatures she smeared on the back. I started to open it, but the lawyer said he would take his leave first. Didn't want to be there when I opened it. He said he gave his word.'

'It was a short letter. Lucid, though. In it she told me in no uncertain terms that I had been adopted. She asked my forgiveness for not telling me before. Said in her youth it wasn't the custom. It didn't matter, she said, because no one knew. Only her and my father. And my father was killed in the war. I read the letter again and again. Kept it on me wherever I went, night or day. Then one day I burned it. I thought she'd been right, that it didn't matter. Nothing had changed. I inherited the name and everything that went with it. But then, as soon as the letter was gone, my problems started. I had lost my peace. My sense of purpose gave way to confusion. I lost interest in everything. I began to have nightmares. I'd get blackouts. Dangerous when you're supposed to be a pilot. I began to think of running away from myself. To find myself. Aren't I a scream?' He seemed on the verge of tears, Bernadette thought. 'Why didn't you go and see someone...a doctor...a....''

'A shrink you mean? No. I couldn't do that. They would have retired me out of the air force. Believe me, a shrink would have decided I was mad. Because I was mad then. I started hallucinating about things. Called people by names that weren't theirs. Made a few real booboos in flight planning and stuff. Luckily there wasn't much action, so no one got killed. I knew I would have real problems on a serious mission. I took a few trips to Bangkok. Screwed myself to death downtown. Walked down the road talking to myself. I tell you, I was going mad.'

'Couldn't you talk to someone? Your wife? Anyone?'

'I have never been a great talker. Silent Clay they used to call me. Thought I was a snob. Maybe I was, but I suppose I was just a tortured soul without knowing it. I hid it all behind a wall of arrogance. Maybe it's got something to do with being adopted. I don't know. I began to float. Then, about a month ago, it came to me. I had no life, right? I didn't get on with the only woman I really wanted. I was no good for the air force anymore. I figured I'd fake my own death. Take time off. Disappear without a trace. I started to plan this. Used every bit of concentration on the plan. The planning was keeping me sane. And then I took off. Now I've screwed up real good. Your people shot me down. I can't go back anywhere now. I wouldn't even if I could. I'd go nuts.'

'You have children?'

'A daughter, but I haven't been much of a father to her. At first she was too little and I was away and then this business came up inside me and I lost interest. Sometimes I forgot she existed. By cancelling my own life out, I cancelled hers, too. It's selfish, I know. I can't help it. I keep telling myself it will all be better when I find out.'

'What do you want to do? Die and disappear and find out whatever it is you are looking for, then come back again as if nothing has happened? Couldn't you talk to your wife? Your friends?'

'I have no friends. My wife won't listen. Maybe she's afraid of me. I don't understand her and she would never understand me. She married my name, not me. Christ, I am talking too much.'

'I don't mind. You said we have time.'

'It's not fair to you. And I'm tired now.'

Her heart went out to him. How could she have been so selfish? She didn't have a worry in the world. He needed her. More than anyone ever did. Not just as a guide. There was something worthwhile for her to do now. A personal cause she could excel in. He made her think of the little children she had cared for years before in the convent. She stretched her arm and touched his head. He recoiled.

'Don't do that,' he said.

'Are you afraid?'

'I'm not very good with intelligent ladies,' he said. 'You feel sorry for me, I know. Please don't do that. I have only one thing on my mind. To find a way out of here and then, you know, sort things out. There's no room in my life for anything else just now.'

'And what if you fail?'

'I'll be dead, that's what. But never you mind. Let's sleep a bit now. We can stay here until evening. We're better walking at night.'

He lay down and closed his eyes. He thought nothing could ever be the same again. The tree and the shrubs and the grass melted into the shadows. The world slept somewhere and it took them there too.

CHAPTER TWELVE

———◾———

Howard Jelinek pulled the main sheet in closer. The boom was almost above the centre of the deck. The boat heeled over sharply as its long keel cut through the South China Sea. The foresail was not quite where it should have been, but the craft moved fast enough. The last leg from Manila had been slow until now since the winds had been late in arriving. The water had been calm all week and the fresh breeze that had started earlier that morning was a welcome change. He might not make it on this tack, but taking a general south-westerly direction he would hit the coast within thirty-six hours. Maybe less.

Howard set the automatic pilot and settled down to continue mending his storm jib. He was not very good at sewing. His large hands and thick strong fingers got in the way. But this would have to do for now. The sailmakers in Manila were not available because of some local holiday. As he pushed the heavy needle into the canvas, he hoped he wouldn't need that sail again before he landed.

His destination and the purpose of his solo trip lay in the long strip of land beyond the horizon. He was getting close and in his mind's eye he could already see it all. How he'd announce the reason for his voyage all the way from Vancouver. How the journalists and television crews would swarm on to his wooden deck to hear him. He would tell them everything and they would spread the word of God.

Never in all his years as a lumberjack did Howard Jelinek forget his origins or his training. In his country of birth, his name was Horvac Jellinek, and before learning how to cut wood he had been trained as a man of God. But his innate call to adventure proved too strong for him to resist. He had always been convinced there was some other purpose, some mission to his life. When he left his native land for Canada after the war, he was guided by disappointment alone. His strong convictions, his energy and his curiosity propelled him into riches without the remotest intention. With his own hands he had built his first home on a large piece of land by the sea, overlooking Victoria Island. He was going to move in there himself, but that did not happen. A local realtor persuaded him to put up ten more houses on the same plot. That marked the beginning of his career.

In ten racing years, he had become one of the best known land developers in western Canada. If anybody had asked him then what his goals were, he would not have been able to answer. And yet, like the salmon's voyage back up the river to spawn before dying, there was a purpose. So he waited for God to see fit to reveal that purpose, and he worked hard while he waited.

He had never married and reached the age of forty-one still on his own. He had brought his love of the ocean from his landlocked native Czechoslovakia. Always a strong swimmer, Howard then took up sailing in the Bay of Vancouver. He enjoyed the peaceful hours on the water. The cool, clear air relaxed his enquiring mind. Somehow, he knew, all that was but a means to an end. A way to propel him, one day soon, to an unknown destination. Howard had always remained a deeply religious man and he waited for a sign.

It came one evening as he watched the nightly news. The story was about Vietnam. It occurred to him that while he was looking for new ways to enrich himself, people were being maimed and killed, and children were made to grow up alone. He had heard the name of that country before, but the next day he went to the library and looked for its whereabouts in the big atlas. That morning, as he sat in the library and read, a fire broke out in the building and he was urged to leave by the fire escape with the others. When he reached the ground, the building collapsed. No one was hurt. The sign he had waited for had been given.

Howard sold his company and all his properties. He moved into the Vancouver Hotel to plan the next step of his mission. What he had to do was clear. He had been preparing for that for years. He was going to Vietnam. By himself. By boat. What God wanted with him once he got there was still a mystery, but he knew the Lord would give him a clue when the time came. While his new boat was being built and the charts prepared, Howard read all there was about the sad divided country he was travelling to. He was profoundly shocked by what he had discovered.

The trip he was undertaking was ambitious. People had tried to talk him out of it. To cross the Pacific single-handed, they said, with hardly any sailing experience was madness. His knowledge of navigation was minute, they said. He'd get lost. But he had the boldness and the courage to do it. The most ferocious enemy of all, loneliness, did not threaten him at all. He would never be alone on the high seas with God at his side.

He had been sailing for twelve weeks and three days through variable seas, but he had witnessed only one storm. On one occasion, he took a swim alongside the boat which rolled lazily with the waves. He had to climb the ladder hurriedly having spotted a big fish nearby. It turned out to be a dolphin, but he took no more chances after that.

The needle broke in his hand, entering his palm. Howard sucked it, looking for blood, but it was only a small scratch. He folded the sail into its bag and went down into the cabin to have his breakfast. He ate a hearty meal. He would need all his strength. The great moment of truth was twenty-four hours away, or less if the wind prevailed.

After his coffee, he went up on deck again and scanned the horizon with his binoculars. The sea was calm and only a few spots of rippled foam revealed the presence of the wind that propelled him forward. God had made the seas large, he thought. During the weeks he had spent on the water he had not seen one other ship. He had been warned of pirates and cannon fire, but he was on the verge of the greatest adventure of his life so he paid no attention. Pirates were a thing of the past anyway, and the mines and warships he was told to watch for were nowhere to be seen.

Satisfied that all was well, he decided to rest for a few hours in the cockpit. He set his alarm clock and lay down, looking up at the wheel and the sails and the sky. He always slept better in the open air. The slight pitch dulled his thoughts into a dreamless sleep.

He was woken by the flapping of a loose sail and the sound of aircraft passing above. The bell went off at almost the same time. There were six or seven planes, big ones, flying high in a southerly direction. They must be bombers, he decided as he walked up to the bow. The jib needed changing since the wind had dropped somewhat. Howard set about replacing it with the larger genoa to catch more of the air. It was always a hard operation, but work had been his religion for many years. The sun seemed to be stuck in the middle of the sky, right above the mast. It was time for lunch, but he felt no hunger.

As soon as the giant foresail was winched up, Howard looked at the horizon. Right there, some fifty or sixty miles ahead, he could make out the hazy shape of mountains. The boat must have moved faster than he had expected. Perhaps he had miscalculated the distance to the shoreline. At this rate, he would touch land by midnight. His map did not help him much. With no known navigation beacons he would have to wait until he'd arrived to find out where he had landed. Hopefully he was far enough to the south not to hit North Vietnam. He could have used his radio to search for a base somewhere ahead of him, but he did not. That was best left to God. The military might stop him or make him turn back. And nothing was going to stop him now.

Howard felt refreshed. The sight of his destination

invigorated him and hunger came. He went below to cook himself a hot lunch. He always cooked his own food, a habit he had adopted after his mother died. He took great pains in preparing a meal and always laid the table in a neat fashion. Today's menu was canned salmon, corned beef, Filipino eggs and rice, and a can of asparagus. He would spoil himself today, he thought with a chuckle. He laid a can of peaches and some thick Carnation cream on the table. It was, after all, Sunday. A good day to arrive in a land the world had forgotten.

The wind picked up after lunch and Howard let the sails out to keep the boat from leaning too close. Soon the haze gave way to a clear view of the land. Evening was descending and the wind continued to blow. He was still making good time and the hours passed quickly. His excitement mounted. The sign would be coming soon. He wondered what method God was going to use. The thought of proximity to his creator always put him at ease. He sat by the wheel and his head fell forward.

He didn't know how long he had slept when he woke. And then the hesitant flicker of lights caught his eye. These were not electric lights. They were not powerful and must have been close. He did not expect any buoys or other guides for his entry. He would miss those since he had never landed anywhere without them. Perhaps he would come close enough to drop anchor. Wait until daylight before getting off the boat.

He turned on the mast lights. If someone was watching him from the shore, they would see him now. He went back to the cabin and turned the radio receiver on. No one was playing music tonight. Not even the high pitched, rhythmic singing he had heard the night before. It was ten o'clock. The coast was asleep. The fishermen would not sail out for a few hours. By that time he would be at anchor.

Then the touch of the wind died on his cheek and the sails started to flap freely. The boat hardly moved now. He began to take the sails down when he heard the engines and saw the boats. Four small craft, keeping close together, were coming out to sea some distance to port. Four oil lamps were clearly visible. They made the boats seem like a procession of candles. The water was as calm as glass and with all the sails down the boat stood still. He started his engine as soon as the boats went past him. The ship rolled as the engines pushed her forward. He prepared the anchor mechanism and went back to raise the Vietnamese flag. His own maple leaf fluttered proudly at the stern.

There were no more boats. The lights along the shore were scanty. This, he reasoned, must be a tiny village. He made out the shape of a small cove and sailed in there and dropped anchor. He turned the engine off and let the fenders out the side, then sat on the bowsprit to await the sun.

Chapter Thirteen

The dog woke them with an explosion of short, impatient barks. It was late afternoon and the heat of the day had evaporated. Bernadette sat up and straightened her hair. The gun, leaning against the thick tree trunk, seemed ugly and useless and without an owner. It ought to belong to another age, she thought. For the first time in many years, she wished she was somewhere else. Far from guns, fatigues and causes that did not seem to need her. Clay looked like a curious child looking for a new toy, as he tucked into the large kitbag. He couldn't be hungry still, she thought and then she heard him call out.

'What happened, Clay?' she asked. It was the first time she had thought of him as Clay. Why was she so trusting?

'Look,' he said. 'Look at this.' He jumped up with great excitement. He was holding a long, newspaper wrapped parcel in his hand. He peeled the paper off and showed her a gold bar. It glittered in the afternoon sun.

'Where did you get this from?'

'It's our ticket out of here, lady,' he said. 'We can buy a plane. There's three more of them in the bag. They were there all the time. Right at the bottom of the bag. No wonder it nearly broke my shoulder. Good thing I didn't tire of it during the night. I thought of dumping it a few times, I can tell you. It was only the food that made me keep it. This is my lucky day. Hey, we'd better go. We must have taken all they've got. They'll be after us now.' He put the bar back into the bag and looked about. 'Let's get out of here,' he said. 'We better take the gun too.'

She felt she was slipping again. It was the gun. Must have been. It was a source of tension between them. This time he noticed her face.

'I'll carry it if it's too heavy. I don't mind. With all that gold in here we can buy the world. You can go back to France.'

Why was he suggesting that? Why did he feel his gold and his gun gave him the power to dictate to her? No. No. It wasn't fair of her. Not even to think that. He was just being kind. Could she not tell the difference? Had she lost all her sensitivities? But why did he want to carry the gun? Was he wary of her intentions? There was little danger for him here.

'Let's go, lady,' he said. He stood before her, tall and proud and arrogant. He was using her. What a fool she was. She'd even begun to feel sorry for him. He turned to go, the gun slung over his shoulders. She didn't move.

'Let me carry it,' she said firmly.

Clay stopped. He turned and looked at her. Why did she want to do that? Didn't she trust him? Worse, should he suspect her? Was she going to kill him? No. He was being stupid. Surely she knew they were in the south and women carrying guns could only be VCs. Maybe she did intend to kill him before they ran into someone.

'No,' he said. 'I'm going to carry the gun and that's it.'

She sat down on the ground. The dog came back from wherever it had been. 'What's got into you?' Clay said. 'We can leave it here and put an end to this nonsense.'

'No, we can't.' The little girl was back in her eyes. This woman meant him no harm. Just an ego trip.

'You take it then, but stay close to me. If we meet any of your countrymen, you'll have to decide which side you're on.'

'I thought you said we were in this together.'

'I said . . . let's go, Bernadette. Let's go see what's behind that ridge.'

'Could be the sea,' she said.

'Christ, I hope it is.'

They scaled the landscape lightfooted and by late afternoon they had descended on to a little stream. The hills they had come down from were tucked away behind them. A small, thickly set forest surrounded the water. Clay left the bag on the bank, took his clothes off and jumped in. He kept calling her to join him. She hesitated, but then the child in her made her lay the gun down and she walked in, still dressed in her fatigues. They swam and they laughed and she thought the war had never been as he chased her to the water's edge.

They came out and lay in the clearing to dry. The Chinese dog watched them, then started barking. It ran out of the clearing and then they heard the footsteps. Clear sounds of breaking dry branches came from the trees. Clay grabbed the gun, motioned to Bernadette to stay where she was, and disappeared stark naked into the bush. Out of the trees, following the Chinese dog, three men appeared. But for the guns they carried, they could have been schoolboys. They came towards her. One stood over her while the other two went to the water's edge and washed their faces.

'Who are you?' he asked.

'My name is Bernadette,' she said. 'I'm a nurse. I am from Ming Ho's group. I am one of you.'

The young man laughed. He turned to his friends and shouted,

'Did you hear that? This foreign whore says she's one of us.'

'I am not a foreigner. I was born in Saigon and have been fighting the invaders for three years.'

'With what? With this bag? You don't even speak properly.'

Clay watched them from behind the shrubs. The laughter and the monotonous sound of the language hinted they were having a friendly conversation. But her face was drawn. She seemed frightened. 'What's in the bag?' the man asked.

'Food,' she said, 'and medicine.'

'Hand it over,' the man said. She shook her head. The young man kicked the ground and shouted something.

'Get it yourself,' Bernadette said quietly.

'Give it here, you foreign whore,' the man said. Clay felt the menace in his voice. He took aim, but he couldn't shoot. The man was too close to Bernadette. The others looked on.

The young man came forward and opened the bag. He looked inside. 'The whore is lying,' he shouted. He picked the bag up and threw it in their direction. 'Look for yourselves.'

The young man pulled his belt off, then his trousers. He came close to Bernadette.

'What are you doing?' the other man said. 'Just kill the bitch and let's get out of here. We're off course as it is.'

'We can stay a while,' the man said. He stood over her, his naked body aroused. He kicked Bernadette's shoulder and mounted her, screaming something.

Clay's angered frustration was tearing him to bits. Bernadette said something as the man tried to pull her clothes off. The others walked back to the water and watched in silence.

'Get his gun, Bernadette,' Clay screamed as he flew out of the bushes, his gun blazing. The two men fell where they stood by the water. The shots shook her into action. She did not think. She rose and lifted the gun from the ground as the man struggled to his feet. She pointed the weapon at him, but did not fire. Clay came closer, but the young man ran naked into the bushes. Clay hit the magazine and the gun came to life. He shot a burst after him, but the man was gone. Clay came to her side, gun in hand. His face was burning. She looked pale and frightened.

This cannot be happening, Bernadette thought with horror. The Chinese dog raced into the bushes after the escaping man, his incessant barking echoing back as Clay surveyed the scene. This is a nightmare, she thought. The young man's spent passion was visible on her shirt. She tore it off. She felt caught in a dream, but the two grotesque bodies lying intertwined by the water were real. Clay turned them over. The muddy faces were young. He opened their bundles and emptied their contents on the grass. Some grenades, a few books, two ammunition magazines and a length of turquoise material.

Bernadette got up and frantically wriggled out of her clothes. She ran to the water's edge and jumped in. She stayed there for a long time, scrubbing the dirt off her skin and crying softly. Clay waited by the edge, his hands holding the material out for her.

At last she came out. Clay came close and wrapped her body with the soft silk. It warmed her and he held her close while she sobbed uncontrollably. Clay looked at her. How beautiful she'd be with a decent dress on, he thought, forgetting his own nakedness.

'I'm sorry,' he murmured. Bernadette was crying still, crying for all the years she had spent proving she was worthy. She cried for her shame. All she was good for was her body. They all tired of her as soon as they had her trust. How long would it take this man to tire of her? All the men in her life had used her. The history professor had gone back to his wife. Ming Ho had brought her to this. She cried and she wanted to die. Her humiliation was final. All he could feel for her would be pity and people tire of pity. But this man's eyes showed concern. He stroked her hair and mumbled things into her ear. His eyes seemed content. She had to resist her acceptance of him. But why? Because it was all too quick. No, it wasn't. Hell could damn her if she was wrong. She had listened to him and what he had said showed he confided in her, and more. He had just saved her life for the second time.

All the way to the coast they kept looking over their shoulders. The man had gotten away and would surely seek help. Now her people would know where she had gone. Soon they would come after her. What would they do to her then? She would have to think about that, but events were moving too quickly for her to concentrate.

They reached the top of another hill as night fell. Below, far down in the darkness, they could hear and smell the ocean. They saw dim lights marking the shape of the coast.

'It's a port,' Clay said, 'a small one . . . there are always boats in a place like that, even if it's only a fishing village.'

'How long before we get there?'

'We could make it by midnight,' he answered. As he spoke, four quivering lights made out to sea, their reflections leaving strips of gold over the water. They headed in the direction of the lights, using them as a beacon.

Later, Clay saw a new set of lights appear in the water. The position and the colours of the lights made his heart soar. The vertical position they held told him they belonged to a mast. They clearly adhered to the standards for American sailboats. He heard a diesel engine running as he watched the craft come towards the shore. Had he been anywhere else in the world, he would have sworn that it was a pleasure craft coming to port after a day out. Walking where he was, down towards the South China Sea, Clay concluded that his eyes were playing tricks on his tired mind.

CHAPTER FOURTEEN

———◼———

The alien sound of an engine invaded his peace. Captain New rolled off his hammock and ran to the centre of the village. The jeep was back. It was a day early, maybe even two. It was surrounded by half the population who listened as the Sergeant talked about his new wife and her wonders.

'Where the hell have you been, you shit chewing rat? I'll ship you back to the front line where you'll soon learn how to use your rotten feet again. Which one of your whores were you trying to impress with my jeep this time? We've been waiting for days. Now get the hell out of this car and get some food. I'll give you five minutes to stuff your face and then we're off. Now get going.'

There was a relieved grin on the Captain's face as the Sergeant jumped out of the jeep. While they were feeding the man, Captain New conferred with the village elders. He was now sure to find his American guest and save him. He would bring the gold back too. The Sergeant had returned the jeep earlier than he dared hope for. The Buddah was smiling down on him still. He gave his people a pledge. He would recover their treasure and would not report back to his unit without it, war or no war. It was not the American who had taken it, it was the Vietcong woman, and she would die for it. Did they not trust his judgement? Was he not the best boy in the village, soon to be made major? Did he not always make good? They should leave it all to him.

The Sergeant finished his meal and came running back. The driver stood at attention by the side of the jeep which was now loaded with food and water. Captain New drank a last gulp of coconut water and climbed in. The Sergeant got into the back and tested the mounted machine-gun by shooting a string of bullets into the air. The villagers clapped their hands as the jeep took off with an impressive, dusty roar. The driver tried to say something, but the Captain told him to be quiet.

'Sir,' the driver tried again, 'this is...'

'You stick to driving and leave the talking to me.'

'But sir...'

'Shut your trap. You'll get plenty of time to talk to yourself when you're at the front, facing the enemy all by yourself.'

'Sir, I must insist on telling you that...'

'For the last time, you frog, shut your mouth or I'll shoot your tongue off.'

The driver looked at the mirror. He eyed the Sergeant who shrugged his shoulders.

By the time they reached the crossroads at the top of

the hill, Captain New had decided to go to the coast. The Vietcong woman wouldn't risk walking about the countryside with the American since she was alone. The Americans would know their man had been captured and their helicopters would be combing the fields. No, the bitch would take him to the coast, where she could get lost. Or steal a boat and take him north by sea. They did not make him captain for nothing, he thought to himself and smiled.

His revenge would be terrible, he swore quietly, and the reds would know all about it. His American guest, his pride and joy, was surely praying for him to catch up with them soon. A real John Wayne rescue mission. Such a success would make him an equal of the great military brains. Did they not sit at night together, exchanging views and solving the problems of the world? And the woman, that red whore, she was surely shivering at the thought of his mighty fist. His fame would spread far and wide and with this daring rescue he might be made colonel. The Americans knew how to look after their friends.

From the bushes by the roadside, a man staggered out, stark naked and dirty. The sight of him brought the Captain back to earth. It was mid-afternoon, and the man appeared from behind the haze, followed by a large Chinese dog. The dog looked familiar.

'Stop the car,' Captain New shouted. They came to a dusty halt and the young man came closer, covering his crotch. He looked frightened.

'Who are you? What are you doing here? Speak!'

The dog rushed up to the jeep, barking excitedly.

'He's from the village,' the driver said.

'Don't be stupid. I've never seen this man before.'

'The dog, Captain.'

'Shut up. Now young man, tell me what happened. Who did you see on the road? Where are your clothes?'

'I was attacked by a madman, an American. Could you spare a drink of water, sir?'

The man had shifty eyes which looked down at the ground. His face was pale and hairless. He looked like an intellectual. A student. His bare feet dug into the dust. He was frightened. He must have been a communist – all students were reds. Captain New got out of the car and stroked the dog's fluffy head.

'Water,' the young man begged.

Captain New let out a loud whistle. 'Open a can of beer for the man,' he told the driver. The young man moved forward and stretched his arm. 'Not so fast,' said Captain New. 'You talk first. You are not from these parts, are you?'

'No. I'm from Saigon. I'm a student. I have been walking for two days. No food or water.'

'You are a revolutionary.'

'I'm not. I was on a field trip with two of my friends. We're doing a paper on local flowers.'

'Flowers, eh? Tell me another.'

'Flowers, I swear to you.'

'Look here, friend. You said you were attacked by a mad American. Was he young, old, was he armed?'

'He was young. I couldn't say exactly how old. Maybe forty. He had a gun.'

'Was he being led by a terrorist woman?'

'He was with a half-caste woman. I don't know what she was . . . I can only tell you no one was leading him.'

'You are lying. I know the American. Of course he was her prisoner. Of course he was being led. Did you see the gold? How many bars were there?'

'Yes, I did see the gold. There were four bars. You see? I'm not lying. There were four bars, right?'

'I'm asking the questions here.'

'Well I saw four bars. The girl tried to hide them when

the foreigner came out of the bushes shooting. He shot my friends in cold blood. She did not move a finger to help. She tried to kill me. He was not being led. They were together.'

'Where are they now?'

The young man pointed at the coastal hills. 'Somewhere in a clearing up there. We went for a swim and he attacked me. He killed two of my friends. I think they are going to the coast somewhere. I don't really know for sure. I just ran. Can I have something to drink now?'

Captain New nodded. He pulled his pistol out of its holster and shot the young man in the ear. He fell without a word and his head hit the front wheel.

'Let's get out of here,' Captain New said. His eyes were angry. 'Start the car.'

'Sir,' the driver said, 'I must talk to you. Orders.'

'Orders? Only I give orders here. What orders? Talk then, you idiot, do you hear me?'

'I have been trying to tell you all day, Captain sir. The Colonel wants you back in the base by nightfall. He called me on the radio himself this morning.'

'Why didn't you call me?'

'You were asleep, sir. The jeep wasn't back. I was afraid to wake you. Anyway, sir, we better get going now. With all this running around, we'll never make it.'

Captain New was too enraged to listen. How could he have been so dumb? Never trust a man who doesn't drink. He would show the American bastard what gratitude meant. He'd cut him to pieces. What a blunder that was. Still, all was not what it seemed. What was he doing walking around with a Vietcong woman? Why didn't he wait to be taken back to his people? He was a spy. Well, maybe not a spy but a deserter for sure, or worse. He and the woman had conspired to rob the village. They turned up right after the bombing, didn't they? Anyway, if he was a deserter, his people would be looking for him. New would catch him and be a hero yet. A major. The American president would thank him personally. Well, maybe it was all different. Maybe the woman had forced him. Maybe the naked man had lied. He had to catch up with them and get to the bottom of things. He climbed back into the jeep.

'Drive to the hills there,' he barked.

'You better forget that sir, the Colonel said...'

'I didn't hear you. Neither did the Sergeant.'

The Sergeant came from his own village. He'd known him all his life.

'No, Captain sir. You did not hear him.'

'Why did I not hear him, sergeant?'

'Because he forgot to tell you about the Colonel's message. He never said a thing.'

'Drive on now,' Captain New said to the driver. 'We must catch them before tonight.'

The driver shrugged his shoulders, got into his seat and started the jeep.

'We'll get the man, the woman, the gold and some fish too. You do like fish, don't you motor mouth?'

He was trying to be funny, but just then a cloud of melancholy hit him and refused to leave. Captain New had always prided himself on knowing people. He dearly hoped he was wrong about the American. He sat there in silence and none of the others dared talk to him. In the dirt track behind them, the young man's body lay where it had fallen. His face was covered with flies. The dog barked, then sat by the young man's side to wait for him to get up and continue their journey.

CHAPTER FIFTEEN

———■———

Mike Carter called Marge from the lobby. They had been seeing each other every day for two weeks now. He did not pry into her relationship with Clay and never dug into her calm acceptance of his death. His even nature and simplicity had made her feel at ease. He was a pleasant man who knew the back streets of the city and every bistro. He was nice to have around. Marge had not asked him to come up to her room before, but now she said come on up as if it was the most natural thing in the world. Soon she heard him knock and said, 'Come on in, it's open.'

Mike's shape entered the doorway and she thought he looked larger than she'd remembered. The room was dark.

'Sorry I didn't come down,' Marge said. 'I was half asleep when you called. Will you pull the blinds for me, Mike? Make it slow.'

It was a personal, almost intimate request, but she felt she had known him all her life. He walked to the window and started to pull the cord.

'It won't make much difference, Marge. The sun isn't out today.'

She had fallen asleep while reading a Harold Robbins novel she had bought in the drugstore. She did not skip the explicit sexual encounters the main character was having. They had held a strange fascination for her, but the wine had sent her to sleep. She was only wearing a pair of panties under the covers and now the soft caress of the sheets aroused her skin. She felt a need and tried to suppress it as she had done over the years, but the tingle in her body held on. She was not sure why she had asked Mike to come into her room. It surely wasn't him who had made her feel that way. She should have asked him to wait. No, no. He was a friend.

Mike sat down and stretched his legs. He had wanted her from the first day, but had managed to keep it to himself. The news he had for her was shattering. He wasn't sure how to start. Outside, the sun came out from behind the clouds and a ray of fire burst onto her bed. The light accentuated the shape of her body. Her generous breasts heaved through the sheet. Lower down, he saw a mound that sent his mind flying. She was a three dimensional living sculpture and the scent that emanated from her set him on fire. Her curves were driving him to the point of pain. He was taken by a mad desire to tear off the sheet and kiss every inch of her body. He tried to concentrate on the reason for his visit, but the vision of his body entering hers refused to leave his mind. A faint smile appeared on her lips and then the clouds covered the sun again and her face was lost. He looked at her again. She seemed agitated. He should get out now, he thought and got up.

'I'll wait downstairs while you dress,' Mike said.

'No. Go lock the door,' she said resolutely.

Mike complied and returned to his chair. He saw her arms stretched towards him. 'We must talk,' he said. 'I have to tell you something.'

'Not now,' she heard herself whisper. What had come over her? Perhaps she was dreaming. Yes, it was all from a passage in the book she was reading. Mike came over and sat by her side. Her bare arm slipped out and touched his knee. He bent over and kissed her eyes and said sorry and kissed her again. This was crazy.

'I'm sorry,' he said again as he probed her neck. 'I can't help it. You better kick me out of here this minute.'

Marge didn't answer. She held on to him and they kissed. She had to stop now, something inside her said, but she couldn't. Why not? She had been on her own for so long. No one had touched her. Clay had other women.

Why shouldn't she please herself? Mike bent down lower and kissed her belly. He felt her pubic hair through the nylon. Her body arched towards him while her fingers caressed him. He pulled the covers off her and bit her. The delicate sour of her hit him. Her legs rubbed against him and her movements were violent. The sweet tension made her groan. He sucked at her and she ached with desire. Then Marge lost control as he hurled himself on top of her and thrust into her. What is happening to me, she asked herself, but she was loving it and could hardly breathe. Mike's own excitement was unbearable. His control was escaping him. He pulled himself away momentarily and kissed her neck.

'Give me...' she said quietly, then screamed the same words. She had no time to be surprised by her own vulgarity as Mike penetrated her again, watching her face. She looked tense and beautiful and moved like the wind as her nails dug into his back. He felt he was nearing the end. Her body raced to him and away from him and she said don't come please and he mumbled he was trying as her relentless thump came against him. Then her release exploded just as his did and a long scream of pleasure came from her. She held on to him and thought so this is what it was all about. 'Stay there,' she whispered and he lay still, looking at her beaming face. 'There,' she said, 'how sweet. How sweet. So sweet.' Mike was spent, but he kept on pressing and moving inside of her. Marge groaned uncontrollably and smiled and cried and then her head fell on the pillow. She looked ravishing. Into the room came a flash of sunshine and he remembered why he was there.

'I haven't known such release before,' she said. And yet it occurred to her that she had used him. She must have been shocked into this. Right now she was feeling too good to think about it. She would work it all out later.

'I wish the world could stop right now,' Mike said.

He was being intense and sentimental, she thought. Why couldn't he just take his pleasure like she did and not think so much about it?

They could never really be together, Mike thought. He would never be able to show her off to the world. 'We have to talk,' he said.

'What about?'

'Your husband.'

'Don't feel guilty about this. I don't. Things were bothering him these last few years. He'd changed. He was never happy with me. We haven't lived together in years. God, I wish he'd known some happiness before he . . . I wish he could have found someone. He used to go with whores, Mike. Whores. He paid women.'

'I wish I was someone else.'

'Why do you say that?'

'I wish someone else was involved here.'

Marge sat up. Her blue eyes seemed cold. 'What are you trying to say, Mike?'

'There's new information about him.'

'Oh?'

'He's alive.' Marge jumped out of the bed. 'The report is not confirmed,' Mike continued, 'but the source is usually very reliable. You can take it he is.'

'What did you say?'

'Clay, your husband. He's alive.'

'Oh God . . . oh my God . . . Clay survived?' Marge thought she would faint.

'Yes, he did. We now know he parachuted out of the plane, but since he wasn't found and did not contact anybody, it was assumed he was killed by the VCs. The new report says he was seen a week ago very much alive.'

Marge seemed to be somewhere else. She lit a cigarette while another was still in her hand.

'My God. . .'

'There's more, Marge. He could be working with the other side.'

'What are you talking about?' She took yet another cigarette from the table and lit it, put it out again, then sat on the floor. 'You're crazy. Clay a traitor? Impossible. Not Clay. Clay loathed everything that was not pure American. He hated the reds with a passion. Hated the liberals back in the States too. Anyone who knows him will tell you. A traitor? You're out of your mind.' Her voice had passion in it. 'The air force was his life, his God. You don't know him, Mike.'

'He may try to contact you.'

'I damn well hope he will. We have a daughter.'

'We think he may ask you for help.'

'Me? Help? What sort of help? And who is "we"?'

'The air force, Marge. I don't know what sort of help. He's been a free man for two weeks now. He was all set to be taken back to his base before he disappeared. We don't understand why he didn't come back. If he contacts you, please let us know.'

'He would never go over to the other side. He doesn't believe in their way of life. . . . He wouldn't do it for money, he doesn't need money. That's one thing he doesn't need.'

'I can't answer that. I've never met your husband.'

'Listen, you take it from me. Clay's no spy. What can he tell them anyway?'

'He's a colonel in the air force. He can tell them plenty. They may have drugged him. At this time we have no more information.' Mike was going to tell her the rest. He was going to tell Marge her husband was not on his own, but he didn't want to hurt her. Her loyalty to him was admirable. The bastard didn't know how lucky he was.

'No, no Mike. He's no spy. I know him.'

'Things didn't work out between you. You said so yourself.'

'That has nothing to do with it, Mike. If you want to know about our love life ... there's dignity in silence.'

'Sorry.'

'Why do you men always try to prove you're great lovers?'

'You read me wrong.'

'You didn't come all this way to talk about my past life with Clay, did you?'

'Anything that may have bearing on his behaviour is important. Stress can lead to things. Some of what you've told me...'

'Aren't you mixing business with personal curiosity?'

'No, I'm not.'

'The air force will be proud of your thoroughness.'

'The air force has orders to find him, Marge, and the air force will. I only hope the whole business can be settled in-house.'

'Is the CIA mixed up in this?'

'I think so.'

'You think? You don't know? Aren't you in charge?'

'Yes, I'm in charge, and they are going to find him. Wherever he is.'

There was a childish smirk on his face, an expression of macho authority. He turned to look at Marge and felt her remoteness. Why did he always have to show people a thing or two? He did not deserve to be near the likes of her. She was a giant, and very much in control of herself. Mike remembered what she had told him about her life and he knew a great change had taken place within her. She no longer suffered any inhibition or stress. She was released. Could be he had done it. She was her own woman now. Her pride was back and it intimidated him.

'One more thing, Marge,' he said defiantly. 'Until you hear otherwise, your husband is dead. These are orders.'

'What are you talking about?'

'This information is classified. As far as the rest of the world is concerned, Clay remains dead. And that includes everybody.'

CHAPTER SIXTEEN

Someone was trying to come aboard. Howard Jelinek heard a scrape along the side and then there was a splash. Whoever it was was welcome, Howard thought. He was washing the breakfast dishes in the galley. Soon the fastidious ritual of the first meal of the day would be over. The bran plate, the egg-cups, the cracker tin would be stored away clean and shiny. The floor would be spotless. He would polish the metal and the wood later in the day. The boat would sparkle on this great occasion. He had not heard the calling of roosters nor the barking of dogs. This was a very quiet village. The silence lasted all through his breakfast and his cleaning chores.

Then the humming of diesel engines shattered the silence. Howard looked out of the window to see the four boats return. He raced up to the deck and then he saw the people. Across the water, on the wooden jetty they had assembled. It must have been the total population of the village. They were waiting for someone to show up and as soon as he appeared on deck they cheered and waved at him and clapped their hands. Howard saw flowers being cast into the water.

They had all seen vessels come close to their coast before, but none had stayed. This sleek ship with a mast as tall as they had ever seen had arrived during the night and had anchored. Also during the night, a rumour spread among the houses. A foreigner was said to have come in the dark on foot, an American. He was accompanied by a woman. The innkeeper was the only one in the village awake at the time and he gave them a room at the inn.

Theirs was a quiet coastal village. The houses were mostly built on stilts. The village had been lucky, too. The wars with the French and other skirmishes that lived on in the memory of the elders had not changed their life in generations. They were too insignificant for any interference. Most people didn't even know that the village was there since the signpost put there by the French had been stolen years ago. No map showed the village, so they were left alone.

The innkeeper was the headman of the village, but he was not really an innkeeper since his establishment consisted of two spare rooms and four beds which the retired seaman rented out on occasion. He sometimes offered a cooked meal with the beds when people stayed for longer than a day. He was an old man now, blessed with a kind heart, a swift turn of phrase and the only flushing toilet in the village. In his youth, a well travelled man, he had started as a deckhand on a freighter before the war and had seen Yokohama, Hong Kong and Manila.

This morning, having some time on his hands, the innkeeper wandered down to the shore to take a first hand look at the new boat. He also hoped to get a glimpse of the owner, who might just agree to move into the inn. Having most probably spent many days at sea, the owner might appreciate the chance of a hot, freshwater bath.

It was therefore with great interest that the innkeeper stood on top of an old chair on the jetty, in front of all the others, to watch Howard emerge on to the deck. In the distance, a thin stripe of gold thickened over the horizon. They waited and still the man did not come to shore. A few children swam out towards the boat, but no one dared to climb aboard. Encouraged by the others, the innkeeper took his small rowing boat and approached the long sailing boat on his own. He got to the long white side and stood up, his hands holding on to the rails, his chin leaning on the gunwale. His parched, smiling face welcomed Howard as he came out of the cabin.

'Permitting I come up?' the man asked with a toothless grin. 'I tie my boat to you okay?'

'You are welcome, my friend,' Howard said. He bent over towards his guest and thought he would give him a hand, but the agile fellow seemed well able to handle the operation by himself. Within seconds, the old man had climbed aboard.

'May I offer you something?' Howard asked.

'I am Mr Ip, innkeeper. You have scotch whisky?'

'No, I do not carry alcohol on board. You can have tea or coffee if you like, or fruit juice.'

'No gin, maybe?'

'No. No gin. I don't have vodka, either.'

'Sorry, no like vodka.'

'Can I offer you anything at all? A biscuit perhaps, or a cup of coffee?' The old man pulled a wet piece of paper out of his pocket. 'I am sailor too, before many years. Now owner of inn. You go see. Hot water and big clean bed. You like hot bath, sir?' The idea did not sound repulsive to Howard. God meant him to get closer to the people. 'You come my boat. Plenty room for two easy. Bath now or tomorrow, sir?'

Howard felt his chin. He could use a shave. No, not before he'd had his sign, but he'd like some fruit and freshly baked bread. 'Do you sell any fruit?'

'Not me. You get fruit in market easy. If you no need bath today, come back tomorrow. Have another American man and woman staying inn. You come tomorrow, maybe?'

'No, no. Please wait. I will go with you now. Let me just fetch some things.'

'Okay. I wait you here.'

The old man was pleased with himself. How sensitive these foreigners were, wanting the whole world to love them all the time. He wanted to see the inside of the cabin, something more to tell the others, but the joy of having his inn full to capacity for the first time in many months had made him forget that. He looked up at the mast. He was amazed at its height and the amount of canvas it could carry. The deck was spotless. There was something odd about a man who would not leave a few crumbs on his boat, a little something for the flies to feed on. A man like that might make demands, but with such a boat he was surely rich.

The people on the jetty were silent. By now the whole village had gathered there to watch the foreigner disembark. Now that Ip's boat was firmly tied to the foreigner's sail-boat, there was no need to wait any longer. He was sure to tell them everything he had seen and heard and as was his way, the story would be embellished and worth listening to. They could really all go home, yet still they waited out of politeness to the innkeeper and his new guest. They watched the foreigner lock up his cabin and come out. He carried a large bag over his shoulder which was stuffed with clothing.

'I'm ready, Mr Ip,' Howard said. 'Nothing like a good hot bath to start God's day with.'

'I tell you before there is American man and woman at inn. They come late last night. I sure they hiding or running away. Why rich American walk at night no car if no running away or hiding? This clothes for poor people?'

The innkeeper pulled at Howard's bag.

'Well, some is. Or all if you need it. We'd have to get them washed first.'

'Can do easy.'

The old man lowered his body through the railing to his boat. Howard waited by the ladder for the innkeeper to push his boat back to the stern. His feeling of anticipation was unbearably exciting. This was the big day. He felt it in his bones. Today, the Lord would tell him what this trip was all about.

Howard climbed into the little boat and sat down. The sun drew golden lines along the water all the way to the jetty and brightly painted the smiling faces of the villagers who awaited him. There was no doubt in his mind that this was the place where great things would happen.

CHAPTER SEVENTEEN

Clay opened his eyes. But for a thin ray of light that sneaked in through a crack in the shutters, the room was dark. He heard Bernadette's steady breathing in the adjoining bed. Last night, before they'd knocked on the door, she'd told him this would be a safe place for a few days anyway. Could they please stay, she had pleaded with Clay. They would find a way out as soon as they had rested.

He had slept fitfully. This was a small village. Grass talks. The presence of a foreigner was as good a piece of gossip here as anywhere else. Someone would talk, Clay had told her, but she just looked at him with a tired smile. As soon as the old man had showed her the bed, Bernadette fell onto it and was fast asleep. He was not sure of anything, but the night had passed peacefully and they were by the sea. The sea had always given him a sense of security and freedom and there were boats around which might offer a way out.

It was a curious little makeshift hostel, yet the notice board in French and English proudly announced it to be an inn. The old man had offered him a plate of cold rice and fried shrimps, but Clay politely declined. He had a hurried wash in the wooden tub outside before he went to his bed.

Now there were voices outside. Clay sat up.

'This is inn,' he heard Ip tell someone. 'Soon you get bath, yes?' The steps Clay heard on the wooden floor were heavy. Then someone knocked on the main door.

'Isn't it your own house?' It was a new voice.

'Sure. This my inn.'

'Why do you knock on your own door?'

'Man and woman inside, I tell you. They get shock to see you.'

Clay slipped out of bed, detecting a sad smile across Bernadette's face. He looked for his gun, then remembered he had left it under the floorboards. He tied his shirt around his waist and walked towards the main door. The knocking persisted.

'We go in now,' Ip said. 'They awake sure. Can go in.'

The door opened and a blinding rush of light hit Clay's face. When his eyes adjusted to the light, he saw the old man standing there, smiling. Behind him stood a tall, slightly balding, bearded man who stared at him with perplexed eyes.

'I bring friend for you sir, see?'

Howard smiled. 'I am Howard Jelinek. I am sorry to get you out of bed like this. It wasn't my idea. I only got here last night and this good man invited me for a bath in his house. I haven't had a proper wash in weeks. Not since Manila.'

'I know the feeling,' Clay said. 'How did you get here?'

'I've sailed here, sir ... Mr...'

'Oh, I'm sorry. I'm Clay Wayne-Turner. Sailed here? Why are you standing out there? Come on in. What about your crew?'

'I have no crew. I've come here by myself.'

'That's incredible.'

This was not the place or time for Howard to go into the details of his voyage. All he wanted now was to wash the salt off his itchy skin. Clay studied him closely. Somewhere in these waters there was a seaworthy craft that could be their ticket out of here. All was not lost, he thought as the man came in. He would have to befriend him. Perhaps he would be willing to sell them a passage to Thailand or Hong Kong or somewhere.

'You've sailed here, that's fantastic. I'm a sailing man myself. What sort of boat have you got? I'd love to take a look at her.'

'All in God's time, my friend.'

'Come have bath,' the innkeeper said. 'We all eat. Talk later, yes?'

Clay thought there was too much resignation in the man's behaviour. He spoke quietly and followed Mr Ip, constantly nodding in amazement. His eyes shone with excitement as the innkeeper led him out to the terrace at the back of the house. The sound of water being poured into the tub followed. Clay went back into the room. He opened the shutters, then came to Bernadette's side and touched her shoulder.

'Wake up, lady,' he said softly. 'We've got things to do.' Her long eyelashes lifted, revealing her bewildered eyes. For a moment she was not quite sure where she was. Then recognition came and she smiled at him. Her face lit up and Clay thought she looked beautiful. He wanted to touch her again, but didn't. She stretched under the covers.

'I slept so well,' she said. 'So well. I thought I slept for years.'

'You have to listen to me, Bernadette.'

'I am listening.'

'Do you want to stay with me? Go with me?'

'Yes,' she said without thinking. 'I have nowhere to go. We cannot stay here?'

'I think I've got us a way out. There is a man here.'

'I thought I heard something. Who is he?'

'I don't know. All I know is he's got a boat. Must be a pretty big one. He's just sailed in from Manila. I'm going to get him to take us out of here. Out of the country.'

'Did you talk to him?'

'Not yet. I'm going to ask him. Do you want to come with me?'

'Where?'

'Anywhere. Hong Kong, Manila ... I don't know. Will you come with me?'

'Yes, yes. I want to come. I have to come.'

'You sure?'

'Yes.'

'I'll talk to him soon. Today.'

'But how ... where ... what will I do after?'

'Trust me, Bernadette. We're better staying together.'

Was he trying to tell her he was fond of her? Was he going to protect her? Was he saying he needed her? She could not read his thoughts. His face seemed taut with determination. She had to run. Her superiors were not going to be generous after her failure. She was tired of failing. Her devotion and her trials and the cause meant nothing now. Only pain. This man was all she had. She must now eat and talk and perhaps sleep with him as long as he wanted her. There was nothing else she could do.

'You look so sad,' Clay said.

'I'm not sad.'

'Then smile.'

'I'm not happy, either. Don't make me smile if I can't.'

'I wouldn't force you to do anything. Just trust me.'

'I have seen war in Europe,' Howard Jelinek said, 'and that was the cruellest war of them all. I did not take part in it because I was very young, but I have seen destruction and death and starvation and civilization killed by people. The whole of Europe was on fire then, and when peace came and with it a struggle for survival, I saw God was not pleased with us. People were frightened and greedy and they had become selfish. I suppose I was selfish too, because I turned my back and left my country. I went to Canada to find my fortune.'

'And did you find it?' asked Clay.

'Yes, I did. It took a long time and longer to find out what my success was meant for.'

'And what was that?'

'Money is only good in the eyes of the Lord when it is used for charity. There are millions of people who deserve to eat and live more than I do, yet I have thrived and they are dying. Still starving and dying. There is little an individual can do to change the laws of nature. I can't stop flood or drought, but wars are made by people and only people can stop them. Take this country here. The earth is good and fertile and the people are willing to work, but war kills all that. I know, I have seen it before. Far away from here.'

'What can you do about this war, Howard? What can anybody do?'

'Without God's word, we can do nothing. I have heard his word and he has commanded me to come here. And here I must wait for him to speak to me again. A sign will come to me.'

'You mean you've sailed here all the way from Vancouver, Canada?'

'Yes, and God was with me all the way.'

'You don't know this country, Howard. This is a complicated situation. History and colonialism and a battle between the superpowers all play a part. You don't know this country.'

'True, and I don't speak the language, but God will show me the way. Even if the whole population ignores me, they cannot ignore God. I arrived late last night. Our good innkeeper came to my boat at first light this morning. God's word is close at hand.'

'We arrived here last night, too,' Bernadette said.

'Perhaps it wasn't by chance,' Clay added. 'We could have taken other directions. There are other ports.' He winked at Bernadette. 'Perhaps we have more in common with our brother Howard than we know.'

Ip the innkeeper had slept through the conversation and when Howard started at last to tackle his food, Clay kicked Bernadette under the table and said, 'Do you think we should let this good man in on our secret? He strikes me as the right man. God does move in mysterious ways.'

At the sound of God's name, Howard looked up and searched Bernadette's face for an answer, but she remained silent.

'Amen,' Howard said.

'I know, Bernadette. I know it's a risk,' Clay said. 'I suppose you feel we don't know enough about brother Howard here, but I have a hunch this is right. How come we're all sitting here around this table? Only one day after we were ordered on our peace mission. I mean, no one knows about it, so why is he here? Could it be we were meant to continue the mission together, brother Howard included?'

'Peace mission?' Howard said in a loud voice. 'What mission?'

'You can't tell him, Clay,' Bernadette joined in. 'It's dangerous. We are sworn to secrecy.'

'God can see through everything,' Clay said, looking at Howard who nodded enthusiastically.

'He does, oh yes he does,' Howard agreed.

'Look Howard,' Clay said in a whisper, 'if you feel I am talking out of turn, if you feel this is not for you, you must give me your word you will never divulge what I'm going to tell you.' He turned to Bernadette, his eyes pleading with her. 'May I, dear Bernadette? May I tell him?'

She nodded serenely, her eyes downcast.

'I am a colonel in the United States Air Force, Howard. Bernadette here is an important official of the North Vietnamese forces. We both belong to a secret group that is trying to bring this slaughter to an end. This beleaguered country deserves a break. There's not a lot of us in on this and we are in constant danger because our governments shun us. We have high ranking connections on both sides. If we are to include you, you will have to come up with some positive suggestions. We're going to hold a meeting in Hong Kong four weeks from tomorrow. The two of us are to prepare the ground for that meeting. The colony is far enough from both Saigon and Hanoi. It is not under the jurisdiction of any of the warring parties.'

Howard's face betrayed amazement. He clasped his hands and looked at the ceiling, then faced Clay, listening attentively.

'Other senior members of our group will be at the meeting in Hong Kong. We are going to try and work out how to stop this madness. Every day some hill or village changes hands with a terrible cost in human lives, only to be taken back the next day. Rice fields burn and forests are poisoned. Factories are razed to the ground. I know, Howard, I know. I have been a part of this destruction. Now I have laid my life on the line by taking the final step. I have deserted my flag, Howard. I am a wanted man. That's why the secrecy. The only solution is for all of us to sit around a table and talk things over, just like we are doing now. We have the will and we have the money.'

Clay reached under his chair and placed the gold bars on the table one by one. 'We're going to pay for this mission ourselves. Months of sacrifice have gone into collecting this gold. You would never guess how many simple farmers have donated their very bread for this. They must be rewarded with peace.'

Clay stopped and the Canadian looked at him with servile admiration. Tears came to his eyes. Howard clasped his hands again, then slipped from the table and knelt. He looked at the ceiling in concentrated silence. Clay and Bernadette exchanged glances while Howard rose and sat on his chair. His eyes shone.

'This is indeed no coincidence,' Howard said. 'No, my friends. This dear old man ... this sleeping innkeeper here ... he was sent to my boat to bring me here. Precisely to meet with you.'

'Could it be, Howard?'

'It is so. Your words to me just now and your secret mission are God's will. I, Howard Jelinek, have been sent across the seas to arrive in this little village today, precisely. You have taken me into your confidence for a reason. It is God's will.'

'In a few days, a submarine will arrive off this coast,' Clay said. 'Perhaps even tonight. One of our friends in the navy has provided it for us. If only we did not need him, he could be better used elsewhere, but we have to get to

Hong Kong and need to leave here soon. We are meeting here today just to part again. I am sure the word of God will come to you and you will serve the cause in your own way.'

'But no, dear friend. I have no plan of my own. It was you all along. Had to be. Why else would I have arrived here at this village, at this inn, today of all days?' Howard could no longer speak. He was overcome by tears.

The innkeeper woke up and rubbed his eyes and looked at his guests. They were hugging each other like they were having a sort of family reunion. He excused himself and left the room.

Clay jumped up after him. 'I think he's arrived at the wrong conclusion. I'd better catch him before he sends a signal to the submarine.'

'Signal? What signal?'

'Ip must be thinking you will be taking us to Hong Kong in your boat. Forgive me for assuming that you'd...'

'But no, Clay, Bernadette, I...' Howard was near hysteria. Uncontrollable, locked up emotions came bursting out and his voice cracked. 'That is what I have been sent here to do. You cannot tempt providence. Don't, in the name of God don't use the submarine. God has provided us with this meeting place. He will provide us with a good wind. I will take you to Hong Kong. Tell him ... this is the word of God...His will.'

'We can't do that to you. You've only just sailed in,' Clay said, 'and we'd have to get provisions. If we sail with you we'll have to get going immediately. I haven't a hope of cashing any gold in this village for the stuff we've got to buy. We need many things. They can all be bought here, but we need cash. We'll pay you back in Hong Kong.'

'Don't worry about that,' Howard assured him. 'I have all the money you will ever need. That is why God granted me success.'

'We couldn't take your money. We've got the gold. We can...'

'This is God's money, Clay. I will take you to Hong Kong or wherever you want to go. Glory be to the Lord. Peace is what I am here for. What a miracle. Will you join me in a prayer of thanksgiving? I know you are people of action, but we must pray now. He will hear us.'

They all kneeled down and concentrated in whispering prayer. Bernadette looked at Howard and prayed in earnest for God to forgive them. They were committing a grave sin. They were deceiving this good man, but they were making him happy. She could see that clearly. Yes, she would pray for the wind. It would take her and Clay and this strange sailor to some promised land beyond the sea. A land where there would be no causes and no mines and no houses of misery they called pleasure.

CHAPTER EIGHTEEN

—————◼—————

The sails were clearly visible as they approached the darkening horizon. They had been gone for hours, Captain New snarled to himself. Too far gone to shoot at with any measure of accuracy, even if he had better weapons at his disposal. His machine-gun was quite useless at this range, but the Captain emptied a frustrated burst of ammunition into the waves. The village bastards were all liars. What could you expect of people who talk to fish? They had hidden the spies all the time and now they pretended they knew nothing. Not even about the gold. They must have been paid with it. That was why they weren't talking.

Captain New coughed with rage, his medals rattling on his heaving barrel chest. That bunch of fishermen had cheated him of his American, the VC woman, his gold and his promotion. And they were going to pay for it.

'You are a pack of brainless, gutless, seaweed eaters,' he yelled. 'Who have I been fighting for all these years, risking my life, watching my friends die?'

'For us,' the innkeeper said, 'to save us from the communists.'

'Save you? You aren't worth saving. For all I care, Ho Chi Minh can come and take you this afternoon. That will teach you shits a lesson. How could you let the foreigner go? Weren't you suspicious of him? Of her?'

'Captain sir, the boat sneaked away without anyone noticing. They've only just gone.'

'Do you think I'm retarded? Look at the sails there. Any child can tell you how long they've been gone. I wouldn't be surprised if all of you stood on the shore waving the spies goodbye. You have no idea of time here. It means nothing to you. No wonder the white man's got so far.'

'We didn't know you were after them. We are simple people. All we know is a good catch from a bad one.'

'I'm going to get you for this, you old shark.'

'If we had only known you were interested, Captain...'

'Interested? Do you realize they were spies, thieves, enemies of our people?'

'Who were they spying for, sir?'

'You're lucky you're too old to be shot, old man. You're going to die soon anyway.'

'Quite right, Captain sir.'

'Captain New had the people rounded up for questioning. They were seated in a circle. No one understood what the fuss was about. The foreigners did not disturb anyone. On the contrary, they had spent many crisp

American dollars in the village store and the American had left a parcel for the Captain. The innkeeper had intended to tell the Captain about the parcel, but with the anger and the commotion and threats he plain forgot. Ip thought to himself that the Captain must have taken a special dislike to him, or perhaps he had a bad stomach. Ip was going to suggest a herbal concoction his late wife used to prepare, but then the Captain did not even want to talk. All he did was shout abuse. He would certainly not listen to any medical advice now.

It was a strange assembly. Nobody present was in the least interested in what the army captain had to say. Uniforms had always meant bad news to them. They were smiling behind his back and he knew it. His mood was becoming ugly. The Sergeant and the driver wished they were somewhere else.

'Well,' Captain New barked at his audience, 'the enemy has gone and you, who could have stopped them, have nothing to say in your defence?'

The old innkeeper moved forward. He lifted his hand to say something, but the Captain slapped his face. 'Not another word from you. What's the matter with you people? Is this arsehole your spokesman?'

To his dismay, the villagers all nodded. They would soon be able to go home. They had better things to do than sit there like a bunch of school children. If the innkeeper was allowed to have his say, this would be over for them. He had been their headman for many years. He had a way with people, and the military upstart who was screaming at them would soon calm down like everybody else.

'Yes,' another elder confirmed, 'the innkeeper speaks for us all. Anyway, no one else had conversations with the foreigners. He talked to them for hours. He knows every-thing. And can we go home now, sir? My wife thinks I am having a quiet screw with some unattached beauty whenever I'm late.'

Everybody laughed, but the Captain didn't see the joke. He was busy thinking of excuses. He was going to need plenty of those for his Colonel, and worse, for his own village.

'Fine,' he said. 'You can all go. Innkeeper, you take me to your inn.'

'Will you grace my house with your custom for the night, Major?'

'I am a captain,' New said with half a grin.

'Really? You certainly look like a major to me. They keep changing uniforms and insignia all the time. A man cannot be expected to follow fashion at my age. I used to know a major once...'

'Just get us in there,' the Captain said. The early evening breeze had cooled his temper a little. The pain in his side had subsided and soon they were seated around the innkeeper's table, sipping tea.

'Think about it, Captain,' the innkeeper said. 'Here we are, exactly where those foreigners were sitting. I couldn't even tell you what they were talking about. I was asleep, you see. Have you anything to drink?'

'Are you trying to upset me? You must remember something.'

'I talk much better with a bit of the hard stuff inside of me.'

'What do I have to do to get through to you, you old fool?'

'Let us see. Old fool, you say. Well not many are lucky enough to reach old age these days, Captain, and around these parts, to be born a fool is considered a privilege. Give me a drink.'

'You win,' the Captain said and motioned to the

Sergeant to put the bourbon bottle on the table. 'There, help yourself.'

'Thank you,' the innkeeper said. He took a long swig out of the bottle. 'That's much better,' he said. 'Now, as I was trying to tell you before, we were sitting around the table and I fell asleep. Later, the American gave me a parcel for you. I thought he was a friend of yours. He spoke highly of you and certainly knew your name.' The old man got up and dragged the heavy parcel over from the other room. 'Captain, this is the parcel the American left for you. It's heavy.'

There was a bar of gold inside, but the other three were missing. The American would not have short-changed him, New thought.

'Did he leave me a note?'

'No. He would have done, because he did ask for pen and paper. To tell you the truth, I did not have one. I pretended to look for a bit not to lose face and in the end he gave up. Then he gave me the message.'

'What did he say?'

'He just told me to give this parcel to you and that he would let you have the rest later. That American must like you a hell of a lot to give this gold to you. He kept this so secret. You know he didn't even want that other foreigner, the strange one who came in the boat, to know anything about it. He was strange, I can tell you. Didn't have a drop of whisky or gin or anything on that boat. He prayed all the time. Talked about God as if he knew him personally. God this and God that.'

'I don't believe the American only gave you one bar of gold.'

'Captain, for an intelligent man you are not being very kind to him. He's a decent man, yet you accuse him. He gave me twenty dollars cash when we left for the harbour.

The money came from the man on the boat because the American had no money at all. And still he returns the gold to you. No one in his position would.'

Captain New sipped his bourbon. He looked at the innkeeper's face. Could be the old man was telling the truth. If that was so, he would be all right. Americans keep to their word and the remaining gold would be sent back to him. The Colonel would not be a problem. New drank some more. Why did the American leave on that boat with the woman? That was a mystery he would solve as soon as he got back to Saigon. But there was time for that later. A childhood song came to his mind and the cool air touched his face as sleep took him.

CHAPTER NINETEEN

———————◼———————

Howard was too alert and excited to sleep. This was surely the happiest day of his life. He wanted to savour the exhilaration in solitude so he checked the instruments and settled down for the first night watch. The stars were out in force and the wind, blowing from the south-west, enabled him to steer straight toward Hong Kong on a broad reach. The Lord's ways are mysterious, he thought as he listened to the bow slicing the swell. He had arrived in Vietnam and had met the very people who would lead him to his destiny. He was given a part to play in the drama of peace, and all in less than twenty-four hours. The Almighty had placed him in the care of the American officer. This was the culmination of all his years in the wilderness. God was truly great.

Howard would take Clay and his partner to Hong

Kong where greater things were sure to happen. They were all in the service of heaven. And yet one sinister thought hung over his happiness and refused to leave. Under the benches, with the sails, Clay had stored an arsenal of guns and grenades that morning. Howard had been taken aback when Clay boarded the boat with the lethal packages. He'd tried to prevent the American from laying the weapons down over the canvas.

'Bearing arms is a sin,' he had said.

'Trust me, brother Howard. There is a very good reason for this. We may have to defend ourselves.'

'God will defend us.'

'I know God will, but I'm afraid the high seas have surprises in store. There are a lot of evil people dead set against our movement. God helps those who help themselves. The enemies of peace are his enemies too, Howard. Americans, South and North Vietnamese, Russians, they all want this war to go on. They would give anything to sabotage this mission. Things will change when we get to Hong Kong. When we reach there, we'll ditch all these guns in the water, I promise you. If you can't bring yourself to accept that, we better part company now. We'll go back to the village and wait for the sub.'

'Oh no. No. You must not do that,' Howard said.

'Even my own people are after me, Howard. They think I'm a deserter. By joining this movement, I've lost everything.'

'Yes, your career and your family. What a sacrifice this must be.'

'I'm no hero, Howard. The woman is, she's the real hero. Willing to leave everything behind, to go with her sworn enemies into unknown territory and all for the sake of peace. All she can expect from her people is a firing squad and we must defend her.'

'Yes, Clay. You're right. As long as these instruments of death are not used in vain. We'll say a prayer for success once we're out at sea.'

'The whole world is against us, Howard. Our presence in this holy boat must be kept secret. We'll have to enter Hong Kong illegally and if a boarding party searches the boat, all will be lost before we even start.'

'I am an expert carpenter. I'm going to build a secret compartment for you. Right under the floorboards. I'll work through the night, while you watch on deck. No one will find you.'

The wind increased and Howard adjusted the sails. His wards were asleep below and he wanted to give them as smooth a ride as possible. He went back to the cabin and started sorting out the provisions and storing them. Keeping busy relaxed him. The thought of Clay's weapons and their possible use was receding.

The sails were in perfect trim with the wind. The boat pitched gently as she surged forward and Howard went up on deck again. He breathed the salty air in. In just a day, he thought, he had been catapulted into the company of giants. He would do anything Clay asked of him, bar killing, but that would never arise since the object of the mission was to stop bloodshed. The Almighty would see to that. If the presence of weapons on board would make Clay feel better, so be it. They were God's messengers. To be travelling along with them was as good as a taste of paradise.

Down under the deck, in the forward cabin, Clay stretched and chuckled. He looked at his watch. His deck watch was one full hour away and he was rested. Up on top, he knew, Howard was fussing with the sails. The boat moved like a dream. He should have felt bad about the blatant lies, but then he had made the man happy. Every part of his face had beamed as they pulled the anchor to leave. He had accepted everything they had told him without question. His naïvety was disarming and his devotion seemed to find new life with the idea of the mission. How could they tell him now it had all been a lie? But all is fair in war, Clay reasoned. He had to save himself and Bernadette. Surely Howard would find happiness in that. They'd have to tell him some time, but the poor Canadian was too besotted with the mission. The truth would only make him suffer.

There was much for Clay to be pleased about. They were well on their way now, going back to the world of cities, cars and sidewalks. To the outside world he was a deserter and a thief. He would need to find a new identity. Nothing was going to stop him now. He would send the gold bars back to the Captain as soon as he could. Anything was possible in Hong Kong, he thought, and then he remembered the Triangle Trading Company of Mody Road. He would be able to get help from them.

A few weeks before, Clay had been put in charge of an investigation into a business deal the Pentagon had made with the Triangle Trading Company for a supply of Japanese electronic equipment which was paid for in advance. He was to inspect the shipment, then turn it over to local representatives of the CIA for deployment in the field. The sophisticated listening devices were to be installed north of the border. And then all hell broke loose. The crates were delivered to the base and he was called in to inspect them. The documentation was perfect and included certificates of inspection signed by the manufacturers. When the crates were opened, all they contained were bicycle parts made in China. A whole delegation of bigwigs came over from Washington in a special plane. They did not stay long. Clay was told it was a large scale fraud that had to be handled without publicity.

Clay remembered the company well and the name of

the man who owned it, a Mr Patel. He was in deep water and Clay would get him to help. He looked at his watch again. Time refused to move. He had plenty to be pleased about, but he couldn't ignore the trouble he was in. Captain New was bound to be interrogated. After all, Clay had arrived in the village a prisoner, was released and given a chance to go back to his base. Now he was roaming the seas with his captor. He could be suspected of going over to the other side. Maybe Captain New might not say a thing. The innkeeper must have given him the message. Nothing was clear-cut.

He looked at Bernadette who slept fitfully, her face smiling at some distant thought. In her sleep, she stretched her hand and touched his arm. He didn't move. Her face seemed confident. Half asleep with the gentle pitch of the boat, Clay waited for Howard's call.

Some miles due south, another vessel was battling harsher waters. The fierce winds shrieked and high waves were throwing her about like an empty bottle. The people who sailed her were used to the sea, having made their living on it. The constant rise and fall of their vessel did not bother them. They were an odd assembly of people, with some Thais, Malays, two Chinese, an Indian and a black man on board. He was an escaped slave whose tongue had been removed by a diamond trader in the Arabian Sea years before. Together they had formed a gang who preyed on traders and small craft which sailed across the South China Sea. They were killers on the water and mostly drunk or in hiding when on land.

Each in his own way had drifted into the world of piracy in the aftermath of the Second World War. The war in Indo-China and the renewed presence of soldiers and military installations brought untold wealth to many. The occupants of the boat sought their fortunes on the waves.

Their base was far away, in the Gulf of Thailand, and they had been at sea for weeks. They were sailing along the coast of Vietnam, hoping to intercept some of the small trading boats that could be found there. These waters were full of small boats, smugglers and rich refugees on their way in and out of the war zone. No one ever reported such boats as missing since mostly they were outside of the law and did not register their movements. It was an easy occupation and no attack ever lasted too long. Their victims hardly ever carried arms. That would have put them behind bars, while smuggling did not mean much beyond a bribe to whichever official came aboard and caught them red-handed.

On this trip they had already had a few good encounters and one near disaster which had forced them to run. A small smuggling boat they attacked had an anti-tank gun mounted at the stern. They took a hit, but their powerful engine had saved them from being sunk. There was little damage to the boat, but one of the Chinese on board had been badly wounded. He lay in his bunk hoping for death to relieve him, while the others waited. There was little they could do except throw him overboard once he'd died. They had exhausted their stock of opium and could no longer do anything about his pain.

The radar they had installed was paying off. The headman had taken to its mysteries like a child to a new toy. He would spend every available moment watching the little screen. Today, the clear signal of a boat had appeared due north. It hardly moved at all, which meant the target was a sailing junk, had a weak engine or had broken down. They were slow themselves due to the weather, but they were sure it would change some time soon. Then they would catch up with the little dot and check it out. If it was a pleasure boat, the reward could be high, just like it had been two years before when they attacked an Australian yawl on her way to Manila. The man was a wealthy jeweller and the woman amused the crew for a whole week before they threw her to the sharks. The headman still wore the dead Australian's diamond-studded watch on his wrist. They had tried to sink the sixty foot boat at the end of the assault, but she refused to go down. They were amused to hear, months after the event, that she was found by a Japanese tanker, masts up and sails flapping, abandoned on the high seas.

A civilian vessel would be a suitable farewell present for this sortie, the headman thought. By now the right palms at Pattaya had been properly greased. The coastguard would not board them there. They could look forward to a safe return. They would have a few good months among the holiday makers on the strip. They could not risk another encounter with the law. Pirates were blown out of the waters by the navy these days.

Bad weather kept them all inside and the headman insisted they use the time to clean and check their weapons. He thought they would catch up with the slower boat at daybreak. The headman loved the wait. The anticipation of action brought excitement into his veins. He watched the screen with great intensity. The expectation of sighting their victim and the thought of what he would find on board brought a broad grin to his weather-beaten face.

CHAPTER TWENTY

When the phone rang, Marge's heart screamed it was him. Perhaps it was what she had wished for. She had yearned for his touch ever since that afternoon in her hotel room in

Paris, three weeks before. He had called her a few times after she'd left Europe, but their conversations had been hurried. Marge was weary of the telephone. It was a legacy from Clay's early years in the air force, especially when he was stationed in Turkey and had flown missions over the Soviet Union. She had difficulties relating to people over the phone and had always kept her conversations short.

She was in Atlanta now and when Mike's voice came on the line, she knew he was near. He had called her the day before to say he was coming, but he hadn't said why.

'I'm at the airport,' he said, 'see you in about twenty minutes.'

A quiver of excitement mounted within her body at the sound of his voice. She was alone in the house with her daughter back at school for the new term. He should have told her what flight he was arriving on and she would have collected him, but then she knew they must not be seen together in public. She was a well-known woman and this was still Georgia.

How she had wished they were walking along some busy Parisian boulevard, unknown and ignored. She was dreaming again. There was no romance in her feelings for him. She was using him, that was all. He was going to find that out some time and in any case, it could never last. They did not move in the same circles. He was a serving officer in the air force and was married. If he wanted to keep his job, he'd stay married.

Ever since his beginnings on a humble Florida farm, Mike had made his mind up he was going places. He was ambitious, but the Carters of Westchester Dairy were not in the same league as the Wayne-Turners. He had arrived in Paris on his own steam, via Korea and other bases around the globe.

Marge wondered how long their relationship would

last and decided it would last as long as they needed each other. She heard the taxi outside and through the curtains she saw him emerge with his briefcase. He had no other luggage. Her pulse was racing as he walked towards the door. He did not get to ring the bell, she just opened the door and he slid in. She grabbed him and pressed him to the wall.

'Missed you, tiger,' she whispered. 'It's been a long time. This is a lonely town.'

'It's lonely everywhere.'

'Are you staying long?'

He didn't answer. She saw there were things on his mind and didn't press him. She led him to the living room.

'Would you like a drink?'

'No thanks. I did little else on the flight over. The way they load you up on these flights...'

Marge shut him up with a kiss. Impatient lust had teased her mind for hours. 'I'm in a hurry,' she said.

'I don't understand.'

'Come,' she ordered him in a husky voice. All her inhibitions were gone. 'Come, I'll show you.'

'Not here, Marge. Not in this house.'

'Don't worry about the house, Mike. Clay's never lived here. He's never even seen it.' Mike looked at her, puzzled.

'I'm horny, but I ain't lying. I must have you, right now. I never thought I'd hear myself talk like this ... and I don't feel guilty.'

She pulled his jacket off and then they were on the carpet. She assaulted him with a maddening embrace. The flight over the Atlantic, the alcohol, the weariness and above all what he had come to tell her were all dismissed as their bodies thumped against each other over and over again. Her passion was fierce and fast and when her explosion brought relief she uttered a loud groan, fell on him and laughed.

'That was inconsiderate of me,' she said with a smile. 'To attack government property like that. I bet you'll want a bath. Let me go fix it for you.'

They walked upstairs and Mike watched her turn the taps on. She poured bath oil into the tub which spread blue foam across the steaming water. He lay in the bath while she sorted out his clothes. All he wanted now was sleep, but he had to talk to her first. There was not much time, yet those hours of tension and the expectation of seeing her again were winning his body over. The heat in the water was forcing his eyelids down. Marge came in and helped him out of the bath. She rubbed his body dry and led him into the bedroom.

'Must talk ...' he mumbled.

'It'll wait, my big bad baby,' she said and covered him.

On her dressing table lay a stack of unopened letters and cables of condolence. She was not about to feel guilty now. They could wait. And anyway, Clay was alive.

It was close to evening when Mike woke up. He touched the sleeping figure next to him as he moved. Marge opened her eyes, turned on the bedside light and looked at him.

'God it's late,' he said.

'No it isn't. The jet lag hit you, that's all.'

Mike sat up. He was fully awake now. 'There's one hell of an enquiry going on, Marge. The air force wants to know what Clay's up to. He didn't return to the base when he had the chance. The latest information we have is that he's managed to get on a sailing boat owned by some Canadian. Got the guy to leave the day after he'd landed. We are checking with the authorities in Vancouver, but there are problems. We have no idea where he is heading. Have you?'

'None whatsoever. Are you crazy? He isn't heading

anywhere. How can he? He is a prisoner.'

'The Vietnamese with whom he had spent the night say he was a free man when he left.'

'What about the boat?'

'We're not sure about anything at this time. All we know is that he was there and they sailed away aboard this Canadian boat with a Vietnamese woman...'

'A woman? What woman? Clay with a Vietnamese woman?'

'Yes, a half-caste, we're told.'

'Where is she taking him?'

'She doesn't appear to be in charge. We aren't sure who is. Clay knows the area pretty well. Planes have been sent to look for them, but there's no sign so far.'

'What do you know about the woman?'

'Not much ... oh, we know she's VC. She's supposed to have captured him after he crashed. She was taking him under guard somewhere. It looks like things changed since...'

'What do you mean? Is she pretty?'

'I mean she isn't in charge now. Clay was free to go back to his base. Then he went off in the night. Now we know he's sailing somewhere.'

'Is she young?'

'I don't know. Tell me, Clay was stationed in Japan and in Thailand ... maybe he's heading there. Did he make any friends there ... real friends?'

'I can't answer that.'

'You're not trying to protect him, Marge? You...'

'You go to hell.'

'You don't understand, Marge, this is the sort of grilling you'll get in Paris.'

'What grilling? Is that what you came over here for? You can't force me to say anything. Nobody can.'

'If our thing together becomes public, they won't let me handle this any longer. For the moment, the air force is running the enquiry from Paris. Washington is too public and the press might pick it up. I'm sorry, I didn't mean what I said.'

She was distant. 'I'm not protecting him. Perhaps I should . . . Christ, the air force knows more about Clay than I do. When is it you're leaving?'

'That's what I'm coming to. Right now, if possible. Tomorrow at the latest. And you're supposed to come with me. They want you out of here and in Paris as quickly as possible. They want you in on this enquiry. They might also ask you to come to Saigon or Bangkok, or somewhere closer to where he might be.'

'Christ, Mike, you know how little couples know about each other. He's not going to ask me to go anywhere. We're separated.'

'Look, they are going to be putting questions to you. I'm trying to help prepare you.'

'The hell they'll question me. A wife can't give evidence against her husband.'

'This isn't a court case, Marge. For all we know, Clay could be a victim of circumstances. I'm only asking you what he would do in this situation.'

'Go ask his friends in the air force.'

'We can't do that. People think he's dead. He must stay dead for now.'

'How long will I have to be away?'

'Until we find him.'

She was no longer listening or even interested in what he had to say. All that worry about using him. Bullshit, he was using her. Using her to find out about Clay. He might not have wanted her at all, but that didn't matter. She had nothing to feel guilty about. He could go to hell. And then it occurred to her that it was Clay who had brought them together and he was heading for trouble. She could help him best by staying with Mike.

CHAPTER TWENTY-ONE

Clay switched the steering to manual and held the wheel in his hand. The wind roared, sending the boat flying through the swell. The clouds, swept aside by the wind, revealed a bright moon that lit the foam and the tight sail in front of him. It was good to be in charge again. He had trimmed the canvas as soon as his turn on deck came, tilting the boat over to run on her cheek. He was competing again, he thought with a smile, and winning. Let them say he was showing off, he was too exhilarated to care. The fresh, cool air bit his face, cleansing his mind. Howard didn't drive the ship hard enough, but then Howard was in no hurry and he was. By now the air force was bound to have put two and two together. They would know he'd survived. They would know he'd spent the night in the Captain's village. They would be puzzled about the woman.

They might keep the thing quiet, but they'd have to tell Marge. Poor Marge, why was he always so hard on her? She didn't understand him. How could she? She didn't know who he was, but neither did he. She had accused him of insensitivity. She said he was distant and there was no communication between them. She said he was intolerant and she might have been right, but then maybe he couldn't help it. Maybe he had been a victim, forced to act out a part that was never his. He didn't want to dwell on it too much. He was on his way to find out who he was. The plan was working again.

From under his feet came the sound of knocking. He jumped up and ran to the cockpit. Inside, under the steps, he saw Howard's back moving. He was working under the scant light of a small electric lamp that hung from the low ceiling. He turned his face, but did not see Clay. In his hand he held a saw. He was doing something to the floorboards at the back, behind the engine. Clay shrugged his shoulders and climbed out. He sat by the wheel and looked at the sails. The boat raced forward.

A feeling of imminent danger sprang into him out of nowhere. It came suddenly, without a reason. The sort of feeling he sometimes had just before a missile approached. He switched over to automatic steering and rushed into the cabin. The radar screen was lit and he examined the phosphorus lights that formed on the glass. Due south, some forty or fifty miles, a moving object was homing in on their path. It was too fast to be a merchant ship, but too slow to be a naval patrol boat. It could be anything. Should he alert Howard, he wondered. Tell him we are being followed? No, he was panicking. Outside, the wind had increased and it howled as the boat tilted steeply. He went up to the cockpit again and eased the sails out a little. If the wind speed continued to increase, he would have to reduce canvas.

The feeling that another boat was chasing them kept nagging at him, but it would take them time, whoever they were, to catch up. The sea was probably rough back there.

In the cabin later, Clay noticed the boat was gaining on them. Perhaps his anxiety was making him see things, but the other vessel was heading straight towards their anticipated route, as if they were planning a collision. He estimated the other ship would come into view by dawn. There were still a few hours left until then and Clay sat by the navigation table cleaning the guns and checking the ammunition. He laid the grenades on the table and smiled. He was not going to shoot at the navy, but if the other boat was red he would. No, it could never be a red boat. It would not come at them from the south. It was probably a motorized junk making for Hong Kong, but it might be smugglers. He mocked his own hysteria. He was being ridiculous.

Back on deck, Clay's eyes wandered towards the horizon, waiting for the first hint of light. The wind had eased. He heard a sound, turned and saw Bernadette coming out of the cabin, wrapped in a rug. She had never been to sea before, but her face seemed calm in spite of the slow pitch.

'It's peaceful up here,' she said. 'Will it be morning soon?'

'Might not be so peaceful then,' he said casually. She studied his face and he grimaced.

'What's the matter, Clay?'

She looked so beautiful there, studying his face. 'Might get stormy again.'

'It's something else, isn't it? The sea looks calm enough to me.'

'It's nothing.'

'You can tell me. You must tell me. You said we're in this together.'

'We're being followed. I could be wrong, but we'd better be ready for the worst. If they're your people, we'll hide under the floor. They wouldn't attack a peaceful Canadian boat, would they?'

'Let me make you some tea.'

As she spoke, Howard's face appeared at the cabin entrance. He was holding a tray. With his windswept hair and ruffled beard he looked like a biblical figure. 'God has blessed us with another day,' he said. 'Your hiding place is ready.'

'You've been working all night?'

'With God's guidance and help.'

'Do you carry any gasoline on board?' Clay asked.

'Sure, high octane stuff. It's for the outboard.'

'You got plenty?'

'Couple of jerrycans...maybe three. Didn't use the dinghy at all.'

'Good.'

Howard's face did not betray his tiredness. He was as excited as ever and his eyes beamed like a prophet's.

'Let us pray,' he said softly. A thin line of silver struggled to emerge where the sea met the sky.

The wounded Chinese died during the night and they threw his body overboard. No one said anything and they all stood there and watched the body float on the pale grey sea for a long while before it disappeared. The Malay remarked that the dead man had always been a good swimmer and the rest of the crew joined in with hearty laughter. They saw the body, face up, bob up and down alongside the ship and then it went under.

Over the horizon, the sun crawled up slowly, as if in pain. Then the sea turned quickly to gold. They could now see the sails quite clearly through the strong binoculars. The sight brought a measure of relief to the headman. The weapons which had been stored in plastic bags during the night were taken out and checked again. The man in charge pronounced the weapons ready. He was an elderly Indian who, having been in the British Army for many years, was entrusted with the servicing of their equipment. He was not a fighting man and over the years he had also drifted into becoming the boat's mechanic and engineer.

The leader of the band paced the deck. He was not sure whether there would be any resistance from the peaceful looking target. He would make short work of killing the crew, then take whatever there was from the vessel before turning back. He knew it was difficult to sink a sailboat and had decided to burn her instead. Very soon now, in an hour or so, he would be able to ascertain how many people she carried. He would then make a proper plan of action.

CHAPTER TWENTY-TWO

—■—

'God has brought us thus far,' Howard said. 'He is not going to allow anyone to stop us now.'

'You may be right, brother Howard,' Clay answered, 'but we better be ready anyway.'

'They may not be after us at all,' Bernadette suggested.

'I won't start any shooting,' Clay told them. 'Still, I wish I had the use of one old fighter plane for an hour. Anyway, a piston engine will do just fine.'

The sea was calm and there was no wind at all now. Howard went below deck. 'Should we start the engine?' he called up to Clay.

'Not yet,' Clay replied. 'Let's wait.'

From the radio came the crackling sound of an American voice talking of the weather and announcing some successes in the field. The disc jockey played requested music. They did not need to look at the radar screen now to see the other boat. Its shape and size grew by the minute as it closed in on them, faster than before. Clay hoisted himself up the mast with his binoculars. He held himself up and looked. She was a black, impersonal ship carrying no flag. She was an old, round wooden steamer. The people on her large deck were all clearly armed. Clay rushed down.

'Start the engine,' he commanded. Howard went to comply and Clay raced below. From the hold he dug out two jerrycans of gasoline and all the old rags he could find. He collected a few empty oil bottles and sat down with Bernadette to turn them into Molotov cocktails. Bernadette worked fast. With the minutes ticking away, the feeling they would have to fight concerned them both, but they were not afraid. She looked at him with trusting eyes. While they worked, Howard busied himself polishing the sink and sweeping the floorboards below. The sails had all been taken down and the boat was advancing on engine power.

'Stop fussing, Howard, and come store the sails. Canvas burns,' Clay shouted and the Canadian obeyed.

They could now see the other boat without the binoculars. Clay watched her crew remove the cover of a camouflaged machine-gun at the stern. She was badly painted in black. The wooden planks were smothered with thick tar. No one seemed in a rush as they went about their business. They could have been a bunch of bored sailors preparing a slow-motion docking operation. The sea all around them was empty all the way to the horizon.

'We've got problems, Howard,' Clay said.

'What do you mean?'

'These men are armed and they're fixing to board us. We'll have to fight.'

'I won't. And nor should you. I am a man of peace.'

'You may be, buddy, but the guys over there sure aren't. Take a look through your binoculars.'

'I believe you, Clay. Still, I won't fight. We can talk to them. Explain. . .'

'You're crazy. We're dealing with evil people here, Howard. Pirates maybe.'

'Pirates? In this day and age?'

'You bet, right here in the South China Sea. God wants them destroyed.'

'Then God will destroy them, not us. We should pray. You must not forget our mission.'

'If they kill us before we get there, there will be no mission.'

Howard looked at Bernadette and she nodded. 'He's right, Howard, but I understand you well. You stay out of it and pray for us. We're going to need every bit of goodwill we can get from Him.'

'Amen,' Clay said. 'I wish I could share you devotion.'

The other boat was even nearer. Its growing dark bulk cast a menacing reflection over the calm waters.

'Bernadette,' Clay called. 'Come over here.' She was by his side before he'd finished his sentence.

'Yes, Clay,' she said quietly.

'I'm going below. You go sit on the bow there, up front, and keep some of your bottles with you. Take this bucket of gas, too. Make sure you don't spill any on our deck. It's meant for theirs, when they catch fire. Don't do a thing until they are good and close. Wait for me to tell you.'

'Yes, Clay,' she answered as Clay went below.

'Ahoy there,' Clay heard Howard shout, but a short burst of automatic fire stopped him. Clay could not see Howard, but he heard the thump of his body hit the deck. He opened the skylight window in front of him and looked outside. The other boat was manoeuvring itself alongside. On her stern, two men came into sight and Clay shot them and watched them fall. One tumbled into the water. A third man, preparing the machine-gun at the back, was hit and hung over the gun, suspended and motionless. There were shouts. Clay ran to the door. 'The bucket,' he shouted, 'the bucket.'

The men on the other boat stood by the railing. The

only person they could see was a woman. The headman ordered a cease-fire. He had all the time in the world, his crew had now been diminished to four. He would exact a terrible punishment. No more shots came from the sailing boat. Whoever was shooting at them was surely with the Buddah now.

'Come forward,' the headman shouted at the woman. The boats were heaving to, a few feet apart.

The steamer's deck loomed high above them. Bernadette nudged the bucket towards the hatch in the bow and walked calmly towards the railing. The boats edged closer by the second. Clay pushed his arm through the hatch and felt the bucket in his hand. Clay looked out. Bernadette was nowhere to be seen. The men were all at their bow, clapping their hands and shouting. Clay lit one of his bottles and held it at the ready. He stuck his head out, but no one saw him. He threw the bottle at the other boat and it fell onto the water. The pirates were gesticulating with obscene movements. One pulled his trousers off, exposing himself. They threw a rope in Bernadette's direction.

Clay pushed his shoulders out of the hatch. He lit another bottle as the other deck rolled towards him. It was close. He could almost touch it as he threw the bottle over. A cloud of black smoke told him it had hit home. Clay emerged from below and picked up the petrol bucket. Then he poured it over the other deck.

'Full throttle,' he shouted at Bernadette and she rushed to the controls. The boat surged ahead. As the sailing boat passed by a gap in the other ship's railing, Clay threw two grenades over and opened hip fire at the pirates. He ran to the cockpit. Behind them, pandemonium broke loose on the other deck. The headman surveyed the damage and then started giving chase. Astern, Clay calmly pulled the pin out of a grenade and waited. Bernadette zigzagged the boat as she moved at full speed. The other boat was right behind, its bow gaining. Clay hurled a full jerrycan of petrol into the water, then threw the grenade in. The sea was aflame in an instant. Smoke from the wooden bow hit their eyes. Then they heard the explosion. Clay pushed Bernadette's hand away from the throttle and slowed down. They watched as the other boat stopped.

Up on their deck, the pirates took their time dying. Their movements seemed slow, as if they were in a daze. They had only one lifeboat, fastened on deck. They were trying to undo it in the ferocious heat. Another explosion shook the old vessel and part of the deck caved in. The pirates disappeared. At the back, the cabin stood out like a lonely bunker in a smoky field. It was quiet for a moment and then a flame shot up from the hold. Ammunition boxes and fuel caught fire. Black smoke snarled up and another explosion followed. The lifeboat took off into the air then dropped into the water. There was no one aboard her as she floated near the wreckage.

'Do you think anyone survived that?' Bernadette asked.

'If they did, they'll have to take their chances with the sea.'

It was all eerily quiet now. Like a sea-borne ghost, the smouldering hull seemed to follow them. The sea was empty and calm, but ahead a small ripple in the water told Clay the wind was coming close. He hoisted the mainsail, then the jib. Bernadette watched as the wind came. Hesitant at first, the air began to fill the sails and Clay turned the engine off. He set his course, switched on the automatic pilot and sat down next to her. For a long while they said nothing.

Later, they laid Howard's body on the bench and Clay went through his pockets. There was a small leather-bound bible and a wooden cross. Howard would want these to go with him, Clay thought. He wrapped the body with a torn sail he had found in the cabin and lifted the dead man and carried him to the side. There would be no one to tell, no one to write to of Howard Jelinek's demise. Here was a man without yesterdays. The 'In case of an accident' section in his passport was empty.   Without saying it, Howard had bequeathed them his boat and his future. With his documents, Clay could now enter the crown colony at the helm. The Triangle Trading Company would find papers for Bernadette soon enough. How little they knew of Howard, Clay thought. They had used him and silently had mocked his intense belief in God and mankind. They eased Howard into the water. Now, as the man floated on the South China Sea towards his creator, a sadness descended on Clay as he watched. This funny, naïve man with his strange voice and foreign accent was closer to him now, even as the sea took him away. He was a man without God, without a family. Was he devoid of a heart, too? Was his mother's drunken accusation the truth?

He had planned an escape to the streets of some oriental city, but now he was no longer alone. Clayton Wayne-Turner was no longer sure of anything. His cockiness vanished with the body out there. What would he do with the woman once they reached Hong Kong? His own search would only start then and there was no room for her. Not her or anyone. He needed a clear head now. He needed strength and conviction. Love and God had no place in a battlefield. Who and where was God anyway?

He turned to look at Bernadette and saw her tears. Perhaps they were destined to be in danger for the rest of their lives. He came to her side and held her close.

'You say the prayers, Bernadette,' Clay said softly. 'There goes a real hero.'

CHAPTER TWENTY-THREE

—■—

With dusk came dazzling lights along the water all the way to the boat. The Christmas tree image of Hong Kong's skyline seemed incredible after weeks and weeks of nothing but sea and sky. The bay that stretched between the illuminated rocks resembled a benevolent dragon. Tall, brightly lit buildings spilled a myriad of lights through thousands of windows. Clay had never arrived there by sea before and they stood by the foresail, watching the city come into view.

'How beautiful,' Bernadette sighed. 'How absolutely perfect. A vertical Paris.'

The wind blew gently behind and Clay opted to pull the mainsail down and sail in under the genoa power alone. He was tired now. The arm of the air force was long and he was far from secure. Bernadette's excitement, he reasoned, must have arisen because at last she was safe. She had seemed confident when they were sailing, looking out at sunrises, sunsets and the reflection of the moon in the water. It had been almost too peaceful after the pirates had gone under, but the way Howard's body was disposed of had upset her more than the bloodshed. She often burst into tears at odd times, saying they had lied to him and had caused his death.

They had not seen any other ships or land until they were some one hundred miles from the colony. She had tried to busy herself with pleasing him. She had listened to him talk about the wind and the swell and the shape of the various sails. She let him teach her how to handle the wheel and pretended to share his exhilaration every time the boat flew over the foam. She always made the right comments. The teacher-pupil relationship came naturally to him and he felt comfortable in her company.

During the long afternoons, as they sailed past the southern part of China, they made love and explored each other's bodies. It had started one night, almost by accident, and she succumbed because she thought he was asleep and did not know what he was doing. Then it happened again, but they did not talk about it. Later on, her sexuality began to assert itself as his desire for her overshadowed his insecurity. The sexual closeness made her forget herself and she indulged herself because at such times she was almost happy. None of the old dark thoughts entered her mind when they were on fire together. If that was his way of loving her, then she accepted it. Beyond that she asked herself no questions.

Bernadette felt no guilt. There was very little thought in her mind when they were close. She began to enjoy him, and with her emerging self-esteem she guided his rhythm. Without words, she caused him to want to please her and he'd learned to do that well. It had been a strange transformation for him. He had been used to spending a few hurried moments with women he had paid for and was never put upon to please them beyond paying at the end. At first, the climax she was achieving brought humiliating memories of what life could have been with Marge. At times it was embarrassing, but later he began to accept the effect the release had on her and he revelled in it. Finally, it made him proud. Bernadette never tried to hide her desire for him and with her body she made him know he had pleased her. Yet sometimes there was still a remote stiffness in him, which she thought was born of mistrust. She never asked him about that. She just withdrew into herself and found a corner on the boat to be alone in. She dreaded their arrival because she believed he would soon tire of her like all the others.

As they neared Hong Kong, Clay's plans for the next

few days were forming in his mind. He was well rehearsed in his new identity as Howard Jelinek. He had grown a beard and with Howard's sun-glasses, Clay resembled the picture in the dead man's passport. He had practised the Canadian's clumsy signature to cash the heap of American Express traveller's cheques he had found in the drawer. He planned to use some of that money until he got to Switzerland. That little haven in the Alps with its banks and clean streets was no longer as far as it had seemed the day his plane was shot down. The number of his secret bank account, along with the jewels he had collected, lay buried in a soggy ricefield back in Vietnam. He would need to go to Lucerne personally and identify himself as Clayton Wayne-Turner. With his passport back at the base he would have to think of a way to prove who he was.

Clay started the engine and brought the sails down. As they folded the huge genoa, he told Bernadette she would have to hide in the place Howard had prepared for them both.

'It won't take long, Bernadette,' he said when he saw the old fear in her eyes. 'As soon as the customs men leave the boat, you'll be able to come out again. I've put some water down there for you in case they take their time. You'll see, it'll be fun to go out on the town after that. I'll take you for dinner tonight.'

Over the radio, Clay identified himself to the port authorities. They were right in the middle of the bay and passed huge moored ocean freighters, cruise ships, busy ferry boats and ancient junks that moved gracefully along the waterway. Halfway through the bay, Hong Kong's lights met those of Kowloon in a colourful symphony. They stood by the wheel, his arm around her shoulder, and followed the route given them by the English voice on the other side.

It was nearly midnight when Clay tied the bow to the berth he had been given. He had thrown all the weapons and his uniform overboard and in the absence of any contraband the bored customs officer completed his examination quickly. The young Chinese immigration officer, smart in his black British uniform, stamped Howard's passport without blinking an eye. He was given a sixty day permit to stay in the colony. A German ketch was moored in the next berth and with her owners out on the town, the immediate vicinity was quiet. As soon as they were alone, Clay opened the hatch and whispered to Bernadette they were safe. There would be no more inspections, he assured her. No more hiding. Nothing but fun now, he said as she came out.

They showered and Clay put on a pair of slacks and a t-shirt he had found in Howard's cupboard. The smell of soap made him feel clean and a new burst of energy buzzed through him.

'This town never sleeps,' he said to Bernadette. 'We'll go get you some decent stuff to wear.'

'Can't we do that tomorrow, please?' she asked. 'Let me have one more night's sleep. It's been a long day.'

Clay was raring to go, but he wanted to please her. He shrugged his shoulders.

'You go,' she said.

'I won't leave you alone here. Aren't you hungry?'

'I'm not really. I can fix you something.'

'I'll stay,' he said and thought he saw the worry lines disappear from her face.

They sat outside for a little while and listened to the city. When tiredness came to him they walked together into the cabin and slept in the motionless bed, oblivious to port and town and the noisy way the people all welcomed the sun.

CHAPTER TWENTY-FOUR

It was mid-morning when Clay woke. He checked his face in the mirror, then made Bernadette a cup of tea and brought it to her. He was courteous, but his eyes were serious. At this time of year, there would be plenty of air force personnel on R and R in town so he didn't shave his beard off. Outside, there was the bustling sound of people and cars and jets taking off and landing at Kai Tak Airport across the water. Then Bernadette came up, dressed in a shirt and a pair of Howard's pants. Her suntanned skin and full lips needed no make up. She didn't ask Clay where they were going. He wasn't smiling and her instinct told her not to challenge his mood.

They walked towards the gate and a friendly guard waved them through. As soon as they were out of the port area, they were surrounded by heavy traffic. A taxi stopped near them and the driver opened the door, inviting them in. His mouth was full of half-chewed rice and he kept eating as they entered. Clay waved a ten dollar bill at him. 'Hope you use these,' he said.

'Dollars US? Okay, okay,' the driver said. He took another mouthful of rice and locked the door. 'Where you go?'

'Mody Road, please.'

Zigzagging between buses and vegetable trucks and the odd rickshaw while avoiding swarms of motorbikes, the driver manoeuvred his taxi like a race-car. There were people everywhere; in cars, on verandahs and sidewalks that lined both sides of the wide road. Decorative Chinese characters hung from the shops and out of the windows, giving the place an air of a permanent carnival. The sidewalks along Nathan Road were crowded with a never-ending procession of people.

Clay wanted to walk so he tapped the driver on the shoulder. 'Soon, soon Mody Road,' the man said.

'We want to walk. We'll find it,' Clay told him.

The driver pointed further up to the right. 'Mody Road there.'

'Stop now,' Clay said. 'We want to walk.'

The driver rammed the brakes, a puzzled look on his face. Clay gave him ten dollars and they got out. They stopped outside a money changer's hut and Clay changed a thousand dollars worth of Howard's traveller's cheques. The man didn't even look at him. He made him sign them in the appropriate place and told him to put his passport number down. Armed with a wad of soft, colourful local bills, they walked up Nathan Road arm in arm. Clay thought Bernadette needed proper clothes right away and led her into Lane Crawford's to get her outfitted. He left her in the care of a young salesman and stood by the entrance to wait. The store had been a favourite of Marge's, and he knew she'd find something there.

When Bernadette came down the escalator, she called out to him. She was transformed. In a light grey dress with a blood red handbag and matching shoes, she could have passed for a rich Latin woman. She certainly drew looks from the other women in the store. Her eyes hid behind a pair of dark glasses and as he took her arm the scent of vetiver reached him. 'You look like a movie star,' he said.

343 Mody Road was a new glass and marble building. The stainless steel lift whisked them rapidly to the second floor. A pretty Indian girl sat behind the counter. The suite was carpeted and a silent blast of air-conditioning blew from the ceiling.

'May I see Mr Patel please?'

'Could I ask what your name is, sir?'

'Colonel Wayne-Turner, United States Air Force.'

'Which Mr Patel do you wish to see?'

'I didn't know there were more than one.'

The girl smiled. 'Mr Jagdish Patel is here, sir. I'll see if he's free.'

They sat down and examined the old prints of clipper ships that hung along the walls. They were framed in gilt and looked original. Bernadette was taken by the deep leather chesterfields and the marble tables. With her frugal upbringing in the convent, the pattern of the rich was foreign to her.

'Who would spend so much money on a place of work?' she asked.

'I guess he's out to impress visitors.'

Soon, a tall, well-dressed Indian came through the walnut doors. He lowered his head for Bernadette, then smiled at Clay. 'Would you like to come in, Colonel? My name is Jagdish Patel.'

He opened the door to his office and ushered Clay in. Patel sat behind his large desk, lit a thick cigar and took his glasses off. 'Can I offer you a drink, Colonel?'

'Scotch on the rocks, if you've got any.'

'For the air force, everything is available in Hong Kong.'

The whisky was brought in while the smile froze on Patel's face. It had been a long time since Clay had had any alcohol and the golden liquid entered his bloodstream swiftly. In the report he had read, Patel had been described as a cagey customer. He would have to think twice before he spoke. The room was lavishly appointed in old English style, with models of old galleons and decanters and family crests all over the walnut walls. A thick, expensive cloud of Havana smoke hung over them.

'What can I do for you, Colonel?'

'I'm supposed to come down on you like a ton of bricks, Patel. My bosses at the air force are furious with you.'

'I expected you earlier, Colonel, still you are welcome now.'

'What do you mean you were expecting me? How did you know I was coming?'

'I have my sources, Colonel, but more to the point, why should your illustrious air force be upset with me?'

'Something to do with shipments you arranged for them. Electronic devices. Wrong shipment in the crates, Patel. You've been a bad, bad boy. I mean, even the air force can tell the difference between electronic equipment and Chinese bicycles.'

'I am sure we can settle all that between the two of us. How much money do you earn, Colonel?'

'You don't have enough.'

'What do you mean?'

'Take a look at last year's Who's Who. You'll find out what the difficulty is. Money is not my problem.'

'Do you have a problem?'

'I didn't say that. I said money's not my problem. I meant I can't be bought.'

'There must be something you need.'

'As a matter of fact, there is.'

'I am sure I can help you.'

'I'm sure you can.'

'What do you need?'

'A service.'

'Are you buying or selling?'

'Neither. I left my passport back at the base in Vietnam and I need a replica of it, complete with entry stamps into Hong Kong and used plane tickets. I also need a French passport for my friend outside, in her own name. Mademoiselle Bernadette Mourniese de la Courcelle. I need these documents in faultless shape and in a hurry. I can pay.'

'Oh there's no need for that, Colonel. I would much rather you did something about my problem with your air force. Delay it a little. My reputation is important to me, you see. I believe they are investigating me.'

'Maybe I have come to the wrong place.'

'No, you are in the right place. Just give me your passport number. As for your friend, we have a contact in the French Consulate. Documents are easily found in Hong Kong. All I need are photographs. What is it the air force is planning to do about me?'

'I figure we can get the necessary photographs ready this afternoon. How long would you need for the passports?'

'How about a hint? You must know what they are going to do. Will they sue me?'

Clay's eyes were cold. 'I guess you know I won't say any more just now. Let's get these passports going. I came to you because I know you'll keep it all quiet. The only people who know why I am here are my superiors. Don't ask any more.'

'Come now, Colonel, you can't blame me for trying.'

Patel took a deep puff of his cigar. The American was unsure of himself. His demeanour was a bluff. What could his problem be? Patel had people in Saigon who would find things out for him. He could have the man followed. No, that was not necessary. He couldn't go anywhere without a passport. The whole thing smelled foul. He must have had some document to get into town in the first place. He might even be someone else. Patel was worried, but a couple of hours at the YMCA sauna would clear his head.

'Are we in business, Patel?'

'Sure we are. Let's shake. Shall we say tomorrow afternoon? You did come unannounced.'

'I'm kind of short of time. You are not the only job they've hung on me here. That's why I need the passports. I'll go see to the pictures. See you later.'

'Why don't you take a tour of the town?'

'I've got that in mind, Patel. My friend's never been here before.'

'Beautiful woman, your friend.'

'Yeah.'

'Sorry you're in a hurry. Lots to do here you know.'

'I'm sure there is. Say, Patel, could you arrange a telephone call for me?'

'No problem.'

'I need to talk to a Captain Nguyen Nang Ding of the South Vietnamese Army. He's better known as Captain New. Here's the unit he's serving with. I'd like him to be at the Hotel Caravelle in Saigon first thing tomorrow morning. You know people there. You can arrange that.'

'What if the Captain refuses to come?'

'He won't. All you have to do is to get your people to tell him it's about the gold bars.'

'Gold bars?'

'You heard right. He'll come. Tell him his American colonel friend wants to talk to him about the gold bars. I'll see you in the morning, Patel.'

CHAPTER TWENTY-FIVE

———————◾———————

'Is that you, Captain?' Patel made a move to leave the room, but Clay motioned to him to stay. 'This is Clayton Wayne-Turner. You saved my life, Captain New, remember?'

'Yes sir, Colonel. I remember well. I remember you any place. How are you?'

'Fine. Sorry I left in a hurry. Did the innkeeper give you the gold?'

'Yes. Some missing.'

'I've got them right here for you.'

'Where?'

'There will be a message for you with the porter at the Peninsula Hotel in Hong Kong, Kowloon side. He will tell you where the gold is. And there will be more.'

'Oh thank you, thank you, sir.'

'You're a good officer, Captain New. You've got initiative and connections. You'll make major soon. I will see to that.'

'You in big, big trouble, Colonel. You can't make major for me. I tell you air force look for you like crazy. I say nothing about conversation today. I am your friend. I save your life and must protect you as old custom. I am responsible for your life now.'

'Don't you believe it, Captain. These people don't tell you everything. I am on a special mission for my country here and I'll tell you more later, if you don't talk.'

'You be sure I no talk, Colonel. You famous man here now.'

'How well you did to find the fishing village. Clever of you, Captain New. You take a few days off and book yourself on a flight to Hong Kong and go visit Mr Patel at the Triangle Trading Company, Mody Road. Mr Patel will have all the details, you understand? You got money?'

'Sure I got. Plenty money.'

'I'll pay you back when you get here.'

Patel listened to every word. He sucked at his cigar and coughed. Sweat ran down his chin. What gold were they talking about? Where in Hong Kong could he be keeping it? All the enquiries he had made during the day got him nowhere. How the Colonel had entered the colony was a mystery. His name did not show up anywhere. He had checked every possible landing strip on both sides of the border. Was the American really doing some hush hush job for someone? Was he in trouble? He didn't sound or look like he was. He could have been acting.

Clay made his arrangements with Captain New. The changing expression on Patel's face was not lost on him. The Indian was greedy. He was after big things. As long as he could keep him interested, he would play ball.

'Do you mind if I call Switzerland, Patel?'

'Of course not. Be my guest.'

'I need to talk to my bank.'

This was getting better every minute, Patel thought. 'What number in Switzerland?'

'Gee, I forgot, it's Saturday. They don't work Saturday. They're rich enough, eh? I guess I'll have to do it Monday night. We're eight hours ahead, right?'

'Feel free to come here any time.'

'I need the passports quickly. When can I have them?'

'Tuesday afternoon, for yours, Colonel. Mademoiselle Mourniese de la Courcelle's passport is here.' Patel took the document out of his drawer and handed it over.

'Overnight delivery, huh? That was quick work. How much do I owe you?'

'This one is on the house, Colonel.'

'No, I insist on paying for goods received.'

'Okay, you pay when you get yours on Tuesday.'

'I'm paying for it now. Strictly cash on delivery.'

Patel capitulated and collected three hundred dollars from Clay. When he left, Patel did not bother to have him followed any more. They had shaken his people off previously and would be back. Patel would be waiting for them.

CHAPTER TWENTY-SIX

London's pearl-like street lights snaked beneath them for miles. The seat-belt sign came on and Mike Carter killed his cigarette. The dry cough that punctured his breathing was getting worse.

'I'm going to kick the habit as soon as this mess is over.'

'I've heard that before,' Marge said. 'I wish I didn't have to come here with you.'

'We need you here. Clay's supposed to be in Hong Kong. The only way to find him there is to contact the authorities here in London. It's a British colony, remember?'

'Why can't you do it yourself?'

'For Chrissakes Marge, this is all unofficial. We can't ask any questions here. You'll have to contact the ministry as a private person. If someone from the embassy starts messing with them, they'll get suspicious. You're a wife looking for a missing husband. It's credible because it's simple.'

'How do we know he's in Hong Kong?'

'We have it from a very reliable source.'

'Who?'

'A South Vietnamese Captain, name of New. He was the last man to see Clay after the crash. He told our people Clay's in Hong Kong, or on his way there. You don't think I'm enjoying this, do you?'

'I don't know and I don't care.'

'And all this when we are just beginning to track him down.'

'Track him down? Are you talking about an animal? The poor guy is being chased across God knows where and you are talking about it like it's a hunting expedition. You keep asking me how he thinks and what he would do, and all the time you're pushing him into desperate corners. Why can't you just leave him alone?'

'We've got to know why he didn't report back after he survived the crash.'

'Maybe someone is blackmailing him.'

'Maybe.'

'And you don't care, I suppose. None of you care. As long as you can go on playing your games.'

'It's a bit nasty to accuse me of that, Marge.'

Under the wings, the city was coming closer and the wet roads reflected the traffic like long mirrors. As the plane touched down, the rain stopped.

'Imagine,' Mike said, 'London without an umbrella.'

'You're so funny. How can you stand yourself?'

'I'm only trying to make conversation.'

'Don't bother,' she said icily as the plane turned off the runway towards the terminal. 'I'm sorry. I guess I'm tired.'

'It's okay, forget it.'

They didn't talk much on the way to passport control. The whole thing was wearing her down. Perhaps Mike was right. Perhaps Clay did have a chance to return to his base and didn't because he wanted to desert. Impossible. Maybe he had changed. His erratic behaviour during their last holiday in Florida was strange. The whole thing was strange. It wasn't like him at all, but maybe she didn't know him anymore.

'How long do you expect to stay in the United Kingdom, madam?' the young immigration officer asked Marge. She looked at Mike who showed her two fingers.

'Well, two days, maybe three or four,' she answered.

Mike showed her his fingers again. This time he whispered something.

'Two weeks, officer. I mean two weeks.'

'Very well,' the man said and stamped her passport.

'Tell me about Captain New, Mike,' Marge said as she stretched her legs in the taxi.

'The man knows quite a bit about Clay. He's intelligent. Clay must have confided in him. Told him things.'

'Surprising, Clay doesn't talk much. What sort of a man is New?'

'An opportunist, I reckon. His loyalty seems to depend on where the cash comes from. A moody man with a lousy temper, but ambitious. He admires Americans and seems to revere Clay. Talks about him like a god. A screwed up adulation that probably developed during the time they spent together in his village. We don't know what happened there. There may be things he is keeping to himself. I suppose Clay promised him something and he's waiting to see if he'll deliver. I get the feeling he consults with someone before talking to us. Maybe with Clay himself. He's cunning. Anyway, the info we get from him seems edited. It's as if he's intent on having a try at catching Clay himself. In any case, New knows his stuff. Everything he's passed to us so far has been accurate.'

'What does he look like?'

'What difference does that make?'

'Don't ever underestimate someone's appearance. It can tell you a lot. What does he look like?'

'He looks like a well-fed Vietnamese peasant. Thirtyish, thick set and short. I think he drinks. He dresses well, like every country boy who's made it. He likes gold watches and chains and big rings.'

'I get the picture. Strange for Clay to get involved with a man like that.'

'He didn't get involved with him. It was an accident. Apparently he saved Clay from the woman who captured him.'

'Clay isn't a prisoner anymore. He would have dropped

him by now.'

'There could be an easy explanation. We'll find out more later. For all I know, they might already be in Hong Kong.'

'They? You mean he's still with that woman?'

'Yes.'

'Would you believe it? How much longer before we get to the hotel? I need a bath.'

'Fifteen minutes. Do you want dinner?'

'No. I'll get room service.'

Marge turned away from him and closed her eyes. She was far from the taxi and farther from him. Mike knew she was not interested in the Captain. Her thoughts were with her husband and the woman. He couldn't blame her for that. He had made her husband into a hero in her eyes. There was romance in Clay's plight and the mysterious presence of a Vietcong woman by his side. Marge was jealous, he thought, and that was fatal.

Later, as Marge emerged from the steaming water in the bathtub, the phone rang. It was Mike. She wrapped herself in a big towel and answered wearily.

'I told you no dinner.'

'Clay's left Hong Kong. We don't know exactly how and when, but above all we don't know where he's gone.'

'What about the authorities?'

'Not much help there. He's got to have some kind of documents. God knows how he's managed that. It probably means he's not working alone. The British can do nothing for us now. We may as well go back to Paris and wait.'

'I'd like a bit of a rest first.'

'Sure thing.'

'Call me in an hour, okay?'

'Okay.' Mike had half expected her to invite him up,

but he knew she was tired. He put the phone down and sat on his bed. His conversation with the man from the embassy had been short and factual. They had been outsmarted. The telex came directly from Saigon and the news was fresh. Clayton Wayne-Turner had shot them all down. Could he have been in the pay of some other US agency? They would have known that in London, surely. A secret mission of some kind? Well that fitted the bill. They would have had his desertion look authentic. They didn't take chances, but why recruit someone with his background and fame? Too high profile. No, he didn't believe that. Maybe Clay was working for the reds, that was more logical.

Captain New had to be working for the reds, too. He would have warned them otherwise. He would have known Clay had left Hong Kong. Yes, Clay was working for the reds, but why? Not money. It was something else. Something driving him. The answer lay with Marge. He would get it out of her one way or another. Marge would know what it was.

Marge had fallen asleep and she dreamt Clay was having a bath in the hotel with Captain New and the half-caste woman. She was soaping the men's backs and they were smiling. Captain New had golden teeth. Next to the bath, in full air force uniform, she saw Mike Carter with a towel, waiting for Clay to come out. Clay was lying full length in the bath, splashing water all over the place. Captain New disappeared and then returned suddenly with a champagne glass in his hand. He raised it in Mike's direction.

'Have a drink, Mike,' she heard Clay say, but Mike declined firmly.

'That's an order, Mike. I'm a general now. You won't get me to jump out of the bath like you did Marge.'

Captain New appeared again from nowhere. He held

an enormous pistol in his hand. 'Drink with the General, Mike, or I tell Ho Chi Minh.'

Marge heard Mike laugh out loud and burst out laughing in her sleep. She was still laughing as the sound woke her. She was still wrapped in the towel and was perspiring heavily. She glanced at her watch. She wanted to lie down again and dream and see Clay. She had not had a dream in years and she remembered every vivid bit of this one. What did it mean?

In Mike's room, the phone rang. It was the man from the American Embassy. 'Look Carter, sorry to disturb you at this hour. We've just got a signal from Saigon. Captain New is going to Hong Kong. He's taken a week off. We got that from a porter at the Hotel Caravelle. He booked the plane ticket for him.'

'What is New going there for?'

'We don't know, but we'll find out. We'll have someone follow him there. Could he be going to meet Wayne-Turner?'

'I thought he had left Hong Kong.'

'We now figure he's still there.'

'Then we'd better stay here for now.'

'Right. Come see us tomorrow at eleven o'clock, okay?'

'All right.'

Mike was apprehensive about Marge's reaction. He took a deep breath and dialled her room. He uttered a careful hello and unexpectedly her voice was relaxed and friendly.

'Come up if you like, Mike. We can eat here. Anything you want me to order?'

'Just some scrambled eggs and toast. I'll be up in a minute.'

When Mike appeared at her door, Marge was taken

aback. 'You look awful,' she said as he came in. 'Fix you a drink?'

'Gin and tonic, thanks.'

She looked so self-contained and remote, Mike thought. He needed her badly. Why can't two people ever feel the same at the same time? he wondered. The waiter came in with the food and while they ate Mike told her the news.

'We stay then, right?'

'Yes, we'll go to Hong Kong if he's still there.'

'I think Clay is not telling Captain New everything. I think he's being chased by others, too. The woman he's with must be important. Maybe she's defected over to us. Maybe he's bringing her in. If that's so, you bet her people are after them now. Or else we're all wrong and Clay is working with her and for the reds in some capacity.'

'You don't believe that, do you?'

'No.'

Marge felt sorry for him. There was a weak, hopeful sparkle in his eyes that gave his face the expression of a child. He needed a boost. She'd take him on her own terms.

'That's all I wanted to hear. Once you're out of your office and uniform you can actually be human. Take your tie off.'

Mike's face flushed at her unexpected concern. He couldn't make her out. She looked almost official and yet her hands were touching him.

As she came closer, Marge saw mist in his eyes. Perhaps her dream wasn't a premonition at all, she thought. Just the extended imagination of a tired mind. Must keep in touch with reality. She was taking charge and she loved it. She could afford to be generous.

'Take me now,' she said gently and all of a sudden they were under the sheets as her hand switched the room lights off.

CHAPTER TWENTY-SEVEN

—■—

Captain New looked at the quivering sunlight on the wing, a flash of fire that came and went as the 727 flew over the South China Sea. The tourist section of the flight served free drinks and New indulged himself. He was going to Hong Kong on a week's leave, and in his pocket he had the list of purchases he was going to make. This was going to be the trip of a lifetime. He was, after all, a hero. Everybody wanted him. Everybody asked to meet with him to talk. They had hinted at great prizes. The man from the American air force was especially friendly. It was only natural, New thought with satisfaction. After all, he had saved their man. He must have been a very important colonel indeed. The air force people fussed about him and asked all kinds of questions. New's answers pleased them, but he didn't tell them everything.

Booking his tickets and the hotel went without a hitch. True, he did tell the Americans he was going to do it and they said his devotion to Colonel Wayne-Turner was commendable. They had offered to give him the money, but he politely refused. Maybe he should have taken it. The Colonel would surely praise him for arranging his leave and coming out to him with such efficiency. After all, what mattered was the end result and he had a duty to his people back in the village. He would soon have their gold bars back. Everything looked good.

The young man next to him was well dressed. He was polite, and his urbane, almost European manner and friendly overtures put the Captain at ease. He had a dark, twitchy face and a scar across his cheek. The nervous eyes behind his glasses showed fear. Perhaps it was a fear of flying, Captain New reasoned. He had noticed the man walked with difficulty when they showed him to his seat.

'Something wrong with your leg?' the Captain asked.

'Motorcycle accident.'

'I prefer four wheels myself.'

'You are quite right. Have you been in Hong Kong before?'

The man had a soft, cultured voice, New observed. 'No. The army keeps us officers busy.'

'Oh, you're a regular soldier then, defending the fatherland...'

'Yes. My name is Nguyen Nang Ding, but the Americans call me New, Captain New. Is this your first trip, Mr...'

'My name is Ming Ho. I get to Hong Kong often. Family business.'

'You rich?'

'We don't do badly, but no one knows how long it will last. Once the communists take the capital it will all be over.'

'They will never see Saigon.'

'If they do, they won't find me there.'

'Where will you go?'

'France. I was a student there. I have a lot of contacts in Paris.'

'Rest assured, it won't happen.'

'You don't know who to believe these days, Captain. The papers say one thing and the television pictures another. If we're doing so well, why are the Americans still here?'

'Do you prefer the Chinese or the Russians?'

'Of course not, but they keep sending people in. Rumour has it they're shipping bodies back to America by the hundreds.'

'Communist propaganda. Still, war is war. I have been a soldier all my life. They are going to make me a major soon.'

'I hope you are right. I'd hate to leave Saigon. Paris is a great city, but it isn't home. Why are you going to Hong Kong, Captain?'

'Oh, just a few days of shopping and fun.'

'Must be a great change for you, a fighting man.'

'Yes. In the field for three years, Ming Ho, living with danger.'

'Hong Kong might bore you.'

'I don't think so. I'm bound to see new faces there.'

'That will happen for sure. It's a city with people from all over the world.'

'You know Hong Kong well?'

'Yes, I suppose so.'

'Perhaps you can show me the ropes?'

'With pleasure,' Ming Ho said and closed his eyes.

Behind them, a plump young American was straining to listen to the conversation. He had taken pictures of the Captain and his friend and would wire them back to Saigon as soon as they landed. They should have sent someone else. All this was done at too short notice. He was weak with the language, but he had the conversation recorded anyway. He had placed the microphone, disguised in a small dictionary, between the two seats. They did not appear to discuss anything of importance. They seemed to have met for the first time, but one never knew in this business. Their constant laughter and shoulder tapping suggested they were telling each other jokes. What the gooks talked about didn't matter. What mattered was what they were going to do. The other man, Ming Ho, seemed serious. His movements and expressions were contrived and intelligent. What possible common ground would he have with the vulgar Captain New? The young American concluded that Ming Ho must have been planted on the Captain. The young American

156

had been told the Captain would lead him to the fugitive. He was not given the name of the man they were looking for, nor the reason he was being chased. He had only been in Vietnam for three months and he missed his Japanese girlfriend and the peace and quiet of the little town not far from Tokyo where he'd spent a happy year. He enjoyed his work in intelligence, but here his information was too limited. He had made some enquiries himself and the answers he was given were vague. He was not sure which intelligence arm of which service was after the man. It could prove to be a no go area if he belonged to a higher authority. He looked out and saw there was not a cloud in the sky. It was going to be a smooth flight.

CHAPTER TWENTY-EIGHT

———◼———

The man didn't look like a banker. His powerful shoulders and arms seemed to burst out of his pin-striped suit. His face was tanned and his healthy smile made him look like a ski instructor. The furniture in the office was sparse and photographs of Switzerland decorated the wall. Through the windows, the calm waters of Lake Lucerne shone in the sun as the banker looked through Clay's papers. Clay was casually dressed and his clean shaven face was pale, but it matched the picture in the passport the banker was holding. He was tired and his body clock kept reminding him Hong Kong was eight hours ahead.

'It is a great pleasure to meet you in person, Mr Wayne-Turner. We seldom meet with our customers in this business, you know. The numbers rarely become human.'

'I won't need a numbered account any more,' Clay

said. 'I'm about to move to Europe permanently.'

'In that case, we should look into an investment account. In dollar terms, your capital has almost doubled and the Swiss franc is strong at the moment.'

'Yes, so I understand. Should we convert the lot into dollars?'

'If you believe the Swiss franc has reached the top, you should.'

'What do you think?'

'It's hard to tell. Interest rates on the dollar are higher.'

'Does that mean my income will be higher, too?'

'It does.'

'In that case, let's do it,' Clay said.

His hotel, an old-fashioned white building, was just visible across the lake. He had left Bernadette to walk around the town. He hadn't had much of a chance to see Lucerne yet, having arrived on the last train from Zurich the night before. Now that his business with the bank was done, he could become a tourist, a luxury he had been looking forward to. He would be able to sit and watch people in the streets and do the things other people did. No appointments, no checkups, no flight paths to plot. Above all, there would be no family name to live up to or apologize for. No more being paraded for visiting congressmen. A large wad of thousand and hundred franc bills was put on the table in front of him. The colours, the sizes of the notes and their design fascinated him. It looked like toy money.

'Your interest for the year, Mr Wayne-Turner.'

'Your English is excellent.'

'I lived for a couple of years in western Canada, in British Columbia. It reminded me somewhat of Lucerne, only bigger, more majestic one could say. Vancouver and the bay, the mountains and the forest and the sea views down on Victoria Island. The people are just like the English, but they dress and talk American. Slower pace though, and not so many people.'

'Ever thought of staying there?'

'I did, but I missed the law and order here. You can get anywhere from here within an hour. You get on a plane and you're in a different country in no time at all. Canada was too big for me, I suppose. What is your room number, Mr Wayne-Turner? I may want to contact you about the investment plan.'

Clay told the banker, then shook his hand and left. Everybody was friendly and he felt at ease. He would lie low for a while before starting to seek his past. A part of his life was over now. He'd find himself a country by the sea not far from here and become a beachcomber. Bernadette was waiting for him by the pier and he crossed the street to join her. Behind the bank, the pale grey rocks of Mount Pilatus pointed at a cloudless sky. Around the lake, green hills rose to high, snow-covered peaks. The Swiss flag flew everywhere, flapping its blood-red colour from boats and tram cars and houses.

'Want to take a boat ride?' Clay asked her.

'Oh yes,' she agreed.

The picture postcard scenery that surrounded the boat on all sides excited Bernadette. White houses, chalets and perfectly shaped trees were visible around the lake. This was the country where her enemies of old, the rich, hid their money from the poor. There were no pirates on this lake and no gunfire. What a beautiful hiding place this was.

Why did she strive to change the world? she asked herself. What was wrong with it? Why did she ... but she had been young and naïve then, when the professor led her and the others to the barricades. She was a pushover. Perhaps the truth was here. No one seemed to go hungry or yearn for change. She had attacked a system she knew nothing about. Well fed, well dressed people sat on the deck. Was there no way to share this wealth out without bloodshed?

The steamer moved proudly, at a slow, elegant speed. How far she was from the choppy South China Sea. Clay paced the deck, then came and sat by her side. A perturbed expression showed on his face.

'What is troubling you?' Bernadette asked him.

'Should have stayed in Hong Kong a little longer to make sure.'

'Make sure?'

'Yes, I left Captain New a note with the porter at the Peninsula Hotel. Told him to go to the boat and collect his gold. Told him exactly where it was and where to find Patel. Left him some cash for his expenses and a note for the harbourmaster in case. I should have made sure it went all right.'

'You did all you could.'

'It's more complicated than that. I asked him to go see Patel after that. I need to talk to him about your people. Make sure he deals with them and gets them off your back.'

'You will never be able to do that. They are dedicated.'

'Patel and Captain New are also dedicated. They will do anything for money. I'm going to make it all safe for you. And I need to talk to the Captain.'

'Patel will get it out of him. He's that sort of man. He'll know.'

'He will need to know. I'm not sure New will understand it all. He's a simple guy.'

'Do you think all Vietnamese are simple?'

'I didn't mean it that way.'

'Why don't you just wait until tonight? You can call Mr Patel then. Didn't you ask Captain New to stay there until you called?'

'Yes.'

'What is the problem, then?'

'I don't know. Maybe he talked to someone.'

'There is nothing you can do from here. We have to accept there
are dangers. We knew that when we started, Clay. Worrying about it will change nothing.'

'I guess you're right.' Her strength and clarity of vision were new to him. He looked at her and wasn't sure what he saw. Was she changing? 'This boat isn't moving at all dammit.'

'You're tired, that's all. Just take it easy. Come and sit here with me.'

Was she becoming too forceful? Clay wondered. He'd have to decide what to do with her. He couldn't keep travelling with her forever, but he must. She was his companion now. He had told her they were in this together. She was his responsibility. He was just being erratic because he was tired. He put his arm around her shoulder and smiled. It seemed the boat picked up some speed, but his mind was still troubled.

The whisky had numbed Captain New's body. His tired, alcohol-sodden senses had sent his imagination flying. He floated in and out of consciousness. He did not feel Ming Ho's hands ease him onto the wooden planks of the deck. They had been sitting in the cockpit of the boat for hours, and they had talked. Captain New said something about the night and Ming Ho's hand felt for the reassuring shape of his knife.

'They came all the way on this little ship,' the Captain said. 'I couldn't do that. I hate the sea. I feel sick just sitting here now. I'd rather fly any time...' His voice was growing weaker. He touched the side of his neck. 'I am so tired Ming Ho,' he said with a sigh. 'It's hot in Hong Kong. Too much whisky ... sleep now I think.'

'Did you rape the woman before you locked her up in the hut?'

Captain New's mind was clouded. The question sounded strange. 'No, I was drunk then, like now. Felt nothing. Didn't rape her. I wanted to. Everybody wanted to. You would have done too. She was beautiful.'

'You said you did. You said you raped her when you told me how you saved the American. Spoils of war you said.'

'No, I did not, I lied. I just boasted. We locked her up and I sat with the Colonel all night and drank. Couldn't rape anyone. Wanted to, though. She was beautiful. Good man, the Colonel. He's kept his word. I must sleep now. Must go see Mr Patel tomorrow. The Colonel said. No more drink. Must wait to talk to the Colonel. Tell him the gold is back with me. He'll call Patel's office. Must sleep now.'

'Have you called Mr Patel yet?'

'No. Not called. Not seen him.'

'He knows nothing of this boat ... of the gold?'

'He knows nothing. I am tired. Must sleep. We had a long day.'

They had spent the whole day together, moving from one sleazy bar to another. The Captain had enjoyed Ming Ho's company even though the younger man did not drink. He had told him his life story more than once. Especially about his encounter with the American colonel and the woman and the young VC he had shot while chasing them. Now he sat on the floor of the cockpit and he was tired.

'Take my shirt off,' the Captain said. His voice was hoarse. 'It's so hot here on the boat. It all happened here you know.'

'Did you rape the woman?'

'I told you no. I didn't touch her. I wanted to, but I didn't. All I did was slap her hard. She became his woman. Not mine. He had her on this boat I tell you. You can still smell them down there. Smell of sweat and woman and man and sex. Strong man, the Colonel. She's still with him now.'

Blind anger assailed Ming Ho as the Captain's head fell on his knee, his sweaty neck exposed. Ming Ho touched it, then pulled his knife out and thrust the needle shaped blade into the flesh. The Captain's body began to wriggle. Ming Ho struggled to keep the heavy man in place. New's legs hit the ground and then he went limp. The humming traffic in the distance mingled with the sound of flapping sails hitting the mast.

Ming Ho undressed the Captain and eased him into the water. The naked body was slowly pulled by the tide and floated towards the bay and the open sea. He would be far away by the morning. Ming Ho went down into the cabin and looked about him. The bag was there where they had left it earlier. So this is where it had happened. Captain New had said he could smell it, but there was no smell at all. This was where Bernadette had given herself to the American. They were both far away now and he would look for her. And when he'd found her, his place in the party would be secure again. They were holding his mother and sister until he returned with Bernadette.

Ming Ho sat there for a while and thought of what the Captain had said. This was where she gave herself to the American. The pain stabbed at him and he climbed out and sat in the cockpit and looked at the water. The Triangle Trading Company of Mody Road. Mr Patel. The Captain had talked of them all day. He had showed him where the office was. Mr Patel was a friend of the American he'd said. He would go and visit Patel himself.

Things could have been so different. Bernadette had been ordered to take the Colonel up north. He had insisted on making her do it to clear the doubts they had once and for all. He could have revealed his feelings to her then. Now it was all over, but he would find them, Ming Ho swore. He would punish her. For being the professor's lover. For becoming the American's mistress. She was a woman, and women were fickle. They should never be allowed to interfere with a man's destiny. And yet still the pain inside him was deep. He would go into town and get drunk. He would look for the soft arms of a whore to sleep with and make believe she was Bernadette.

At the American Embassy in London, the lights burned brightly long into the night. The air attaché and his clerk were huddled over long telex messages from Hong Kong and Saigon. There were endless telephone conferences with Washington all through the early hours.

'Get Colonel Carter over here, now,' the air attaché told his aide. 'We can all take a day off once we've put him in the picture.'

'Does anyone else know the latest?'

'Only the Ambassador. Go on, get him.'

'The poor bastard.'

'Don't feel too sorry for him. He's having a great time of it.'

'What do you mean?'

'Forget it. I want him here inside ten minutes. Washington wants us to handle this from London. Too many Vietcong ears in Paris.'

Mike looked rested and comfortable in his civilian suit. They offered him coffee and gave him the news and his new orders.

'Are you sure?' he asked when it was over.

'You're damn right we're sure. The man's a spy. There's no other explanation to it. He must be located as soon as possible and eliminated. He's well known. We can't take the embarrassment of a high profile defection now.'

'Eliminated? You mean ... you mean killed...'

'Yes. If he shows up somewhere, we're in trouble.'

'Why would a man like that...'

'Carter, no one here or in Washington is interested in why. We don't want him approached or interrogated. Nothing. They were going to take a contract on him, but that's out. It's got to be an inside job. The fewer people who know, the better.'

'You mean I must do it myself?'

'You're in charge, Carter. It's your baby. You are relieved of all your other duties until this is done.'

'I'm not sure he's guilty.'

'Look, Carter, what you or I think doesn't matter. The other side is convinced he is. Clay's friend Captain New went to Hong Kong. He's been seen there all day with a known Vietcong big shot. We must be seen to do justice here. They'll lose respect if we don't. If the reds get into the top floor of the air force, they'll pass information to Moscow and Peking. They know we know. They expect us to act. It's no enquiry Carter, it's an execution.'

'I think we're being hasty.'

'The decision isn't hasty. We've got orders from the very top. Look, we know he wasn't quite himself lately. He changed, talked a lot of shit. Even that last flight of his, he didn't tell anyone about it. Didn't log a thing. There were no orders, no nothing. There it is, buddy. No more than a dozen people know he's alive, and this is how it must stay. Clayton Wayne-Turner died in Vietnam, shot down. He stays dead, understand? He does not surface anywhere.'

'What about the woman?'

'She's no concern of ours. The reds will deal with her.'

'What if new evidence turns up?'

'The case is closed, Carter. Find him and get rid of him, that's all.'

'Yes, sir.'

'Good. We understand each other.'

'I want this order in writing.'

'Forget it.'

'Does the Ambassador know about it?'

'Yes.'

'I want you to repeat the order in his presence. You'd do the same in my place. No one wants to take the rap for nothing. If things turn out to prove us wrong, I want it known ... I insist.'

'Okay, I'll look into it. Now look, you know what you've got to do. Do it yourself. No progress report until he's dead.'

Go get him, Mike thought as he reached Park Lane on his way back to the hotel. Three words that would make Marge a widow for real. Three words that would put an end to the life of a brother officer. Clay had no chance, Mike thought. And yet something was not right here. What could he tell Marge now?

He walked through the underground passage into the park. He'd take a long stroll to the Serpentine and think. What was there to think of? He would have to find Clay, and that needed time. There was no one he could talk to or consult. The guys at the Embassy were messenger boys. He'd be damned if he took it all lying down. In the time it took him to find Clay, something would give. He was no killer. Why couldn't he just take it and do what he was told and enjoy that delectable woman? No, he couldn't. Why? Because he was not that kind of a man. The scruples that had brought him thus far were beginning to hurt. Clay was guilty. Had to be. The people in Washington were no butchers. They wouldn't order him to kill a man without proof. They didn't tell him everything. That's what it was. They had their reasons, they always did.

In all his years in uniform, Mike Carter had never questioned his orders. He had taken the oath years before and had believed the flag could do no wrong. Killing was a young man's job. They'd believe anything. People had gone through the centuries destroying each other in the name of progress and religion and liberty. Maybe they were using him to find Clay. They'd stop him as soon as he was found. This could be a cover-up for something bigger. Or maybe Clay was doing something under cover–and it blew up. Now they were going to do away with him because he knew too much. Destroy the evidence. He must not ask too many questions. It would drive him mad.

Perhaps it was time for him to retire, but they wouldn't let him. They might disinherit him once he'd done it. And Marge? What could he tell her? How could he face her? Mike had always abhorred lying. Ever since he was a child. For the first time in years, he wished he could be a child again. The death sentence that now hung over Clayton Wayne-Turner was clear and cold. It hung over him, too.

CHAPTER TWENTY-NINE

—■—

'Someone is following us,' Bernadette said. 'There, by the window.'

Clay waited. He looked at her face and tried to read it. Her lips twitched. They had come off the boat at

Küssnacht, a quaint little town adorned by a statue of Wilhelm Tell that stood proudly, surrounded by flower beds. Gleaming red buses spilled out tourists into the square. They sat in a small restaurant overlooking the lake. On the walls, a herd of stuffed gazelle heads stared with sad eyes at the smoky room.

'He is looking at us,' she said. There was terror in her voice.

'Sure he is. Everybody is looking at you.'

She did cause a stir. She was well-dressed and made up and looked exotic. 'Look now,' she said.

Clay looked. The man by the window was large and had a red, puffed, sweaty face. He was wearing heavy tweeds. 'An Englishman,' Clay said. 'Have you never seen an Englishman?'

'I saw him on the boat. I saw him walk behind you when you came out of the bank. He was looking at you then.'

'You're being childish. Your imagination is going crazy.'

'Don't patronize me.'

'Dammit, I've got problems too. Can't a man crack a joke?'

'You're hiding things from me.'

'Christ almighty, if that's the case I must be hiding things from myself.'

'Why did you let me go?'

'What are you talking about now?'

'The hut, back in Vietnam. Why did you release me? You could have gone back ... I am going to cause trouble for you.'

'I don't want to talk about that now.'

'You must not worry about me. I can look after myself. You shouldn't cut yourself off from everything because of me.'

'Don't be so heavy. Come on. Let's get back to Lucerne.'

'You can't call Patel before midnight.'

'Let's go. This place depresses me.'

As they boarded the boat, Bernadette saw the big Englishman race down to reach the gangway. He was gasping for air.

'Look,' she said quietly. 'He's after us. I told you. I know.'

'Oh stop it now. Too clumsy for that. Just an over-weight guy trying to pick a boat. It's a free country. People travel. You're seeing things.'

'Have it your own way.'

On the boat there were holiday posters on the polished walls. Summer scenes with palms and beaches and Swissair planes. Yugoslavia. Greece. Italy. Mallorca.

'Should have thought of it before,' Clay said. 'Mal-lorca.'

'What about it?'

'We can go to Mallorca. It's a small island and you'll love the weather. Spent some time there years ago.'

'Okay, if you like.'

Mallorca. Fifty-five minutes from Zurich, the poster said. He was becoming restless. Could go to Zurich tonight. The money would last. And there was Howard's money too. He couldn't do that. Why not? Howard had no use for it. Clay still travelled on his passport. What was he so worried about? He looked at Bernadette. Maybe her anxiety had rubbed off on him.

The sun was still out when they docked at Lucerne, but the air had cooled. 'We'd better get you some sort of a coat,' Clay said. The bulky Englishman walked straight past them and disappeared. 'I told you no one is following us.'

'I don't need a coat. Aren't we going to that sunny island?'

'I need to call Patel tonight. Maybe we'll go tomorrow.'

'I'll stay in the room then.'

They walked over the famous bridge. Bernadette looked flushed and again she drew glances from passers-by. The tram cars and their bells sent ringing into the early evening air. Clay was momentarily happy. He was not trained to look for an enemy on the ground. Bernadette's worries seemed to have subsided as she glided under the wooden canopy of the ancient bridge and its paintings. The man was nowhere to be seen. Perhaps Clay had been right. Perhaps she had been seeing things.

They reached the hotel entrance in darkness. The street lights had come on in town and around the lake. Clay took a shower while she unpacked. They would take a rest before calling Hong Kong.

Patel's voice came through clearly on the line when Clay placed the call.

'You sound as if you're next door, Patel,' Clay said.

'Good morning, Colonel. Your voice is tired. You far away?'

'That would be telling. Has the Captain turned up yet?'

'Yes, Colonel. He's right here with me.'

'Can you put him on?'

'Right away,' Patel replied and handed the phone to the other man.

'Colonel Wayne-Turner?' The Captain never called him by name, Clay thought. 'Good to talk to you again, sir.' Something was different. Captain New's voice was always warm. It had enthusiasm before. This man sounded cold. Perhaps he was tired.

'Did you collect the gold, Captain?'

'I did. Thank you.'

'You know about the woman I am travelling with. . .'

'Sure, Colonel.'

'She thinks her people are following us. I need help from you.'

'Anything you say, Colonel. Your wish is my command.'

The man's English was too eloquent. Something was wrong. He'd better stop. 'I trust you are having fun in Hong Kong?'

'Sure, Colonel, sure.'

This man's answers were too short. 'Has the dog come back to the village, Captain?' There was silence on the other side. Clay waited. The Captain didn't sound drunk.

'Yes, it's back. So is everybody else.'

'You should tie him up next time.'

'No harm done. He was only gone for an hour. You said you wanted help with the girl?'

That was not Captain New. He was guessing. Something was different. English too good. The accent? That's it, the accent. 'Don't worry about it now. May I speak to Mr Patel again, Captain?'

While Patel was coming to the phone, Clay told Bernadette of his suspicion. She asked him to let her listen in.

'Hello,' said Patel.

'The man with you. Can he hear me?'

'No.'

'That is not Captain New.'

'Are you sure?'

'You bet I'm sure. Get rid of him. Tell him nothing more. Get him out this minute.'

'Oh, I can't do that, Colonel. Yes, of course I'm looking after Captain New. I know he saved your life.'

'You can't get rid of him?'

'You are quite correct.'

'Just look at him carefully. Memorize his face ... anything. Put him on again in twenty seconds, okay?'

'Sure, Colonel. I will do just that.'

Clay covered the mouthpiece. 'Will you recognize Captain New's voice?'

'Of course.'

'This man speaks like you, like a Frenchman, but his English is near perfect.'

'We used to be a French colony. Everybody over thirty speaks French.'

'The Captain's English stinks. His accent, if anything, is American.'

'Let me listen.'

'Are we ready, Mr Patel?' Clay asked.

'Oh sure. You want to speak to the Captain again?'

'Yes. Tell him to recite the national anthem. It's an agreed signal between us.'

He handed the phone to Bernadette. In Hong Kong, the man began to sing. Bernadette's face fell. Her skin went taut and pale. She covered the instrument with her hand. 'I know this man well. I know him,' she whispered. 'Here, take it.'

'Okay Captain New,' Clay said, his eyes fixed on her terrified face, 'I hope you forgive me, but you do remember we had agreed. I will never forget what you've done for me. I had to be sure you remembered our signal.'

'It's okay, Colonel. How is your woman? Is she happy?'

'She's in Paris. May I speak to Mr Patel again?'

'I will go and get him. He's left the room. Will you wait?'

'Sure,' Clay said and covered the mouthpiece with his hand. Bernadette told him who the man was. His name, she said, was Ming Ho. He was her mentor, a man she'd known for years. From way back in Paris. She was afraid of him. Clay put his hand on her shoulder and winked reassuringly. Patel came back on the line.

'You happy now, Colonel?'

'Can the man hear me?'

'No. Only me.'

'That is not Captain New. His name is Ming Ho, and he's a Vietcong, a dangerous, ruthless man. This can only mean Captain New is dead. What a mess. Your agent in Saigon talked too much. It's your fault, you know Patel, all your fault.'

'I don't know what to say.'

'Say nothing. Just get rid of him, but don't leave the office until you hear from me again.'

'Okay, Colonel. I will give him a good time. I'll pay for everything.'

Patel replaced the receiver and sat in silence, contemplating the Vietnamese who was looking him straight in the face and smiling. Too smug, too sure of himself, Patel thought. Too secure in this town. Where was Captain New? Could the American have been right? What would a Vietcong want with the Colonel?

In a few hours, he would know where Clay had gone. His own agent, an Englishman named Bloomfield had followed the couple all day. He had briefly reported from the airport where they had booked themselves on the Swissair flight for Zurich. Patel had instructed Bloomfield to get on the same flight. He would call and report as soon as they were settled somewhere. So it was Switzerland. That made sense. The American must have money there and he would know soon. Bloomfield was bound to call him. He smelt money. There was always money in fear and dirt. There was money in spying because governments pay. He wanted as much of that money for himself as he could get.

'I think that will be all for today,' he said to his guest. 'Tell me, Captain New, how long will you stay with us?'

'I don't know yet.'

'Let me take you out for dinner tonight. The Colonel has asked me to look after you.'

'That will be fine.'

'Meet me at the Baron's Table restaurant. It's at the Holiday Inn. Seven o'clock? I shall be waiting for you.'

Ming Ho shook the Indian's hand and was gone. He had noted the shift in Patel's posture. Something might have been worrying him, but then it could just be his way. He was a guttersnipe and a capitalist dog and he held the key to find the woman.

It had been a good day, Ming Ho thought as he stepped into the bustling street. The Americans would be looking for the couple themselves. They had the facilities to scan the world, but they were too careful. They would leave enough clues for him to find them first. In any case, he thought with a smile, Patel knew where they were and he would talk.

Ming Ho didn't like the town much. A show-case of slave labour. A playground for parasites with money to burn. A backstreet printing press for forgeries. The system that had allowed Patel and his type must be destroyed, he thought as he walked down Nathan Road. He was doing his share and when the new order came about his part would be remembered.

The phone rang in Patel's office. It was his English sleuth. 'They are in Lucerne,' the man told him in a tired voice. 'They have been sightseeing and visiting a bank and shopping. I am compiling a report with all the details.'

'Well done, Bloomfield. You sound tired. Get some rest.'

'I have not slept a wink. I can't sleep on a plane and I was never sure what they would do next. Had to stick behind them. We are staying at the same hotel. What now?'

'Get some sleep, but make sure you are up in the morning. Keep following them and call me the same time tomorrow. Are you okay for money? You'll need warm clothes. How is your back?'

'Better, Mr Patel, thank you. Much better.'

'When this is over you can stay in Europe for a little holiday. Go to a health farm or something. A little rest will do you a world of good.'

No one had ever cared for his well-being before. 'Thank you, Mr Patel,' he said.

'Goodnight.'

Patel was a man he could admire. He was a hard working, ruthless man, but he had compassion. His operations may not have been legal, but he had never once broken the law in the colony. As an ex-policeman in the Hong Kong Police, Bloomfield knew Patel's record. He had not been briefed on the background of the case and had no idea why the couple had to be followed. Patel would not waste that sort of effort on a divorce case.

Bloomfield decided to take a sleeping pill. He was overtired. He had seen a light under the Colonel's door only minutes before. Perhaps the Colonel was working for Patel too. But such was his trust of his employer that he did not need to ask any questions. Soon the alcohol and the barbiturate met in Bloomfield's veins. He fell asleep on the bed and slept with his shoes on.

CHAPTER THIRTY

—■—

The thought of having to become an executioner troubled Mike Carter. He needed a bath or something. It had been a long day and he had left Marge a message that he'd be out. As the day wore on, Mike had convinced himself that Clay was innocent. He'd have to dig up some information on his own. The frustration of helplessness was digging into his soul. It was nine o'clock and he switched the television on for the news. Some hill or another had been taken by the Americans near Da Nang. It had already changed hands three times that week. Casualties were reported to be high, the announcer said in his detached BBC voice. They showed archive footage of flag-wrapped coffins at some mainland USA airport. People held back their tears while soldiers fired salvos in the air. The main items on the news were the unemployment figures and the price of oil. They had their priorities all screwed up here, Mike thought, or did they? And then the telephone rang.

It was his contact man in Saigon. He had some more information about Captain New's VC friend and his movements in Hong Kong. Among the places he called on was a company in Mody Road called the Triangle Trading Company. The Captain himself had not been seen since last night, but they had the VC guy followed. He had been at Mody Road on two occasions and on both he had introduced himself as Captain New. Could Colonel Carter make anything of that?

The company name rang a bell. Mike called Washington and within an hour they came back with the answer. The company was well known to the Pentagon. It was being investigated, especially the head of the company, a Hong Kong resident of Indian origins by the name of Jagdish Patel.

The enquiry was headed by Colonel Clay Wayne-Turner. Colonel Carter was advised to leave it well alone.

Mike was hopewell as soon as he heard the reply. Perhaps Clay was doing a job for some other branch of the armed forces. Could some wires have been crossed? Was he supposed to disappear in order to continue the investigation? Washington did tell him the enquiry was still in progress.

The answer lay with the Triangle Trading Company. A few enquiries with the hotel operator gave him the company's number. He asked the operator to place the call, but she told him it was busy. She would try again soon.

He was frantic. He could still prove something. The man Patel was bound to tell him why Clay did not report to his base when he'd had the chance. On the second try, he reached the company. Patel's secretary said he was on an overseas call. He had visions of Clay on the line himself right that minute, talking to Patel and ignorant of the mess he was in. That was it, Mike concluded. Clay must still be on some official job that required him to disappear. And the air force wanted him dead. One hand didn't know what the other was doing. Not unusual.

The girl in Patel's office came back to ask whether he wished to hold. He said he would. She clicked him off the line and he waited.

'Sorry to keep you waiting,' she said, 'he's still on the line.'

'Your Vietnamese friend is after more than just my enchanting company,' Patel said to Clay. 'I feel it in my bones.'

'You could be right.'

'He wants to know where you are and it seems he's not the only one. What is it you've got that people are after, Colonel?'

'You tell me, Patel. I must be in some trouble.'

'Maybe I can help, Colonel, but you'll have to make it worth my while. You said Ming Ho is dangerous. What's that to me? It's not me he's after, it's you. Does your life have a price? I could talk to him. He might pay to know where you are.'

'You can't tell him a thing. Once you do that, you won't be around to collect. Not even from me. What can you tell him?'

'I could start by telling him you're in Lucerne.'

Clay did not expect that, but he revealed no shock. 'There's nothing more to say, Patel,' he said.

'Of course there is, Colonel. Two heads are better than one. We can still do business.'

'Let me sleep on it. I'll be in touch. Whatever you do, keep addressing Ming Ho as Captain New. Don't let him know you're on to him.'

'Call me at my home if you like,' Patel said and gave him his private number. They hung up.

Clay looked at Bernadette. 'We're leaving,' he said curtly. 'You were right. He knows where we are. The puffed-faced Englishman works for Patel.'

Bernadette got up and calmly walked to the suitcases. 'Thank you for a lovely afternoon,' she said with a faint smile, 'I'd better pack.'

'Why would Patel follow us?'

'Not us. It's me. Ming Ho wants to find me. You must get rid of me now, Clay. I'm going to cause problems for you. You don't know Ming Ho.'

She must have been frightened, but her voice was steady, as if she accepted the doom. He would protect her, he thought as a rush of warmth came to his face and he blushed. The woman was trying to shield him. She cared. He got up and took her in his arms. He should learn to listen – to her and to others.

'You're not going anywhere, lady. Unless you're sick of me, you're not going anywhere.'

'But...'

'We're in this together, Bernadette. Remember?'

He picked the phone up and asked for a porter. They wanted to check out. No, the hotel was very comfortable indeed, the food was excellent. So was the service. No, nothing and nobody had offended him. They just had a bit of bad news and had to leave town. Were there any trains this time of night? No? Well, could they hire a car? No? How about a taxi? The porter said he'd see what he could do.

The cab took them as far as the town of Zug. They stopped in front of the railway station and Clay asked the driver about trains to the south and Italy. The little man, armed with his timetable, rattled the information off with a serious face. Bernadette kept looking over her shoulder.

Clay tipped the driver. As soon as the car was gone down the empty street, Clay took Bernadette by the hand. A sluggish dawn crawled through the misty peaks and they saw trains being washed and polished for the day.

'I reckon they'll trace us to this town,' Clay said. 'We won't take a train from this station.'

'What are we going to do?'

'We'll get another cab. Take it two stations up the road, then get another. We'll board a train closer to Zurich, or we'll steal a car if you prefer.'

Bernadette laughed, and his spirits lifted with a new sense of danger. The woman looked up to him. She listened to every word he said. There was none of the bitterness he had associated with Marge. He was in command again and this was as good as any dogfight.

'You can fool a missile,' he told her, 'if you know where they hail from. At least we know who is following us, even if we don't know why.'

CHAPTER THIRTY-ONE

Patel sat back and looked at the wall. The man he was talking to was friendly and open.

'My name is Colonel Mike Carter. I won't beat around the bush, Mr Patel. I am looking for Colonel Wayne-Turner.'

'Why are you asking me?'

'We both know why, Mr Patel. You've got some dealings with Wayne-Turner. We know he came to see you. Do you know where he is?'

That could only mean the enquiry was still on, Patel decided. The Colonel had not done a thing to stop it. He was not working for the air force anymore, he was running from them. This man Carter was looking for him, but what had he done?

'Let me call you back, Colonel Carter,' Patel said. 'Give me your number.'

'I will. There's another thing, too. We need to know about a Vietnamese army officer called Captain New. Can you find out where he is? We know he was in Hong Kong yesterday.'

'Let me look into this,' Patel said. 'Give me your number.'

Mike told him and they hung up.

He should have never told Wayne-Turner he knew where he was, Patel thought. Bloomfield would be exposed. Still, he must not let it frustrate him. He had tried to reach his Saigon agent all morning, but the man was out. They said he went up country to check on some delivery and he'd soon be back. That could mean an hour or a month, he thought as he lit another cigar. In the old days, he would have gone to Saigon himself, but not now. There were too many personal accounts settled by murder in Saigon these days. They blamed every shooting on the war down there. A man could be gotten rid of for fifty dollars, and one never knew who held a grudge. You couldn't rely on anyone. No one except for Bloomfield, he sighed, and he wasn't even family.

Uncertainties tormented Patel. This was a puzzle that had no answer. Where did the real Captain New get to? What possible business could he have had with the likes of Wayne-Turner? Who was now running the enquiry into his business? Mike Carter? The longer he thought about it, the more confusing the picture became. Patel took a drink of scotch. Gold prices never rose in tranquil times, he remembered as the alcohol took effect. Secure businesses needed to pay no protection money. Uncertainty was good for business. He should have been grateful, but uncertainties made him nervous. He lived with fear of the squalid poverty he was born into. His success only served to remind him of where he had started.

The phone rang, but Patel didn't make a move to answer it. He couldn't bring himself to make conversation with anyone. Ming Ho came to his mind. The man was dangerous, Clay had said, and he looked it. He was certainly intelligent. He would have to make sure he never saw him alone again. What did he want with Clay? The colour of gold kept crawling back into Patel's mind. Gold and money. There was a payoff somewhere and Clay was involved. He was going to see Ming Ho later that night and he knew the man would never tell him a thing.

Patel lifted the phone and called the Souchang Martial Arts school. The voice on the other side knew who he was. They had done business before. 'I need two of your best this evening,' Patel said.

'Bodyguard operation or a kill?'

'Could be both. Holiday Inn Golden Mile. Baron's Table restaurant. Seven o'clock tonight.'

'Fine.'

'They better watch me like hawks. If they see me ask the waiter for a light, they must act immediately.'

'Understood. Thank you, Mr Patel.' He felt secure again. These people were professionals. Nothing could happen to him now. The intercontinental clock on the wall said it was ten o'clock in the morning in England. He picked the phone up and booked a call to London.

'Carter here,' the voice said.

'It's me, Patel.'

'You've got some news?'

'I had no luck in locating Captain New.'

'He's in Hong Kong. He's got to be. He was there yesterday.'

'I promise you he isn't here now.'

'Are you going to tell me where Colonel Wayne-Turner is?'

'Are you making me an offer?'

'Look, you've got a big problem with the air force, right? I might be able to help you if you help me. I can't promise anything.'

'You colonels are all alike. Wayne-Turner said he'd. . .'

'I figure I can do better, but I need to find him first. You seem to be the only one who knows where he can be found.'

'You're not the only one who wants him. You have competition. Someone followed Captain New to Hong Kong.'

'Yes, our man, a young, plump guy.'

'If your people are in the field, you don't need me.'

'We've lost him.'

'There's another man after them, a Vietnamese.'

'You know anything about him?'

'Maybe. He, too, is very keen on your colonel. I am a businessman. I sell to the highest bidder.'

'You'll have to tell me what they offer.'

'And you'll match that?'

'To use your phrase, let me say maybe. You know the Vietnamese?'

'I've told you too much already. You have not committed yourself.'

'My people won't move until I can show something concrete.'

'I'm meeting with the Vietnamese tonight. Let's leave it until tomorrow. I'll know more by then. We'll talk.'

'Good enough. I'll find out what can be done about that enquiry.'

'Goodbye, Colonel Carter.'

Patel felt better now. He sipped the whisky slowly and puffed at his cigar. It was six o'clock. It only took five minutes to get to the Holiday Inn from his office. He would be there in plenty of time to welcome his Vietnamese friend.

How many more people could the system cram into this stinking town, Ming Ho asked himself as he climbed the gangway to the ferry for Kowloon. Despite the crowd, he enjoyed the short ride across the bay. Out at sea, the lights made him forget this was a city without a future. He had visited Repulse Bay and Aberdeen where he saw discarded humanity at work. He saw places where children were born, grew up and died without ever going further than the next ridge. He saw sampan helmsmen who had never seen more than one Hong Kong dollar at one time. This was where people worked to support the pockets of the greedy.

In his bag, he carried the gold bars he had taken from the boat. He could use them later. Where was Wayne-Turner in all this? Where did the Indian fit in? It didn't make any difference, Ming Ho concluded as Kowloon approached. Patel knew where Bernadette was and nothing else mattered beyond that. It was six o'clock. He would get himself washed and shaved and would dress up. Suddenly, Ming Ho began to lose his patience. The docking of the ferry seemed to take forever.

The Baron's Table was packed and Patel's decadent smile welcomed Ming Ho into the restaurant. Johann Strauss's waltzes pulsated through the air. Austrian delicacies served on flowered wooden trays were whisked about by attractive, dirndl-clad, blonde waitresses. They settled down into their table and Ming Ho studied the complicated menu while watching the Indian from the corner of his eye.

'This looks like an exclusive place,' Ming Ho said. 'Everybody knows you here. How does it feel to be rich?'

Patel squashed his wet cigar end into the ashtray. A waiter came from nowhere and replaced it. He lit a match in anticipation, but Patel shook his head. 'It's hard work, Captain New. That's all it is, hard work.'

Ming Ho had bought Patel a box of Monte Cristo cigars. He handed them over. 'Difficult to find something for a man who has everything.'

'You are very observant, Captain New, and very kind. Let's see now, what would you like to eat?'

'You are a man of the world, Mr Patel. You order for me.'

Ming Ho had noticed the two young men at a nearby table. Their muscles bulged under their blue business suits. One ordered coffee while the other watched Patel from behind the menu. Ming Ho thought he saw the man nod.

'Would you like some wine, Captain New?'

'Yes, but would you order it for me?'

'To tell the truth, I am no expert...'

'Let me tell you the truth, too, Mr Patel. I am not Captain New. My name is Ming Ho. I suppose a man of your intelligence would have found that out long ago. I'd like to be open with you, be your friend. We can do business together. You choose the wine.'

Patel's surprise overcame him for a moment. He emptied a glassful of water. 'Where, Ming Ho, is Captain New?'

'The Captain's duty has been discharged, Mr Patel. Your Colonel owed him something. Now that he has collected, he's gone back to Saigon.'

'I don't understand that. The Colonel explicitly asked for the Captain to be here tonight. How do I know you are telling the truth?'

'You need proof? For your information, the Colonel had borrowed gold bars from the Captain. He had brought two of them to Hong Kong for safekeeping and now that he has gone and the Captain has collected his gold, Captain New has no interest in the Colonel. He helped him leave the colony, you know, and so did I. The Captain gave me one of his gold bars to show his appreciation. He asked me to find a safe place for the rest, here in Hong Kong. He doesn't believe Saigon will hold much longer, you see. Our Captain New is a very rich man.'

'Show me, Ming Ho, show me the gold.'

'Just pick up the parcel under the table, Mr Patel. Go on, take it to the bathroom and take a good look.'

Patel jumped up. He grabbed the parcel and took off. From the other table, one of the blue-suited Chinese sprinted after the Indian. Ming Ho dug into his hors d'oeuvres and carefully poured his wine into the flower vase.

When Patel came back, his face beamed. He seemed relaxed. His speech had slowed down and he was smiling.

'Is there more of this, Ming Ho?'

'Plenty, Mr Patel. Our Captain was a collector of gold bars, you might say. He didn't have much faith in his paper money pension.'

'How much more?'

'You are asking premature questions, Mr Patel. You should enjoy your meal first.'

'What do you want?'

'How do you mean that, Mr Patel?'

'You wouldn't offer me all this for nothing. There must be something you want of me.'

'Yes, but there's no hurry. The night is young and the gold won't run out on us. The South China News says it'll reach three hundred dollars an ounce. While you were out, I noticed the strawberry cake there on the dessert trolley. It looks delectable, Mr Patel. I also noticed those two men there. They finished their coffee a long time ago. Shouldn't they go home?'

Patel wrote a short note and called the waiter who, accepting the paper with a two hundred dollar bill, walked over to the other table. Ming Ho poured himself a glass of ice water.

'Wine makes me thirsty, Mr Patel. I have walked around all day. Sweated like a pig. I don't think we need any more partners, do you? You could become the major shareholder in this deal.' The table across from them was now empty.

'That's better,' Ming Ho said, nodding in that direction. 'We can deal now.'

'What do I have to do?'

'Do you know where the Colonel is?'

'You know I do. You heard him on the phone.'

'He called you. That does not mean you know where he is.'

'Come on, of course I know where he is.'

'I shall have to verify that statement.'

'You are very eloquent. You are articulate and thorough, Ming Ho.'

'I was going to be a journalist in my youth, but I'm sure my life story isn't what we're here for. Are you going to prove your claim?'

'I'll do better than that. We'll go call the Colonel now. You can speak to him yourself.'

'That would only frighten him off.'

'No worries there, my friend. One of my best people is tailing him right now. He hasn't left his side since they left. Shall we go?'

'Let's have some strawberry cake first.'

'You're a cool customer, Ming Ho. We will go places together.'

'Thank you.'

This was only the tip of some rich iceberg, Patel thought. The Colonel had something too many people wanted. Something of great value. Ming Ho was not offering him a partnership just for an address in Switzerland.

'What do you want with the fellow anyway?'

'This, my dear Mr Patel, will have to remain a secret until I make sure you know where he is.'

'I believe he had a woman with him. I saw her in my office a few days ago. A beautiful girl, I must admit.'

The statement brought a painful thump into Ming Ho's chest, but Patel had consumed too much wine to notice. The bill came and Patel signed it.

'How the rich live,' Ming Ho said with a grin. 'It's nice to be popular.'

'Shall we go to the office? My man Bloomfield is waiting for my call. He's the best detective I know.'

'An Englishman? I thought you only employed locals.'

'Not in Europe, Ming Ho, they stand out too much among the white faces. It's not too far and I have eaten too much. Mind if we walk?'

Bloomfield's voice was hoarse and it cracked with embarrassment.

'The birds have flown, Mr Patel, I have lost them. They have gone. I am sorry. There's nothing else I can say for the moment.'

'Stay there until you hear from me. Look after yourself.' The Vietnamese whispered something in his ear. 'Bloomfield, listen. Don't leave Lucerne. A Mr Ming Ho will be joining you there within a day or so. He has my full authority. He will take over. Co-operate with him, Mr Bloomfield. Obey him.'

'We all make mistakes, sir,' Bloomfield said. 'I'm sorry.'

'Don't worry about that now.'

'Yes, sir. I shall look forward to seeing Mr Ming Ho.'

'Are you okay for money?'

'Yes, sir. Thank you, Mr Patel. I am all right for money.'

'Ming Ho will bring ample funds out. You work on a plan to find them meantime. We'll be in touch, good night.'

'It seems you have a problem,' Ming Ho said. His expression was dark.

'Temporary hiccup, I assure you. Mr Bloomfield is good. He used to be a police officer here. He'll soon find them again.'

'Where did you say he was staying?'

'At the Grand Hotel in Lucerne.'

'What about a visa for Switzerland?'

'Just go see Mr Hartmann at the Swiss Consulate and give him one of these.'

From his drawer, Patel fished out a visiting card and made two crosses on it. 'You'll have no problems there. I think we should talk terms before you go. You know, who gets what and so on.'

'That will not be necessary, Mr Patel. We trust each other.'

Patel did not understand what the man meant. Bloomfield had failed him and there was little for him to sell now. With all the wine in his system, Patel did not worry as he usually did when he couldn't deliver. Colonel Carter was going to call, but Patel had decided he would decline whatever he had to offer. This man was a better bet. Ming Ho got up and stood by his side. He picked the phone up and dialled the operator.

Patel sat back and closed his eyes. He puffed at his cigar and his mind wandered back to the Ganges. He did not think of his childhood. The river radiated warm thoughts and the shadows were gone. He did not see the needle-like blade, nor feel it penetrate his neck and then the room went dark.

Ming Ho wiped the cold metal. It was only a small slash by the side of the throat. Patel's usefulness to him and the world had ended. He wondered where the man's soul would go. From Patel's drawer, Ming Ho took a large wad of bills he had noticed there before. He stuffed the money into the bag. Outside, the overcrowded city seemed to go on forever. No decent man would miss the scum who had been his host.

CHAPTER THIRTY-TWO

—■—

How can I ever forget that morning? I had hardly slept after that last telephone conversation with Mr Patel. I had failed him, yet he said nothing to scold me. There was warmth and concern in his voice then. Even when he told me about Ming Ho. Obey him, Mr Patel said. He'll tell you what is to be done. Look after yourself, he added, we'll be in touch. My life was going to change forever, but I did not know it then. I felt depressed. Sleeping pills always did that to me. I swore I would never take them again. I waited for news, but none came. I didn't dare leave the hotel. I had every transport schedule in the country brought up to my room. No trains, no planes and no roads out of Switzerland were going to be a secret to me. I had arranged the living room in my suite like a command post. There were maps and schedules hanging all over the walls.

Three days I stayed inside. I was tired and bitter. I had tried to call Mr Patel, but there was no answer. I didn't dare ask any of my former colleagues in the Hong Kong Police to take a look. My confidence in old friends was gone. It is strange, that after ten long years with the Hong Kong Police, I was made to feel like an outsider to a force I had helped to reorganize in the post-war years. There was little respect for us then. The Japanese occupation had been a calamity. People felt they had been let down by the empire on which the sun supposedly never set. Europeans who could escape went to Australia and the locals were left to bear the brunt. The bravery of Chiang Kai-shek and Mao Tse-tung resisting the Japanese became a legend that put us all to shame.

After landing in the colony with the army, I joined the police and I worked hard. It was going to be a career for life, the recruiting officer had said. I rose to the rank of inspector and had a number of impressive catches under my belt. I did well. My crime, I suppose, was being caught. A shipment of cocaine that was seized by customs was stored in a warehouse by the port. The place had been entrusted to members of my unit for the night, pending action. They were going to have the stuff burned the next day. That night, in the Miramar Bar, I was approached by a Chinese who owned the apartment in which I lived. He offered me a large sum of money. All he wanted me to do was get my people out of the warehouse for one hour. He said the politicians were going to sell it for cash in any case, so why worry. I don't know what came over me. I have never worked it out why I agreed, but I did. Every man has his price, I suppose. We arranged a party in the warehouse. The most beautiful girls the Chinese could find were brought to the place. There was a band and trays of delicious food. Someone suggested we leave the place for an empty tea house two streets away to continue the celebration there. We were gone for two hours. The lads had a good time and by the time we got back the drugs had vanished. The next day I was discharged from the force. My commander said I was lucky to get away without a jail sentence.

Hell, why pretend? I am old enough now to admit I was after the money. Others made fortunes out there. What I was not aware of then was that my chief was involved in the deal. He made more money out of it than I did. He left the force a rich man soon after. For a few months, I wandered the streets of the city without much to do. I used to go to the gym at the YMCA to keep myself fit and it was there that I first met Mr Patel.

Within days of our acquaintance, he offered me a job. I did well for him. I was running the security operation of the company and we saw each other often. He helped me invest my money and within a few years I had become quite wealthy. I did not seem to put a foot wrong until I got to Switzerland. And that was where I sat, locked up inside, waiting for new instructions.

And then, in the morning, three days after I was first told about him, Ming Ho walked into my room unannounced. He was a short, wiry man who wore glasses, but did not look like an intellectual. He had smooth, darkish skin and a hard face. He also had a slight limp. He looked straight at me, through me, perhaps. His presence sent an ice-cold gust of wind into me as his eyes measured me. I think I took an instant dislike to him then. Maybe it was fear.

'Please sit down,' I said. 'Would you like a coffee?'

'I am Ming Ho,' he said without niceties. 'I am taking this enquiry over.' He handed me one of Mr Patel's signed visiting cards.

'I was going to collect you at Zurich Airport,' I said, but he seemed uninterested. He had a small suitcase in his hand.

'I'll stay in the bedroom,' he said harshly. 'You put a bed for yourself in here.' He seemed accustomed to giving orders. 'We don't need to waste Mr Patel's money on unnecessary comforts.'

'Would you like some breakfast?'

'No,' he said. 'What were the American's last movements?'

He might have wanted to upset me. I don't know. From the first moment he came into my life, he had me agitated. His nervousness was infectious. He could not have been a very happy man. I had no idea where he had sprung from, but Mr Patel's judgement was always sound and he must have had his reasons. Mr Patel had told me himself Ming Ho was taking over. There was something about Ming Ho that mesmerized me. He was intense. He seemed angry most of the time. He was curt and gruff and stiff. Nothing pleased him and he made me feel stupid.

I went through every detail. I gave him a copy of my report. He made me take him for a boat trip on the lake. We went to Küssnacht, just like the Colonel did. We sat in that same restaurant, but Ming Ho didn't eat. He didn't like us being there, but food was important to me in those days and at the beginning I did not let him stop me from enjoying it. From that first day, he began to take control of me and he did that quite expertly. Bit by bit. I didn't even notice he was taking me over too and not just the investigation. In the evening, having walked back over the wooden bridge, we sat in the room and he said, 'You shouldn't have let him escape, Bloomfield.'

'Yes, that was bad. I guess he knew I was here. I think she noticed me.'

'Were they close?' he asked. That was quite out of character. This was a personal question and I said I wasn't close enough to them to hear. I couldn't help reading the intense curiosity that had taken charge of his face.

'I don't know,' I said.

'You could have watched their movements. Their body ballet towards each other. Did he take her in his arms?'

'I didn't notice.'

'Mr Patel said you were a great detective.'

'I've been with him for five years.'

'Do you think they would stay in Switzerland?'

'I don't think so. It's a small place. They know we are here.'

'Are they still together?'

'Fifty-fifty, that. I wonder why Mr Patel is so interested in them.'

'That is not your concern.'

He was right, of course. My orders had been clear.

Follow Ming Ho's instructions, Patel had said and that I was going to do. During that first day, Ming Ho made me feel useless. I talked and he heard what I said and I am sure he took notice, but his uninterested face dismissed me as if I was an idiot.

'Where would they go, do you think?'

'Summer is coming. They could go anywhere. They would go somewhere crowded. The Mediterranean coast, Italy, North Africa, Spain maybe. The whole continent belongs to the sun in summer. The Colonel is a seaman. I should think they'd go somewhere where there are boats.'

'That's not good enough. It could be anywhere.'

'If we knew the name he is travelling under, it would be easier. Do you want me to go back to Hong Kong?'

'When I do, I'll tell you,' he snapped. 'I think the man is travelling on a Canadian passport.'

'How do you know?'

'The boat he sailed into Hong Kong on was registered in Canada. If we can find out in whose name it was registered, we might work out what name he's travelling on. The owner disappeared. I'm sure the American killed him.'

'How do you know there was an owner?'

'Captain New told me there was. The man sailed out of Vietnam with them, but he never arrived in Hong Kong. The American killed him.'

'A tall story. He wouldn't do that while on the run. Too many clues.'

'They sailed all the way to Hong Kong, Bloomfield. He could have thrown the Canadian overboard any place. The man could have had an accident.'

'Yes, perhaps an accident. That I'd go along with.'

'You find out about the boat.'

'I can call Lloyd's in London in the morning. They may have a record of the insurance.'

'No, you go to London yourself. I will wait here.'

'We could check at the bank.'

'What bank?'

'The American visited a bank here.'

'Find out in the morning.'

'It's not so simple. There's banking secrecy in this country.'

'We'll see about that. You better go to England then.'

'What was the name of the boat?'

'Peace for the Lord,' he said. I couldn't help smiling.

'I'll be off in the morning. Would you like some dinner?'

'All you think about is food,' he scolded me. I pretended not to take any notice and left the room to go out. The fresh air outside cleared my head and I walked into town. I hoped he would be asleep when I got back. I had had just about enough of him for one day.

I had not been back to England since the war. I cannot say I enjoyed my visit. Perhaps it was too short. Perhaps it was because I had no one there. It was a big, impersonal place with dirty streets and people who seemed too serious. Lloyd's of London were polite, but could not help me at all. The insurance, they said, must have been done in Canada. The man I spoke to said he would make enquiries for me. It was a wasted trip. I only stayed in town for one night. I tried to reach Hong Kong from there and came up with nothing. There was no answer. Mr Patel's private number was unobtainable.

Ming Ho's tense figure awaited me at Zurich airport when I got back. We took a train to Zug and looked around the railway station for an hour. Ming Ho chatted to passers-by in French.

'Try to enter his mind,' Ming Ho told me. 'He is an

unusual tourist. He is on the run. Unfortunately, he has seen you. That narrows your usefulness for now.'

'Do you want me to go back to Hong Kong?'

'I told you before, when I want you to do something, I'll tell you.'

'To start with, we ought to work out how he got out of here.'

'For once you're using your head. What do you suggest?'

I loved it. Finally, he'd noticed me. I had become a human being at last. It's funny how you become a slave to someone in authority. How you want to please them, how you obey and take abuse and humiliation. And then, out of the blue, when they pay you a compliment, you settle down. You forget everything, every thought of rebellion. You lie down and you purr like a satisfied cat.

'He couldn't rent a car and no one had seen him board the train. He must have taken a taxi. This is a small place. The man would remember him because the ride must have been unusually long. Or maybe he did rent a car. We could soon find that out.'

'He'd need a passport for that...'

'They could have used her name. He could have used his own name, too. Mr Patel got him a replica of his own passport. He wouldn't have been able to visit the bank without identification.'

'Could be, but he didn't use his passport in Hong Kong. No Wayne-Turner has either entered or left Hong Kong. Mr Patel has checked that. I think he used the Canadian's name. He got rid of him. The man's a killer.'

'What makes you say that?'

'He was a fighter pilot.'

'That's different. I tell you, I saw him. He didn't look like a cold-blooded killer to me. The woman was with him, too. She wouldn't have stood for that.'

'She is a Vietcong. She is trained to kill.'

'I still think something else happened to the Canadian.'

'Yes, he was murdered.'

'You keep saying that. Why?'

'I didn't want to tell you. I know you were close to him...'

'To whom? What are you saying, Ming Ho?'

'Your American killed Mr Patel.'

I was in too much of a shock to think. 'When?' I asked.

'The day before I left. He had him stabbed in his own office.'

'How? He wasn't there. He was here for Christ's sake.'

'You know he had a friend in the Vietnamese Army, Captain New. The Captain did it for him. He was paid for it. Patel was a gentleman. As far as I am concerned, the American Colonel killed him himself.'

'We've got to find him now, Ming Ho. I wonder what it was Mr Patel wanted with him.'

'It doesn't matter. We'll complete the job. We'll get him for this crime if nothing else.'

I stormed out of the room and walked to the central post office. I booked a call to Hong Kong. One of my old colleagues, with whom I was still on talking terms, confirmed what Ming Ho had said. Mr Patel was dead. Stabbed in his office. There were no clues at all. No one was going to send me Christmas cards anymore, call out of the blue to ask how my back was. Patel was like that. Now he was dead.

'I'm sorry,' he said. 'I know you were close to him.'

'He was my family,' I said.

'If there's anything I can do, let me know.'

I think I wandered the streets all night. I walked from one bar into another. I could hardly walk when Ming Ho found me at dawn, sitting on a bench by the lake. He walked out of the mist and sat by my side. At first he said nothing. He just watched me. Dark thoughts bedevilled me. I had never been lonelier. I had left my pistol at the hotel, otherwise I would have certainly done some damage to myself. Patel was dead and in what had been our last conversation I had failed him. I sat there and sucked at the whisky. I was talking to myself.

'You want to kill yourself?' Ming Ho asked. His voice was gentle and his arm was on my shoulder. He seemed almost human then, but I was paralytic. In my need for sympathy, I could have imagined it. I cried like a child.

'I don't know.'

'Trust me, Bloomfield. Get even. Don't get angry.'

CHAPTER THIRTY-THREE

◆

Ming Ho had traded the arms of the Buddah for Lenin's years before. I knew he was a communist. The way he talked of money and the rich and factories had convinced me. I never asked myself how such a man got involved with Mr Patel. I was now caught by the fever of the hunter. Not only because Mr Patel had ordered me. I had a personal reason, a sort of vendetta. The Colonel had caused Mr Patel's death and the woman was with him. That made her an accomplice. Finding them became the most important thing in my life. It was to be my mission. I was burning inside. Not once did I give a thought to the original reason for this chase. Ming Ho was the leader, but I was going to be the powerhouse.

We combed Europe in our search for them. We

travelled by trains and buses. We visited many places, but saw none. We crossed borders at night. Sometimes, I posed as a policeman bringing a prisoner to justice. Sometimes I was a businessman touring Europe with a prospective customer. On one occasion, we acted the part of two missionaries out of Hong Kong on our way to Rome. Mr Patel would have been proud of my inventiveness. We went along the coast of France from Cap d'Agde to Cassis and all the way from there to San Remo in Italy. We checked every hotel and every marina and every holiday camp along the Gulf of Lyon and the Côte d'Azur. The old Mediterranean had warmed up by the time we reached Cannes.

Frustration and loneliness were getting me down. I had put on ten pounds of further flab. I was only able to button my trousers up when stretched on my back. My flannel suit still fitted me, but with summer around the corner I was sweltering.

Ming Ho was mean with Mr Patel's money. He made me hire a tiny Fiat 600. Sitting with my bulge behind the wheel along the fashionable coast, my belt undone to help me breathe, was most humiliating. Ming Ho made fun of me. He said I resembled a Chinese bear. I didn't think of all that then. The adrenalin was high in my system and I was working out what I was going to do to the American when I caught up with him. I thought of nothing else. Lived for nothing else.

Of course, I was not young any more, even then. The daily, sweaty slog and the cheap hotels and oily food were taking their toll on me. I could have had some money cabled from my private account in Hong Kong, but that didn't even enter my mind. I allowed Ming Ho to take our finances over. I found relief in food and mealtimes became corners of tranquillity to me. Ming Ho never talked much and often he disappeared to make strange telephone calls to people in places unknown. He always took his little suitcase with him and, somewhere, a curiosity developed inside of me. I imagined all kinds of things lurked in there and I thought of looking there at night, but Ming Ho never appeared to sleep.

When we arrived in Genoa, Ming Ho announced we were going to stay there. This was going to be our base. It was there, sitting in a small spaghetti house that a brainwave hit me.

'I'm going to call Switzerland,' I said.

'No you will not,' Ming Ho snapped, making notes on his eternal pad. 'You stay here. What do you want to call Switzerland for?'

'I have an idea.'

'Since when do you have any ideas?'

I don't know what possessed me then, but I had nothing to lose. I was rude to him. I called him names, but he did not notice. My anger was coming out. I could have hit him. He looked at my face and then smiled 'What's on your mind?' he asked.

'I'll tell you later,' I said and rose to walk across the road to our hotel. 'If you want me to do anything further for you, you better stay right here. If you don't, I'll go back to Hong Kong.'

'Why don't you order some more food?' he suggested.

'When I get back.'

I think I ran across to the hotel. I must have looked ridiculous in my suit among the bikinis. The reception chief smiled at me.

'Give me the international operator,' I said, out of breath.

I soon got to speak to the porter at the Grand Hotel in Lucerne. The man remembered me. I asked him for the name of the bank by the lake, across the road from the railway station. He gave me the number. I was excited when they answered. I put on a perfect American accent and told the girl my name was Clayton Wayne-Turner. Would she put me through to the man who looked after my account? I hit gold that time. A man's voice came on the line and he was most co-operative.

'Where are you?' he asked.

'In Genoa, Italy,' I said. 'Have you made all the arrangements?' It was a long shot, but I could always put the phone down.

'You'd better give me your new address Mr Wayne-Turner,' the banker said. 'When did you leave Mallorca?' So that's where they went.

'I can't hear you very well,' I said, 'it's a lousy line. Let me call you back.'

'Did you contact the American Express office in Palma?'

'I can't hear you at all. I'll call again,' I said and hung up. I was too excited to talk. The man I had been chasing was only across the water from me. I took a deep breath. I was earning my keep at last. Mallorca. Why didn't I think of that before? It was an island and popular enough for them to get lost in. There were boats there and the Colonel would not be able to leave without being noticed. I could make contact with the Spanish police. I still had my police union card. Mr Patel would have been pleased with me, I thought. I must have beamed with pride. The hotel receptionist smiled at me as I walked past him. 'Good news?' he asked and I nodded and flew out.

Ming Ho was still there, where I had left him. I was seized by an enormous appetite. I ordered a bottle of red wine and another plate of spaghetti. I looked at him, but his eyes were distant. He just sat there and I thought he was in one of his morose moods. He did not say anything when

I ordered a huge plate of ice-cream. He didn't talk at all.

'Got them,' I said. I would have given a lot to know what went through his mind then, but he hugged his little case and remained silent. It could have been I was gaining the upper hand on him, but his sadness and silence took all the pleasure out of it. 'Give me some money,' I said when the meal was over. 'I'll need some clothes.' He didn't argue and just handed me a large wad of those beautiful Italian bills without making a note of the amount.

'Want to come with me?' He shook his head. 'We're leaving town,' I said. 'I have found them.'

There was a flash of light in his eyes, but it didn't last. Something was definitely wrong with him. It was as if he never wanted to find them at all. 'I'll be a couple of hours,' I told him. 'You pay the bill.' He nodded. 'I'll see you back at the hotel.' He nodded again and I walked out.

Hindsight is a mister smartass. Now, all these years later, I know exactly what had happened to him. What it was that had driven him. What torment his smitten soul had gone through. Ming Ho was born to be a poet. How and when his verses gave way to hate and war and the struggle for causes, I didn't know. Not then.

Ming Ho never let you know he was listening. His face seemed bored and uninterested in anything I had to say. At best, his expression was vacant. Only now do I realize that he knew. He knew we were closing in on them and he wasn't sure what he was going to do. Was he ever going to get her back to where she was the day Clay fell into her life? Was he going to save his tarnished reputation? He was a tortured soul. I must have suspected, even then, that there was more to it. He was after her for something else. Maybe she did something awful to him way back in Paris. He became strange and remote every time I talked of her. He was becoming weak and I was taking over. He hardly mentioned the American Colonel. At that time, I was blind. I was too full of my own importance to notice any of it.

I splashed out on a heap of summer clothes. I got shoes and suits and shirts and a hat. I bought a suitcase and aftershave lotion and hair oil. There is a large choice for big men in Latin countries. No one looks at you or mocks your size. No one tells you to go on a diet. People there enjoy themselves and are certainly not as critical as we are. That is why I am going to live out my life on the shore of this ancient sea.

Ming Ho was hiding things from me. He played with my pride to cover his frustrations. God, how much simpler life would have been had I known all this then, but I didn't. He had humiliated me almost daily. I hated that man with a passion. I forgave him nothing. The only emotion in me was the desire to avenge Mr Patel.

I booked a passage to Palma via Barcelona. We were to depart three days later on a ship belonging to the Kangaroo line. The ship, I was told, was modern and I bought first class tickets. I felt like a naughty schoolboy. When I told Ming Ho about it, he did not argue. His chronic misery persisted all day and I went out and saw a film. Mallorca was a day and a half away and soon the Colonel would be in my hand.

CHAPTER THIRTY-FOUR

◆

The mist patches that had shadowed the Mediterranean lifted as the sleek ship cut her way through the dark, calm waters of summer. The *Cabo de San Sebastian* of Barcelona was gliding into the bay of Palma. Up on the bridge, the duty officer called the Captain in his cabin. He liked to be in personal command of the large ferry boat for her entry into Palma de Mallorca. The ship was not full to capacity as the tourist invasion was only due to start some weeks later. A party of school children from Holland who had started the trip raising hell and roaming the decks deep into the night were now exhausted. Their soft, innocent sleeping faces turned upwards towards the ceiling, they lay dead to the world.

'The old sea is a swimming pool today,' the first officer commented to his Captain who yawned in agreement.

The first rays of morning sun entered their cabin and landed on Clay's cheeks. He opened his eyes, rose and drew the thin curtains. Bernadette was still asleep and he got dressed and tiptoed out of the cabin to watch the docking. He still had to decide what to do with Bernadette. He enjoyed her dependence on him. The way she looked, open-eyed, every time he said something, as if he was the smartest man in the world. And everywhere they went, people looked at her with great admiration. Perhaps she might like to go back to France. She had lived there for many years, but whenever he broached the subject, she seemed frightened. At such times, she would come close to him and snuggle under his arm like a child. Protecting her made him feel important. Marge used to talk of his lack of compassion, but Marge did not need him. She was always her own woman. The only mystery was Bernadette's dark moments of depression. They would come suddenly. Her eyes would darken and her face would fall. And then she would get up and go somewhere and sit by herself. During those moments, she didn't want him near her. She wouldn't talk or smile. She would just sit where she was. It did not last too long. Something was missing from her life, he thought, and he was going to find out what it was and give it to her.

The wide bay of Palma spread out ahead, its rocky walls and pine-strewn hills stretched open like beckoning arms. The grey waters turned emerald green and under a gloriously blue sky the last morning clouds evaporated. Ahead, the old city began to take shape as the unmistakable structure of the cathedral rose to welcome the eye. In the cabin below, Bernadette awoke. She felt for Clay's body and her hand stretched into nothing. She sat up with a fright. Why did he go without telling her? She heard the voices outside and looked out of the window at the sea. Rays of sun had set it alight. The heat calmed her nerves and she went back to bed and lay down. There was new excitement on the shore. It was a small island. No one would find them there.

Why did she always have to find new places? Was that why no one stayed with her? What did the future hold? Nothing. She had no future as long as Ming Ho was after her. And he had been her friend. He had saved her life and she had repaid him by betraying his confidence. She had failed him like she had failed everyone else. Nothing good would ever come of her, she had been told by the big girls at the convent. They had been right. With her being around Clay's neck, he would get into trouble. His people could not be far behind. Soon she would sink into darkness. If only she could just lie down and die. But Clay had been kind to her. He seemed to really care. She must at least try. She must not allow the black void to take her. She must not dwell on her problems. Other people were worse off and they had faith. Howard had faith, but Howard was at the bottom of the South China Sea and all because of her. No, no. She jumped out of bed and went to the shower cubicle. Soon the cold water made her shiver and washed her anxieties down the drain.

It had taken them two weeks to reach Palma. As soon as they had arrived in Zurich, Clay called his bank and made arrangements for them to find him a corresponding bank in Palma. In the meantime, they could contact him at the American Express branch office there. From Zurich, they had flown to Lausanne where they took the train to Dijon in France. Clay was travelling as Howard Jelinek and the passport control on board the train was casual. At Dijon, Bernadette hired a car under her name. They drove through France and across the Spanish border to Barcelona where they had boarded the ship.

Clay stood on deck and watched the city. The cathedral and Bendinat Castle grew closer as the ship approached. He thought of the time, years ago, when Marge and he flew down from London to visit a friend who was stationed aboard the Saratoga, anchored in this same bay. Those were carefree days. Perhaps the only happy time he had known. Marge was interested in everything they had seen and they had rented a small car and travelled the length and breadth of the island. They ate in quaint little tapas bars and seafood places and saw the villages that had remained in the Middle Ages in spite of the tourists. They went shopping through the narrow streets of the old city and visited the caves in Porto Christo. They swam off deserted beaches in the moonlight. They were an attractive couple and life stretched ahead with optimistic youthfulness. When did all the bitterness come in? How? Was he doomed to spend his search for his past running away from people?

If only he could have turned the clock back to the day before his mother had told him he was not her son. He would then rewrite the script and exclude that sentence. Life would have turned out differently and he would not be here, in his middle years, in search of a lost identity. His mother had never spoken of that again and all the enquiries he started had drawn a blank. The letter she had left him was no longer there. Could he not burn the memory of what she had said?

He had been born in Germany. That much he knew. It even said so on his own passport. The documents relating to his actual birth would have been destroyed during the war. Perhaps there were none. Perhaps they had ordered him from his real mother. Perhaps he had been kidnapped. Only God knew. Perhaps his mother had lied. Perhaps he had been her son all the time and she just wanted to hurt him. Maybe that was why no one else knew.

Clay paced the deck. Where he was now, it didn't matter a damn. His mother had been dead for years and he, adopted or otherwise, was a wanted man and as such his roots didn't matter. If only he'd been able to contact Patel or Captain New. He could get the Captain to change his story. Say he had been killed. It would have been easy for the Captain to say it had all been a mistake. To say he had never left the village alive. He would have been paid handsomely for that. But no, he was dreaming.

Face facts, Clay told himself. Someone was looking for Bernadette. Of course her people would want her. The mere mention of Ming Ho's name never failed to shake her. There must have been terror in her past, but she never talked of it. It was as if her life had started the day he fell into her field. She did see things, though. She had been right about the plump Englishman, but they had not seen him again. They were both fugitives now. The air force was looking for him. Together with Marge they would dog him back into the land of the living. Perhaps he should make contact with them. People are not bad. Since the crash, he had seen other travellers. Howard's faith had impressed him greatly, but he had God to trust in. People would have failed him,

Clay thought and a bitter smile appeared on his face.

The ship was closing in on the ancient stone walled pier. Clay watched the cathedral extending into full view on the other side of the port. There was fun ahead. He could rent a boat and sail again. He ruffled his hair and felt the heat caressing his face. He took one more look at the palms along the Paseo Maritimo and went below.

CHAPTER THIRTY-FIVE

A solid line of car lights moved along the curving bay below them. Hulls and masts and the illuminated cathedral were reflected in the water. A coloured Christmas tree of bulbs in the shape of a cruise ship approached the harbour. Bernadette and Clay sat at Tito's night-club watching the cabaret, and Clay had his first scotch since Hong Kong. Trumpets, drums and a piano-led orchestra played a forties routine as two black tap dancers appeared on the stage. The small hotel they had been staying in was a few blocks away and only half full. The porter had told them that the big rush of tourists would start in a few weeks. He liked them, he'd said, and would see that they got a special price. They would have to leave later, though. The place was sold out for the season, but he would find somewhere for them. If they wanted to tour this beautiful island he could recommend a cheap car hire firm. Or maybe they wanted a scooter. It was cooler and easier to park. It would be fun riding the Vespa up and down the narrow cobbled streets with the trees flying by alongside.

The porter had promised he would find them somewhere to go well before they had to leave. It would be cheaper for them to stay outside Palma, he said. If they were careful with their funds, Clay calculated, they would be able to stay on the island for a long time. His banker in Lucerne knew where he was. For the moment, he could sit back and relax. Clay clapped his hands as he watched the tap dancers perform a miracle of movement on the wooden floor. He took another sip of his drink. The cool air and the whisky made him forget why he was there. He decided he should try not to think, now that he represented no one but himself. Whoever he was.

'We are throwing good money away,' Bernadette said as Clay called for another drink. 'I can get a bottle to keep in the room.'

'Just a little fun once in a while,' Clay answered.

And then the stage was flooded in red and a magician appeared. His tricks amused Bernadette and she began to laugh out loud.

From his office in Paris, Mike Carter tried once more to talk sense to the operator. It couldn't be, he said, that the number in Hong Kong did not exist. He had gotten through to it from London. And not just once. He had even called it collect on occasion. An argument ensued. She said he didn't need to be rude and he told her she should get another job. Then he was put through to a supervisor.

Ever since Mike had left London, all signs of life concerning Clay, Captain New and Patel had vanished. No one could, or would, tell him anything. The office next door to Patel had little to say. Yes there used to be an Indian company there on the second floor, but they had moved. His man from the air force flew in from Saigon and combed the area. He was told The Triangle Trading Company could have gone back to India. There was a new government there now. People do not stay in Hong Kong forever. They come and make their money, then they leave. They don't write letters or leave forwarding addresses.

'It must have been an unlisted number,' the supervisor said. 'I am sorry. Hong Kong says there is no record of it.'

So the Patels were no longer in Mody Road. Perhaps they were never there in the first place. It was all crazy. Three people could not disappear just like that, and all at the same time. The air force man had said he'd managed to get inside. The offices were empty and they looked dusty, as if they had never been occupied. No, he didn't doubt Mike's sincerity or sanity. It was just that things were different in that part of the world. Nothing was permanent. The population was nomadic and fluid. Companies were born and died within weeks. Often they were only formed for one deal. It was normal here. Sorry.

Mike had not seen Marge since London. She had planned to take a tour of southern Europe before the summer. She had kept her room at the Paris Intercontinental, but was hardly ever there. Now that the French were preparing to leave Paris and the Germans, the Swedes and the British were coming, the attraction of the city was lost to her. She did write him a short note. For now, she had told him, she did not know her own mind or what she wanted or what she had expected of him. He would understand, she said. Then the phone rang and it was her.

'Long time no see,' she said. 'How are you?'

'Never better,' he answered quickly.

'You're lying.'

'You're right.'

'Want a bite to eat tonight?'

'Okay. Where are you?'

'At the Intercontinental. I'm planning a little cruise. Thought I'd pick your brain.'

She sounded friendly, Mike thought, too friendly. He could detect none of the tension her voice had when they were lovers.

'Where are you thinking of going?'

'It's going to be hot in town. A boat trip before the summer comes down on me. Then back home.'

'There are a few cruises around the Mediterranean. They stop in many ports.'

'I want to see people, too.'

'I hear they do have people on these boats.'

Marge laughed. 'Can you ask around?'

'Sure thing. What time?'

'Six-thirty?'

'Fine.'

Marge was pleased with the way he'd sounded. She'd book herself an appointment at the beauty salon. Not for Mike, she thought, for herself. Her bags were more or less packed and she needed to get away from her room. It was creepy.

She emptied her pocket-book onto the bed. With the coins and her lipstick she saw Clay's driving permit. His rugged, handsome face stared at her from the colour photograph. It felt like an omen.

Marge started thinking about him. He must have changed a lot. He had been on the run and danger alters people. He had to fend for himself. Was he cold or hungry? Where did he get money from? Was he afraid? Did he need anyone? And the woman with him, what about the woman? Was he in love with her? Nonsense, Clay wasn't in love with anyone. But what if he'd changed? What if he'd become all the things she had wanted him to be?

She called the front desk and said she was planning to go on a cruise. Would they send up some leaflets? She would like some things cleaned. Yes, she would keep her room.

Marge looked at herself in the mirror. She was an attractive woman, but a bit of a tan would not go amiss.

A few hours at the salon would do her good. They always spoilt her there.

If only she could see Clay, just for a bit. See what had happened to him, how he lived, where he slept. How he saw the world now that his uniform and family name were not there to shield him. See what being chased like an animal had done to him. He would have learned some humility and consideration. Mike had not said a thing. Perhaps they were no longer interested in Clay, but what if they were? They could not seriously believe he had become a traitor. What if he'd gone mad? If only she could see him now. Could they work things out between them now that they had seen other worlds?

CHAPTER THIRTY-SIX

——■——

The hotel porter was sorry. They'd have to leave in three days. There was an apartment nearby, but it would not be free for ten days or so. It was best they left the city. Go to some other resort. He'd find them something. It seemed the whole world was coming to Mallorca this summer. The hotels were already overbooked.

There was a new hotel in Cala d'Or, a small place, quaint and fashionable. It had wonderful beaches. It was forty miles away, no more than an hour by taxi. They would be better off by taxi. Anyway, the Vespa was booked from the following week.

'I better let the banker in Switzerland know,' Clay said to Bernadette.

'I always worry when you tell him where we are.'

'Banks over there are sworn to secrecy,' he reassured her.

At the American Express office downtown, they were very obliging. There was only one thousand dollars for him, the man said. You may call the bank from here if you wish.

'I'm sorry to call you collect,' Clay said to the banker, 'but I'm not at my hotel. Thank you for accepting the charges. I need more money. I seem to keep you people busy, eh?'

The banker laughed. 'You've been busy yourself. You're back from Italy, are you?'

'Italy?'

'Yes, I remember you said you were calling from Genoa. We make a note of everything here.'

'Oh?'

'You said you couldn't hear me very well. The line was bad or something. I suppose with all the travelling you do you forgot. When did you get back to Palma?'

'Well ... I....' Clay thought he'd better not say too much.

'No matter, we're talking now. Can I be of service?'

'Yes, I need another four thousand dollars. Spending a fortune.'

'We're here to help, Colonel. I have prepared the investment plan for you.'

'Put that on hold for a while, will you? I'm moving about a lot right now. Perhaps we should communicate in writing until I know where I will settle. They have strange regulations on foreign currency in Spain.'

'All right. Don't hesitate to contact me any time. The four thousand will go out to you today.'

'Thank you.'

'Enjoy Mallorca.'

'Goodbye.'

Who the hell could that have been, Clay wondered, Patel? The air force? How did they find out about the account? Marge would have told them. Of course, they were all talking together, all buddies. They were all looking for him. Good thing he was getting out of town. A small place would be much safer. Who knows what the banker had told them, but he wouldn't tell them much. Clay assumed the others would soon follow, whoever they were. He had to act accordingly.

Bernadette was waiting for him outside. 'Bought you a *Tribune*,' she said. 'What's wrong?'

'Nothing.'

'I can read you Clay, don't shut me out.'

'Someone spoke to the bank in Lucerne the other day, said he was me. Said he was in Genoa.'

'People are looking for us ... for me. I told you I was bad for you.'

'I think it's my people this time.'

'Don't be silly, they know nothing. There hasn't been a sign of anything from them.'

'You're underestimating them.'

'Maybe, but I know Ming Ho.'

'Ming Ho? The guy who got it in the leg when I crashed?' Bernadette nodded. 'Not in a million years. His accent wouldn't have fooled the bank...'

'You don't know him, Clay. It was him. He was in Hong Kong with Patel. And the Englishman in Lucerne, remember?'

'Yes, could be.'

'Patel and Ming Ho and the Englishman are involved. I'm not stupid.'

'Don't be so touchy. If your Ming Ho is such a genius, he would have found us already. He was with Patel when I spoke to him and Patel knew where we were. He had a hell of a head start. We know someone was following us. Well, I figured we had left a good smokescreen, but now there's this guy who called the bank.'

'The screen wasn't thick enough.'

'It's just a hiccup. I'll have to think this one over.'

'If you let me think with you, we could get somewhere.'

'What's eating you, Bernadette?'

'I don't know. Maybe there's no escape for me. It's all been too good to be true. Perhaps I was too happy. I have no right.'

'Everyone's got the right. We're getting out of here. All they know is we're in Palma. Maybe they don't even know that. The banker said I called from Genoa. Maybe Palma wasn't mentioned. It'll take them months to find us out in the sticks. We'll see them long before they track us down. What does Ming Ho look like?'

'You saw him.'

'I don't remember.'

'Do all us orientals look the same to you?'

'Hold it, I remember him now. Short tight guy with the clean shirt and the glasses. Spoke like a Frenchman. He'll never know me.'

'Ming Ho will remember the size of your shoes.'

'Don't panic. We can't be sure it's him anyway. If he's joined forces with Patel's man, all he'll want is money. I can get hold of some.'

'He hasn't joined forces with anyone. Ming Ho is using Patel. He isn't interested in money.'

'What does he want you for? What have you done to him?'

'He wants to bring me back to punish me. I was his disciple. His...'

'Mistress?'

'Never. Don't talk to me like that.'

'Whoever is after us is in Italy now. If they ever arrive on this island, we'll be lost in Cala d'Or.'

'I'm scared.'

'We'll just have to take it easy for a while. Get a boat and go to sea, grow another beard. We'll watch carefully. Ming Ho knows you and he knows how frightened you are. He feels good about that and he will be walking out in the open. We will see him first. He can't just pounce on you. This isn't Saigon. There's order here. Police.'

'Nothing will stop him. You don't know what he's like.'

Perhaps the bank manager had not mentioned Palma at all, Clay thought. They might be worried about nothing. Anyway, it could be the air force. All they could get him for was desertion. Send him to a shrink or something. They wouldn't touch Bernadette. He wanted to tell her that, but she was becoming hysterical and that made her aggressive. He could almost feel her tension.

Ming Ho's face came into Bernadette's mind. She heard his voice. She tried to think of their early friendship, his youthful dreams and his clean-shaven, scarless face. But the old Ming Ho refused to materialize. The new Ming Ho was there, breathing down her neck. His angry eyes looked out of everyone's face, accusing her of failure, of betrayal. He was going to punish her for allowing the American to escape. It was not for her, this sweet life. She had no right. She had sinned.

They reached the Paseo Maritimo and walked under the palms, watching the boats. Clay pointed out to the sea.

'Look at that one with the blue sails. They're running before the wind, Bernadette. It's blowing from the shore and it'll take them far in no time. I wonder where the lucky bastards are going.'

'Let's get our bags and get out of the hotel. It's after one.'

There is no escape for sinners. Didn't she remember what they had taught her at the convent? Bernadette stopped and sat down on a stone bench.

'What's the matter with you?'

'Nothing. I don't want to talk.'

'Yeah, okay. We'll go now. Let's grab the first cab we see and get our stuff. I'm going to miss this bay though. All good things come to an end. I guess we can come back here anytime we want to.'

A taxi stopped by the kerb. It was letting passengers out. Clay flagged the man, then ran up and put his head into the window. The driver spoke English and Clay gave him the name of the hotel.

'You can walk. It's only five minutes' walk from here,' he said.

'We're not stopping there. We're going to Cala d'Or right after. Just picking up our luggage. You know where Cala d'Or is?'

'Oh yes, beautiful little place. Rich people go there. I know it well. My family come from a village just near Cala d'Or. Went swimming there as a child. Before they built it up. Beautiful little beaches, you'll love it.'

Mike Carter looked at his watch. It was six o'clock. He didn't want to be too punctual. He would seem too eager. Did she make all men feel insecure? Was Clay running away from her because of that? She was hell-bent on going on that damn cruise. She was attractive. She would meet someone. There were rich people about, handsome, cultured Europeans out for an adventure. Art lovers and connoisseurs of fine wine. She would try to use them like she used him. She might fall in love. What sort of man would she meet? Some Italian playboy?

The phone rang. It was the man from London. His

voice was sharp and cruel. 'You done it yet, Carter?'

'I'm afraid. . .'

'Don't bother with the details. Time's running out and if our guy is seen alive by anyone we're in trouble.'

'I've got a good lead.'

'Don't tell me about leads. Just let me know when he's dead. You've got another three weeks. Washington takes over after that.'

The telephone went dead. Mike sat in a pool of cold sweat. He needed to compose himself. That husband of hers was putting him on the spot. He resented Clay for being her man. He was jealous of the nights and the years they had spent together. Maybe the bastard did go over to the other side. That was it. He would do it. He'd find the man and do it himself.

CHAPTER THIRTY-SEVEN

Patience has always been my best quality. Perhaps the only one. I think it came about because I was born clumsy. You need to watch every movement you make when you are that way. Put a glass back on the table slowly, in case it drops. You make sure of things before you act. You control your impulses and above all take your time. Maybe this is why I have always felt at ease in the Orient. You wouldn't imagine the patience the Chinese have. With patience, hard work and tenacity they have managed to make that small island of Hong Kong into an industrial power to be reckoned with. Even in the field of crime I had seen opposing clan leaders wait years for their opponents to fall into an intricate trap set for them. Revenge is never immediate and many murders have their origins in events that happened years before.

A detective needs patience. The glamour of the Hollywood private eye who always finds the culprit before the picture ends is crap. There's no glamour in it at all. It's a long, tedious slog, examining details and going over testimonies and places until you get a break, if you ever do. If people knew how many crimes are never solved, they'd worry themselves to death.

Ming Ho was not a patient man, but he must have believed in destiny. My ability to find Clay and Bernadette had thrown him completely. During those last few days in Genoa, he had changed. I did not expect him to stay that way. I think he was depressed because he had treated this as his own private affair, and I was the one who had discovered they had gone to Mallorca. He certainly had lost most of his self-confidence. Maybe he never had any. I made the best of Genoa and hired a larger car and toured the area. I found I wasn't eating as much as I had been. Ming Ho came along with me everywhere. He and his case.

There was a bit of comic relief when we went to the Spanish Consulate to get a visa for him. I had the relevant visiting cards printed for the occasion. I posed as a wealthy British tourist from Hong Kong and Ming Ho was my manservant. While the interview with the Spanish diplomat went on, I got him to carry my briefcase and hold my hat. I ordered him to help me off and on with my jacket. My performance seemed acceptable.

'How long will you stay in Palma?' the diplomat asked.

'Haven't made plans yet,' I said. 'I have never been there before.'

'It has become very popular,' he said proudly. 'there are seven tourists for every native of the island during the summer.' I showed the right amount of admiration. 'Do you travel with your servant everywhere?'

'Yes,' I said, 'I don't know what I'd do without him. He cooks for me. I need a special diet. Diabetes, you know.'

When we left the Consulate, Ming Ho smiled. It was the first time I had seen him smile.

'You were good,' he said. 'You should have been an actor.'

'Not handsome enough for that,' I said curtly.

That afternoon we went to see the Medrano Circus. Ming Ho was interested in a bored sort of way. The show was lavish and varied. I have always held a fascination for lion tamers. I am not a coward, but I doubt if I'd ever have survived sitting inside a cage with a lion or a tiger. There was a family of acrobats who performed dangerous flying exercises without a net and a group of clowns that had me on the floor. We drank coffee laced with brandy and by dinner time we were both drunk. At the table, in a very fashionable restaurant, Ming Ho drank a bottle of wine all by himself. It seemed to raise his spirits. He talked a lot. It was the first time he seemed to open up a bit. And the last. Except for that other time, much later, at the end of our time together.

'When this is over, I'll go back to Paris before I leave Europe,' he said.

'You know Paris?'

'Yes, I was a student there.'

'What did you study?'

'Literature.'

'You?'

'Yes, I used to write poetry myself.' There was a strange, sad pride in his eyes.

'Could you let me see some?'

'You can't read French.'

'You could translate it for me.'

'It's too private, too personal.'

I was a little high myself. I couldn't believe my ears. The man was talking in a manner I did not imagine possible.

'You know the woman with the American, don't you,' I said to him.

'Yes.'

'Long?'

'We were students together in Paris.'

'You go back a long time then.'

'Yes,' he sighed. 'A very long time.'

'Do you hate her?'

He looked at me as if I was mad. 'Why do you say that?'

'You seem determined to get her.'

'It's the man I am after,' he said without conviction.

'What has he done to you?'

Ming Ho fell silent. He held on tightly to his case and drank more wine. I had to carry him to the taxi. I think I provoked him because I wanted him to come out and admit what I had suspected, that the American did not interest him, that it had nothing to do with the war or her dedication for the cause. He was after her alone. Perhaps for something dark she had done. It would have made no difference to me then. Mr Patel had told me to follow and obey Ming Ho and I would have continued to do that regardless. He did not tell me a thing. That would have been too much to ask of him. He was a very private man.

A few days later, we climbed the gangway to the ship. She was modern and sleek and we were welcomed aboard like kings. Two porters carried our luggage and Ming Ho held on to his case as usual. It was late afternoon. We would reach Barcelona in the morning and Palma on the next day. There were many people on board and we stood on the side deck and watched Genoa and the hills beyond.

I was thinking of the future. We were getting close to our target. Ming Ho always said he would tell me what to do once we had the two of them in our hands. Patel was dead. I would have to find a new job. Ming Ho stood there with me and I saw his face harden. Perhaps the little honeymoon we had had was over. I didn't know. I caught his eyes staring at me and I saw a cruelty on his face I had never noticed before. He looked determined and mean, like a merciless killer. The sincere murderers, those who believe in what they do, are the most dangerous. I felt the cold come into my bones again. I wondered what plans he had for me.

It was there, as the siren sounded and the boat started to move, that it came to me. If he was going to kill the American and take the woman with him, he would need to put the blame on someone. He wouldn't risk having a witness. That was why he never told me what he intended to do. I may be slow sometimes, I deliberate and analyse forever, but in the end I do get where I am heading. Behind my back they used to call me Bulldog Bloomfield. I can't say I minded the name. It rather suited me.

My relationship with Ming Ho took a turn. Something happened that day. I am sure now, but the feeling that I could be in some danger must have hit me then. I wasn't aware of it, like a toothache that starts with a faint tang of pain when you drink something and then it's gone. You feel so relieved you forget all about it. But then it comes back and they tell you the tooth needs to be taken out. It was something like that. Something began to nag me without identifying itself. Of course I found out all about it later. For the time being, I felt a little uncomfortable. It was nothing more sinister than that.

'Why did the American have Patel killed?' I asked.

'You do not need to know that,' he said. His voice had assumed that curt hardness. The old Ming Ho was back.

The city retreated into the haze as we sailed out. Darkness seemed to come quickly and I strolled to the upper deck cafeteria and sat down. Ming Ho followed. I must have been frustrated by something. I ordered a large ice-cream.

'When we get there, you'll stop that,' he said. 'We'll need to look for them. And no more drinking until it's over.'

I drank a lot that night. I am not a great sailor and I wanted the trip to be over and done with while I was asleep. I slept like a dead man all the way to Barcelona and then again on the way to Palma. I must have slept for almost twenty hours.

I woke to the touch of a hand on my shoulder. It was Ming Ho. I saw at once he was his old self again.

'Get up, Bloomfield,' he barked. 'We're here.'

'It'll take them time to disembark,' I said. 'Give me another ten minutes.'

'Get out of bed now,' he ordered. In his hand he held a steaming paper cup of tea. 'I brought you this,' he said. He smiled down at me the way one smiles at a dog who's just been offered a bone. I was too tired to say anything. I sat up and took the cup.

'I'll wait for you by the gangway,' he told me. 'Don't leave anything behind.' He held his case tightly under his arm. 'They are on this island,' he said. A cloud settled across his face.

'They and millions of others.'

'I am not interested in the others.'

'Don't you ever relax?'

'Not until we get them.'

He went out and I got up. I looked out of the window. Outside, the sun hit the pale, weather-beaten stones. Fenders in the shape of black rubber tires moved about as great iron gates opened below. Squeaking, overloaded cranes, car engines and people's voices came from the open door. The hum of engines died as the great ship stopped. We were there. The hunt was on.

I am ashamed. My throat is heavy. Old age gives you the luxury of truth. You can admit things to yourself and others you'd never do as a young man. I was excited. I was eager. Never once did I spare a thought for Bernadette and Clay. How they must have felt, being chased all over the place. Perhaps it did not occur to me. They were, after all, the enemy. I like to think they were not aware of us. When you're flushed and consumed by the heat of the kill, you don't think of the hunted. Only God does that, if he's there.

It was the first time I had been to Spain. I think it was love at first sight. There was something happy and light about the place. People were smiling and friendly and eager to please. No one rushed. I knew then I was going to enjoy the battleground. I didn't imagine how it was going to end. I certainly didn't think I was destined to end my days in that country.

CHAPTER THIRTY-EIGHT

It seemed a relaxed resort. They told Clay there was a small port there and a marina where boats could be hired. He noticed expensive foreign cars and well dressed people browsing in exclusive boutiques. The houses were white-washed. He didn't get a chance to see everything during the short stroll he had taken. He wanted Bernadette to come with him, but she was asleep when he woke. They were staying at the Hotel Tucan and he liked it. He bought the local English language paper and had a coffee at the terrace café on the main street. The place was called Fernando's, after its bearded owner, an amateur sculptor whose statues lurked between the trees.

Across the way from Fernando's, there was a small pension. Fernando told him the owners were an unlikely couple. He was an Italian count and she an English Jewess. They had met in Bulgaria in the thirties, while they were in their respective countries' diplomatic service. When war broke out, she went back to England and in 1945 he wrote to her from a prisoner of war camp. The Count was an unrepentant fascist, Fernando said. She came out to him and since they could not live together in either of their own countries, they chose to live in Spain. The Count even tried his hand at bullfighting before settling in Cala d'Or.

Nowadays, Fernando said with a smile, the Count got drunk quite early in the morning. He would often stand outside his establishment and talk politics in a loud voice. They were a strange couple. He gave her hell, but in spite of her long-suffering expression, she stuck by him.

Clay paid for his coffee and promised to be back. The hotel was just two minutes down the road.

Bernadette seemed to make a habit of sleeping late these days, Clay thought as he came back into the room. The sun blazed into the room, but Bernadette was still dead to the world. He slipped out to the verandah and looked down at the pool.

Cala d'Or was built around a quaint group of coves which gave its beaches a feeling of intimacy. Years before, he had been told, the place was known only to a few. Mostly they were smugglers who had used the narrow, accessible bays to bring in cigarettes and whisky from Tangiers. It was only a night's sail away to the south. They used to earn twenty-five pesetas a night for carrying sacks full of forbidden contraband into a waiting cart on the sand. The smugglers were all gone now, Clay was told. They were replaced by restaurants and cafés and shops. Money now came to Cala d'Or with the tourists. Some bought themselves villas to settle there.

Down by the pool, people began to congregate. He was not sure what to do today, but it didn't matter. He came back to the room and sat on the bed, waiting for Bernadette to wake up. She always knew what was best and lately he had been waiting to hear what she had in mind before making any plans. Leaving it all to her, the planning and the decision, gave him a strong sense of freedom.

Later, they went to the beach. It was a small cove, just down the road from the Tucan. It was swarmed with people speaking several languages. Sun worshippers sprawled on the sand. White pedalos mingled with bronzed bodies in the emerald waters of the cove. Bernadette had put on cream against the sun and lay on the white sand by his side. She drew glances from all directions. Clay watched the people around him. Most spoke German. He smiled to himself as he thought someone here might be related to him. He wasn't going to dwell on that now. He would embark on his search when the summer was over.

Clay watched a small sailing boat tacking into the wind. He could almost feel the tiller in his hand. Bernadette's body was getting darker by the moment. He thought he might go for a swim to cool a little.

'Do my back, will you?' her deep, hoarse voice said. She handed him the bottle and turned over. 'Undo my top first.'

Clay obliged and rubbed the oil deep into her soft skin. The pink Scandinavians behind them watched in quiet, envious admiration.

'Could you wipe the bottle and put it back in the bag.'

'Sure,' he said. The perfect escort, he thought to himself. He was going to go get her a drink when she sat up.

'Can I have a coke?' she asked.

'Great minds think alike.'

Definitely the perfect escort. The sunny terrace back in Palma had given his own skin a healthy looking colour and his hair had grown. The Germans had tried talking to him in their language, but all he could muster was 'Nix verstehen.'

Dammit, he was born in Berlin and had his parents not adopted him he would have been sitting there with them instead. He would be sipping endless lukewarm lagers, listening to nagging wives, playing with unruly children. God bless America, Captain New would have said.

Maybe he was his mother's natural child. She could have been drunk or angry when she said he was someone else's child. What did that matter? What difference did it really make? It was a beautifully sunny afternoon and he had been brought up to be an officer and a southern gentleman. The chatter, the sea air and the smell of overdone hamburgers brought peace to him. Why did he worry so much about who he might have been?

Things could have been so different. Where had he been all these years? Why did he allow that intensity to rule him? Marge loved the sun, he remembered, and she talked a lot. He liked people who talked a lot. She would have enjoyed being here. If only things had worked out better. He wouldn't have looked for an escape then. He would have never taken off in search of unknown galaxies. Maybe he would not have been shot down. No one would have been looking for him then.

He thought he should make contact with her one of these days, for the sake of their daughter if nothing else.

But it was Marge he caught himself thinking of, not their daughter. Strange. Why strange? They had been married for fourteen long years. Yes, he would make contact with her. She would never believe her eyes. A male chauvinist pig spreading suntan oil on a woman's back.

The lazy afternoon lulled him. He'd soon be out of the mess. He would think of something. He would talk to people and make friends and listen and learn. He was thirsty again, but he didn't get up. He didn't want to leave Bernadette there all by herself. She always went funny when he did. The fear that lurked somewhere in her never left. Or she'd get angry and shout as she did these days. It seemed to take little to get her to lose her temper. Or maybe he only thought so because he was so relaxed. He could take a sip of her drink, but then she sat up and finished the bottle off with one long swig. She turned herself, top up to the sun. Someone behind them whistled.

The Scandinavians were leaving. One young woman smiled at him and another waved. Perhaps the blonde had made him think of Marge. It was a long afternoon, he thought. Perhaps Bernadette would agree to go out on the town later.

CHAPTER THIRTY-NINE

Mike stayed at the airport long after Marge's plane took off. He had insisted on driving her to Orly and now he sat in the bar sipping a Pernod. He felt empty. He hadn't said anything about Clay and she hadn't asked. She seemed so happy about the cruise. She showed him the leaflets and told him of the books she had read about the places they were going to call at. She'd never been on a big ship, she kept saying. It would put some distance between her and the world, she said, but she didn't explain.

Mike's thoughts drifted back to the night before, after he had dropped Marge at her hotel. He had to erase the episode from his mind. The shape of that other woman, her scent and her false smile kept creeping back into his head and with it the images of defeat. What had made him do it? Marge's rejection, that's what. No, it was all Clay's fault.

It was quite late when he said goodbye to Marge by the main entrance. He kept hoping she'd invite him to come up, but she had an early start and so did he. It would have been so much simpler if they'd spent her last night together. Centuries seemed to have passed since the last time they were intimate. Perhaps it was doomed from the start. Perhaps his usefulness to her was over.

At dinner she had been friendly and correct, but distant. When she disappeared inside the hotel he decided he did not want to drive home. He would stay at the Grand Hotel instead. God, did he have to remember it now? Yes, he did. Maybe then he would forget it for good.

At the reception of the Grand Hotel they had said he could have a room for the night. They wanted to be paid in advance because he had no luggage. He said he had stayed there before. They could check their records and see for themselves. Too late for that now, they said. He paid, took his key and said he did not need to be shown to his room. He felt so alone he wanted to cry.

At the end of the marble corridor, by the lift, stood a young, oriental looking woman. She waited, watching the numbers light up. The lift came and they got in.

'Which floor?' he asked and yawned and apologized.

'Any one,' she said. 'It's not important.'

He pressed the third floor button and moved into the corner.

'You alone?' she asked.

'Yes.'

She moved closer as the doors closed. 'Need company?'

'Who doesn't?'

'Who doesn't,' she agreed.

When they reached his floor, he stepped out. She followed. It could not have been his charm, he thought with a bitter smile. He'd hardly said a word. He found the number on his door and opened it. She stood right behind him and as he walked in she followed. He switched the light on and she sat down on one of the beds.

'I thought you were staying in the hotel,' he said. 'Isn't that a key you are holding?'

She didn't answer immediately, but looked at him, her full lips curling into a smile. She was small and dark, with slightly slanting eyes. God, if Marge knew. What if she did? She wouldn't care.

'You American?'

The accent sounded familiar. Spanish perhaps. 'Yes, he said.'

'We have lots of Americans in the Philippines.'

'Are you a tourist in Paris?'

'No, a student,' she said. 'You like sex?'

'What?'

'Paris is very expensive. I can be very good to you and make you happy if you help me a little.'

'How little?' Mike was surprised at his own question, but it was too late to take it back.

'Four hundred francs. A hundred dollars maybe. I can make you happy for sure.' She smiled again. It was a sickly, blatantly false smile. She looked at her watch.

'I don't have a hundred dollars on me.'

'How much do you have?'

'Let me see ... maybe fifty ... anyway, I'm tired.'

'I can wake you up. Don't worry, if all you have is fifty, I'll do it for that.'

He could not remember the last time he'd been with a hooker. This one was not entirely professional. Her smile seemed forced and she looked a little frightened. She kept looking at her watch and at the door. He hoped she'd change her mind and go.

What the hell, he thought. 'You'll have to do it for me . . . all by yourself.'

'Give me the money first.'

He counted out four fifty franc notes.

'It's better to get the business out of the way. More relaxing after that,' she said. She got up and took her clothes off. She had a short plump body. Her skin was white. Mike lay on the bed and she took his shoes off, then his socks and trousers.

'Get under the sheets,' she told him. 'I go take a bath.'

He did not mind if she ran off. He hoped she would. He picked the phone up and asked the operator to call him at seven. The girl came back from the bathroom.

'What's your name?' he asked.

'Lola,' she said. 'Lola Martinez.'

There was nothing exciting about her. She set about to arouse him in a mechanical way, like trying to start a flooded engine. She kissed his body and sucked at him. She pulled and caressed and all the while she was talking. How life in Paris was hard for foreigners. How she missed the tropics and her family. Her voice was scratchy. His body did not respond.

'You're trying too hard,' he said.

'Do you want your money back?' she asked.

'No,' he said sheepishly. He wished she'd disappear, but she came into the bed and pulled him over. She lifted her short legs and surrounded his body and he was touching her there. He tried to penetrate her with his soft manhood. It seemed to take forever, and then he felt himself inside her. She started to move. He tried to imagine she was someone else. It was hot and he felt sticky and dirty and her breath smelt of stale tobacco. A bitter-sweet relief came to him with his climax. She uttered a false groan and said, 'Ooh you are great.' The she jumped up and got dressed and was out of the room before he could apologize.

It took hours for him to fall asleep and even then he slept badly. The morning call came long before he was ready for it. He had a cold shower and raced down to met Marge.

Now she was gone. She must have landed in Marseilles by now, he thought. He looked one more time at the runway, paid his bill and left. In the car driving back to the city, he felt deceitful and cheap. It was all Clay's fault. He stepped on the gas and the road came forward faster. He had two weeks left and Clay had the whole god damned world and his wife's unwavering sympathy. Mike hated him.

Why did all that have to happen? Why did Marge come into his life to confuse him? Why didn't her husband die? No. He must not even think that. He was suddenly aware he was driving his car. The sign for the city said 10 kilometres, but the returning Sunday traffic was heavy. By the time he was back, it would be lunchtime. She was boarding the ship at eleven. He hoped she'd have a lousy time.

CHAPTER FORTY

The ship was a twenty thousand tonner with Italian waiters, French food and Swiss management. The burly, bearded Greek Captain told his table at lunch she was more of a floating luxury hotel than a liner. There were two swimming pools, five sundecks, saunas, a gymnasium, a cinema and other trimmings. He suggested they discover the ship by themselves. This was better than the brochures Marge had seen. She would write and tell Mike about it when she settled down.

The passengers were as mixed as the crew, all looking for a change of routine before summer. A few famous faces caused excited whispers in the dining room, but these subsided as the meal progressed. The ship was going to Sicily, Sardinia, Mallorca and back to Marseilles via Monaco. The thought of seeing Palma again excited her. The name of that place never failed to bring sweet memories to her mind. They were going to stay there for a day, just enough time for her to recapture some old happiness.

They were going to spend the first afternoon at sea getting to know each other, but Marge was tired. She had had a late night and an early morning. She felt bad about Mike. She should not have allowed him to take her to the airport. He'd seemed sad and there was nothing she could say to help him. She could not pretend things were the same between them. She knew there had been a change in her. What it was she couldn't put her finger on. Maybe she had outgrown whatever it was he was able to offer her. Clay had accused her of being frigid. She now knew she was not. If only Clay had more patience with her.

Mike was a friend now and would remain so. Why could she not sustain a relationship with him? Was the recurring image of Clay in her mind responsible for the drift? Mike was a good man. She felt responsible because she had seduced him. He had helped her to find herself at a difficult time. She wanted to think of him, but couldn't somehow remember what he looked like.

When coffee came, Marge excused herself and left for

her cabin. She would meet them all later, she decided. After all, she was there for a rest. Her stateroom was dominated by blues and beiges, her favourite colours. It was spacious and sunny. The Intercontinental Hotel had sent her a bouquet of flowers with a note. She lay down on the big bed and dozed off.

That seemed to be the order of things for the first few days. Marge came to the table for meals, lay in the sun for a little and read. Mostly she slept. At the dining table, she usually sat with a Japanese lady whose husband produced dry fish in Hokkaido. The woman was shy and her silence suited Marge, who did not feel inclined to make too much conversation. As the days passed, the Japanese lady began to come out of herself and proved to be a chatterbox.

'Lovely food,' the Japanese lady said.

'This stuff is too rich for me,' Marge said. 'Very bad for my diet. You are lucky to be slim.'

Her companion acknowledged the compliment with a shy smile. 'I have never been on a ship before. My husband wanted me to have a rest. My son has just passed his university entrance examinations. I have worked with him for almost a year to prepare. It was exhausting.'

'They say there is nothing like sea air. So far I've been too sleepy to enjoy much of it. These five courses would do me for the rest of the day.'

'There is a big party on board tonight. Will you go?'

'I don't know yet.'

'Will you dance?'

'Sure, if I'm there.'

'With a strange man?'

'They won't let you dance with a woman.'

The Japanese lady laughed quietly, cupping her mouth with her hand. 'Do you think we should dress for that?' she asked.

'I wouldn't worry about it too much. This is the Mediterranean. Ask the Captain if you're not sure.'

Marge's limbs felt heavy again and her face was flushed. The bordeaux and the côte de rhône danced in her bloodstream. Having promised to have tea with the Japanese lady, she went to her cabin and took a bottle of water with her. She lay down and thought of Mike's haggard face that last day at the airport. Then Clay came back into her mind. She stretched on the bed. The boat rolled gently and she yawned and then dozed off. She dreamed.

A squadron of low-flying jets was buzzing her garden. Marge couldn't make out which of their houses she was in. She saw Clay sitting on the tail of the last plane, pulling a coloured Chinese New Year kite behind him. The kite was moving violently in all directions. Clay's face was dirty with soot and he wore green battle fatigues. The plane was stationary. Stuck in mid-air, it hung suspended between heaven and earth, its huge fuselage directly over the house. She was out on the lawn, in her white Bermuda shorts, watering the flowers. Her daughter was there, and another woman, a pretty little oriental lady who seemed a darker version of her Japanese friend from Hokkaido. She was tiny, not much larger than a doll. Marge had to strain her eyes to see her. In her hand, the oriental lady held a miniature machine-gun. She was wearing a long evening gown and she blew kisses to Clay, who laughed as he caught them, one by one, in mid-air.

Marge heard herself plead with him to get the plane moving. It was dangerous just sitting there, but he paid no attention. Any minute now the plane will crash, she shouted and he could hear her because the engine was out. The other planes flew about like mosquitoes, the pilots shooting their pistols at Clay. The oriental lady had doubled in size now and she had a new face. She laid the machine-gun on the grass and calmly she took her clothes off. She kept growing until she reached a normal height. From somewhere a band started playing and the woman moved her body to the rhythm of the music. She stood there and sang, smiling a voluptuous smile, her body stark-naked. In her hand, she had a thick rope. The rope was tied to the plane and kept it from flying. She pulled the rope about and the flying machine with Clay on it moved up and down like a kite.

'Don't scream,' the oriental lady said to Marge, 'or I'll let go and he'll fly away. You will never see him again.'

Clay was crying. His tears came down on Marge's face. 'I don't want to go dancing,' he said. 'Let me stay please.'

Her daughter was playing tennis on a small ping-pong table. Her partner had no face. He wore an air force uniform. He turned and pulled a pistol out of his pocket. While hitting the ball with his racket, he shot missiles at Clay. None hit the plane, but they came closer all the time. Some exploded dangerously near to Clay's head. Marge started running towards the air force man and her legs moved faster and faster, but she did not advance at all. He hit another tennis ball at her daughter.

'Fourteen-love,' someone announced and then Marge saw the man's face. It was Mike. He smiled at her and shot another missile at Clay's plane.

'What are you doing?' she heard herself shout.

'The air force wants Clay down,' he said. 'Orders.'

Marge's feet were planted in the gound. She could not move at all. The oriental woman grew as high as the trees. Her face was near to Clay's They kissed.

'Tell your father to be careful,' Marge urged her daughter, but the girl answered her in French and she did not understand a word. Her body shook. She tried to grab the rope from the oriental woman, but it kept slipping away. The neighbours were all there, pointing up at the woman's nakedness. They laughed as they whispered to each other. Then they pointed at her. Marge was embarrassed. In the mirror that suddenly materialized right in front of her, she saw herself. Her shorts and top were gone. She was naked. She tried to lie down on the grass to hide herself, but she still couldn't move. Her legs were stuck in the soil. The oriental woman's face grew some more. It nearly covered the sky. She emitted a shrieking scream and dropped her end of the rope on to the lawn. Clay's plane came to life. The engine spat fire and the machine took off vertically into the sky.

'Now see what you have done,' the oriental woman's voice roared. As the plane disappeared into the sky, her size began to reduce. Soon she was normal again. She put on a set of dirty battle fatigues and grabbed her machine-gun and ran off into the woods. Shots could be heard and Marge saw exploding puffs of smoke over her garden. Then she woke. The room was dark. She closed her eyes to see what had happened to Clay, but no pictures came. Her eyes were heavy and soon sleep took her again.

CHAPTER FORTY-ONE

That must have been one of the worst days of my life. You know, when suddenly the very earth you have been walking on starts shaking and then it slips away from under your feet and you are suspended. A free fall is a terrifying experience, and that was how I felt.

The day had started as days usually did for us in Palma. We stayed at the Melia, a big luxury hotel on the Paseo Maritimo overlooking the bay. We had two adjoining rooms and Ming Ho had the key for the partition door. He would walk into my room any time he felt like it. During the last few days he had become strange and remote and his shifty eyes looked at me from everywhere.

I had been living on handouts ever since we had landed. He wouldn't let me sign for anything at the restaurant. We ate in small, cheap cafeterias. He made me wash my clothes to save on laundry bills. My size grew again and I was in need of new pants since those I had bought in Genoa no longer fit me. I took to wearing a belt and had my shirts hanging out to hide my bulge. It was unbearably hot. We spent hours watching passers-by. We took bus tours to Formentor and Andraix and many other resorts, but there was no sign of the American Colonel and the girl. I had asked someone at the American Express office downtown to let me know as soon as the Colonel was there. I had promised him ten thousand pesetas for that. I said I had a surprise for Clayton Wayne-Turner and did not wish him to know I was looking for him. He must have had a lot of money on him, wherever he was, since he had not been back there at all.

That morning I had suddenly had enough. Something exploded inside of me and the patience I have always been so proud of disappeared. I lay in bed feeling sorry for myself and then anger replaced self-pity. It was early, perhaps six o'clock, and I asked the hotel operator to get me my bank in Hong Kong. Ming Ho had gone on one of his mysterious morning walks. He would not be back for some while yet. He insisted on having breakfast with me every day and that usually happened at nine. I made the call collect.

The manager came on the line. 'I am in Mallorca, Spain,' I said. 'Thank you for accepting the charges.'

'Think nothing of it, sir,' he said. I remember thinking there were still some decent people around. Some who remembered me before I became a dilapidated shadow of myself trailing behind a cruel, vindictive Vietnamese.

'I require some money,' I said. 'Could you arrange for that? You can send it to the American Express office in Palma.' I gave him the address.

'No problem at all,' he said. 'By the way, I was sorry to hear about Mr Patel. He was a good customer of ours. You will be amazed to hear that the last payment into your account came from him.'

'I suppose it was my salary.'

'No, he said it was a sort of bonus. A hundred thousand Hong Kong dollars. He made the payment himself, in cash, on the day before he was murdered.'

'Have they found his killer yet?'

'No, but they know all about him. There was an artist's impression of the man's face in the paper only the other day.'

'I imagine so. A Vietnamese army officer. Short and thick-set, right?'

'Not at all. The man they are looking for looks different. He is a Vietnamese, but far from being an army officer he is a suspected Vietcong. They know all about him. It was in the papers. He is small and thin and nervous. Wears glasses. He was seen with Mr Patel at the Baron's Table restaurant, you know, the one at the Holiday Inn. They were observed leaving together. The funny thing was Mr Patel had suspected someone was about to kill him. He had hired two bodyguards from the Souchang School of Martial Arts. That was in the papers too.'

'Why didn't they follow him?'

'He asked them to leave in the middle of the evening.'

'Are the police on to this?'

'They must be. The paper quoted police sources.'

My blood pressure was running high. Anger and suspicion spread through me. I thanked the bank manager and had the operator call my friend at the police. It was a strange conversation.

'Fancy hearing from you, Bulldog,' he said. 'What are you doing in Spain?'

'It's a long story. Tell me, regarding my old boss Mr Patel ... are you people still looking for his killer?'

'We are.'

'Do you have any more details?'

'Plenty,' he said. 'The bugger's a cool customer. He left Hong Kong under his own name. He is known to have boarded a Swissair flight to Zurich two months ago. Since then, he's disappeared. We have been asking the Swiss for help, but these things take time.'

'I think I can help,' I said with great excitement. 'What is his name?' There was a pause. I felt the proximity of doom.

'Ming Ho,' he answered finally. 'A dangerous fellow. A body found floating on the water suffered an identical wound. Identified as a Vietnamese army captain by the name of Nguyen Van something. I don't remember. He was tipped as the killer before we got on to the other Vietnamese. Someone called the police about him. Probably Ming Ho himself. The record at Kai Tak Airport shows they both arrived on the same plane. Anyway, Bulldog, can you really help us?' The mention of my old nickname was gratifying.

'Oh yes I can, but keep this under your hat for now.'

'A policeman is always a policeman, right?'

'I suppose so.'

'Strange your old boss going like that. He was a crafty customer. We had nothing on him, but we kept trying. The joke is even the Americans were interested. Some air force colonel named Carter. Stationed in Paris, I believe. Another air force chap from Saigon was snooping around his office for days after his death. There was some enquiry going on about Patel. The Yanks didn't tell us a thing. In any case, they dropped everything after his death. Be careful, will you?'

'Don't worry. I've got my old pistol,' I said.

'I didn't hear that,' he said. 'Let me know how you're doing.'

'I shall,' I replied and we said goodbye.

I was sweating like a dog. Anger numbed me. I must have been pale as hell. Then the partition door opened and Ming Ho walked in casually, like he owned the place. He looked menacing. I could have shot him there and then.

'I was trying to call you from downstairs. The operator said you were talking to Hong Kong. Who did you talk to? How dare you do that without asking me? I won't pay for this call.'

'You don't have to. I called my bank. They will send me some money today.'

'Oh,' he said. I was not sure he'd believed me. 'Shall we have some breakfast?' he asked.

I was fuming inside. I did not feel hungry at all. In front of me stood the man who had killed Mr Patel. I fought to keep my emotions buried inside. Everything had changed now. I needed to think.

'What is the matter?' he demanded.

'I am sick and tired of being treated like a boy.'

'We have to conserve our funds. This hotel is expensive.'

'Let's go down,' I said.

We sat in a small café a few doors from the hotel and had coffee and croissants. I nibbled at the food, but my mind was racing. I was next, I thought, but not before we had found the American and the girl. Ming Ho would try and get me somewhere outside the hotel for that. I was pleased I had kept my old service pistol. I was well known at Kai Tak Airport in Hong Kong. No one checked me there. It had travelled with me all over Europe. In those days they were not as strict about searching you as they are today, certainly not on buses and trains. I had wrapped the gun in plastic and hid it inside the water cistern above the toilet. He did not know about it and if he did, he did not say.

'What is new in Hong Kong?' he asked.

'I don't know. My bank manager isn't a gossip. I did not discuss the weather with him.' I gulped the coffee down and it burned my throat.

'Let's go out to the plaza,' he said. 'I have a hunch we'll see them today.'

He had said things like that before, but I did not comment. He was not working for Patel. He was after the pair for his own reasons. I'd have to work it out. A moment to sit there and look at the people would enable me to make a plan. I knew I would have to find them first and warn them, especially the girl. Without knowing it, they had become my allies.

It is surprising how quickly events can change your attitude to people. I think my affection for the fugitives started that morning. Now that I knew the Colonel had nothing to do with Mr Patel's murder, he had almost become a friend. Had my rage for Ming Ho not been consuming me, I would have started feeling guilty about them right then. Perhaps I did. I don't know.

All the way to the plaza, Ming Ho watched me. I could feel his cold eyes trying to enter my mind. I hoped to God we were not going to see them that day. Nothing was ready.

I passed through the American Express office. Ming Ho came in with me. The man said he had not seen the Colonel yet. I told him I had come in for something else. They were going to receive some funds for me later that day or the day after. Would they call me at my hotel and tell me when the money was in?

Ming Ho walked out before the man had a chance to

answer. I followed him into the tree lined avenue. His small nervous figure stood out in front. His walk was assured. He had said we would see them today. He must have believed so. We sat down and I ordered a cup of tea. His eyes relaxed.

'I want some money,' I said.

'What for?'

'I need a pair of trousers, if you don't mind. I'll give it back to you when my money comes. Don't do me any favours.'

'I'll go with you later,' he replied with a smile. I think he believed me. I had to talk to my friend at the Hong Kong police again. My mind was busy thinking of ways to achieve that. Perhaps that was why my anger had subsided. My breathing was easier now. Get even, Ming Ho had said. Not angry. I was going to follow his advice. I think he had suggested we go to a show. While checking the place out we could enjoy ourselves, he had said. I pretended not to listen. He did not persist.

CHAPTER FORTY-TWO

———■———

'Oh that was fun,' Clay said, sipping his third Fundador brandy. They were sitting at Fernando's bar watching the main street. The Italian Count across the road had just ended a long, loud speech about the lack of discipline in the world. The fascists knew how to keep things in order, he had said before his wife persuaded him to come inside. He could hardly stand on his feet and stumbled on his way.

'They never learn,' an Englishman said from the next table. 'They weren't hit hard enough in 1945.'

'I suppose you're right,' Clay said.

'Of course he's right,' Bernadette joined in. 'Fascists

never learn.'

'Where are you from?' the Englishman asked.

'The new world.'

'What brings you here? You've got California and Florida and Hawaii right on your doorstep for God's sake.'

'I'm a Canadian. I lived in Switzerland for a bit. Thought we'd have a look at Spain before going back to Vancouver.'

'Employed, are you?' the Englishman questioned Clay.

'Not any more,' Bernadette said with a gruff voice. Clay turned away in embarrassment. The Englishman looked closely at her. She had really caught the sun that day. In her white cotton dress she looked ravishing. The waiter could not take his eyes off her. He zoomed round them all the time, spilling beer on people in the process. He had made sure Clay's glass was never empty until Bernadette told him to stop.

She sipped her iced tea and looked at Clay's face. He was an attractive man, she thought, but he was drinking a little too much these past few weeks. She had never seen him drink that much before. The smell of stale liquor was abhorrent to her. It always brought back the memory of Saigon's back street brothel to her mind. The white bodies. The vomit. The fire.

Not the same man, not the same place. Not the same anything. When would her doubts die? Passers-by were looking at her, pointing at her. Some took pictures of her. She felt as if she was sitting in a cage. She did not remember such staring in Paris. Europeans think we are inferior, Ming Ho had told her years ago, but she had laughed it off. That's why we must fight for our independence, he had said. And he must have convinced her, she thought. She did follow him to Vietnam, but then that was not why she had left

Paris. There were other reasons for that.

'They are looking at me,' she whispered to Clay.

'Sure, they're jealous.'

The women were dressed to kill. Perhaps she should go into the shops herself. She felt a little cold, probably from too much sun. She thought she should get up and go back to the hotel. He would agree. He always agreed these days, even when she wished he wouldn't. God Bernadette, you are a negative woman, she said to herself. There was music in the street and Clay seemed to be enjoying himself. The waiters and a few locals all knew him by name. He was talking to the Englishman again. She couldn't be jealous of that, but she was. Not jealous, just afraid. Afraid Clay would see through her and find out she was impossible to please because she never knew her own mind. Because she was always afraid. Because no good would ever come of her. She had sinned. Her father had sinned. Her mother was a whore and God makes children pay for the sins of their elders.

Clay had always been considerate. He always made sure there was a drink for her, a pillow on the straw chair. Would she ever learn to accept the friendship he was offering? Women kept staring, more than the men. Perhaps they were thinking she was his mistress. They certainly did not look like a married couple, but what was she surprised about? She was his mistress.

Bernadette did not like thinking of herself as a mistress, a cheat. The other woman. Stealing time that belonged to the man's family. Women like her were for sale. Wives hated them. She looked at the women and read all that in their eyes. No, he has no other woman now, she wanted to say. It is not the money that keeps us together, just the fear of remembering a tormented childhood and a dangerous journey that will lead nowhere.

Did she love him? She had often asked herself that. No, not while he looked happy and carefree and independent. Soon, after a few more brandies he would be drunk and sloppy and talkative. She took his glass and emptied it into the geranium bed. He did not notice. He was too immersed in his conversation with the Englishman. They were talking about boats.

The Englishman said he had a boat in the port. Would Clay like to come out with him? How about the lady? She might like it, he said. Clay assured him she would. She was an experienced sailor herself, he added. There was pride in his eyes. Why do men always brag, Bernadette wondered.

'Let's do it one day,' Clay said and looked at her.

'Sure,' she said. 'With pleasure.'

'Good,' Clay said as if he owned her.

The waiter came and Bernadette ordered two coffees.

This is what life should be about, Clay thought. No tomorrows, no yesterdays and no one to give orders to. No one cared who he was. He wondered what Marge would think of all this. He drank his coffee and paid the bill. Bernadette got up and he followed her. He would have dearly loved to stay, but she did not like late nights.

The telephone rang. It was late at night and the man did not introduce himself. 'You're working late.'

'Yes,' Mike Carter answered.

'Change of plans,' the voice said. 'Hot stuff. You're off the hook. You are to act as a finder. Once you positively locate him you call us in London and tell us. Another guy will finish the job. He's a professional. I don't mind telling you we're relieved here. It's out of our hands. Now Carter, this is a favour because your record is good. Get rid of the heavy stuff in your bag and call me when you know where he is.'

'I sure appreciate this...'

'You have one week, Colonel, remember. Goodbye.'

Mike was left on his own again. The room felt stuffy and hot and he got up to open the window. He had not advanced one inch. All his sources of information had run dry. He had a packed case with two automatics in it. Saigon and Zurich and Hong Kong were waiting for his instructions, but he had none to issue. He sat back and stretched his legs. So they'd finally taken pity on him. No, not pity. They had given up on him. They needed expedience. They needed cold-blooded efficiency he could not deliver. Clay was now further away from salvation. No cavalry for him.

'Mike would have to find him. And then the idea came to him. Clay had to live on something. The gold he had stolen would not have lasted that long. He was in Europe. There were rumours from Hong Kong he had gone to Switzerland. Maybe he had money there. That could be a beginning. Or Monaco. Mike knew just the man who could help. He dictated a memo for his secretary. No appointments from now on. For the time being he would sleep in his office. In any case, he thought as he finished, he could see the moon better from there.

The band played Latin American music late into Sunday night. The theme of the ship's party was black and white. People were happy. They drank exotic drinks out of glasses decorated with tropical flowers. The Japanese lady had shed her shyness and was seen on the dance floor, smiling nervously at her partner.

Marge sat at a table near the dance floor. She felt rested and happy. Her feet tapped the floor with the rhythm. She was curious. She wanted to see her husband. Perhaps the jungle decorations on the wall had brought it on. It didn't matter. Her dreams of him were very much on her mind still. They could have been an omen. The Captain came over to ask her for a dance, but she declined.

The Japanese lady was back, her face flushed. 'My husband cannot dance,' she said.

'You're doing great,' Marge told her.

'We had lessons at my school. A long time ago.'

'It's like cycling. You never forget how to dance.'

Drinks were on the house. There was a floor show and a second supper at midnight. For a small woman, the Japanese lady had a big appetite, Marge thought with amusement. She got up and went for a stroll on the deck. The moon was out, drawing a long silvery line from the stern of the ship to the horizon. Couples cuddled in dark corners.

She got talking to an elderly titled English lady who came and stood by her side.

'Love the nights here, my dear.'

'Yes, they're charming.'

'Been on the Med before?'

'Once, a long time ago.'

'I take a cruise at least once a year,' the lady said. 'These days there is hardly anyone to talk to. In the old days, you could make real friends on board.'

'I'm glad to hear that. I came for a rest, myself.'

'They feed you too much for that.'

'Good food is a part of a holiday, don't you think?'

'Food's far from good here, my dear.'

She would try and avoid Lady Breckenbridge in future, Marge thought as she proceeded to criticize the ship and her contents from stem to stern. Everything was frightfully this or honestly that and she was certainly not coming back again. She had a lot of friends who'd settled in Jamaica.

Marge sat and listened and nodded. On the lower deck

she noticed the Japanese lady walking clumsily on the planks. She was held closely by a large man who had a glass in his other hand.

'Look what the Major's picked up down there,' her ladyship remarked. 'His wife is one of the most beautiful women in London. He could really do better than that. He says she stayed back in San Trop this summer. Silly fool.'

The swell was rising and the ship's roll became more apparent. The Major and the Japanese lady were embracing. They kissed.

'Fast worker, your Major,' Marge said and got up.

'Going already, my dear? I can't blame you. They could find a calmer stretch of water for this cruise.'

'They can't help that, can they?'

'They should consult the weather man.'

'Well, Lady Breckenbridge...'

'Call me Beatrice, my dear. All my friends do.'

'I have never met an aristocrat before. It kind of amuses me to call you that. Good night.'

'Perhaps we can have another chat some time. You Americans can be such fun.'

'Terrific. Good night, Lady Breckenbridge.'

'Good night, my dear.'

In her cabin, Marge's thoughts wandered towards her husband again. Ever since she had the dream, she kept hoping she would dream again. In the dream she could almost touch him. It was such a long time since he'd disappeared. She wondered how much success Mike had in his search. He had promised he would cable her on board ship if he had any news. She said she'd come back to Paris any time he needed her.

There was a lot she was going to say to Clay. Perhaps he had things to tell her, too. The thought he was still alive and still married to her brought peace to her mind. She particularly looked forward to Mallorca. There was part of her youth on that island. That gave her a feeling of well-being. She would sleep well tonight.

CHAPTER FORTY-THREE

———————■———————

I was sitting on a time bomb. I didn't know how long I'd be able to keep this charade going. Ming Ho was a sensitive man. I had taken handouts and humiliation and mockery from him and all for nothing. The bastard had murdered the only man I was ever fond of and he was sitting right there, with me. Frustration was killing me. I wanted to strangle the little runt in the dark and slip away. He was going to stick that long needle into my throat as soon as we'd found the American and the girl. I had no illusions about that. But when was that going to happen? I thought of calling the bank in Lucerne again to tell the man the truth. Arrange a meeting with the Colonel. He was probably not guilty of anything beyond desertion.

Desertion. If he was a deserter, the American air force would have been looking for him too. That was why they had sniffed around Patel's office. Of course, that was easy. I could get in touch with the American embassy somewhere, tell them what was going on. Tell them the Colonel was in mortal danger from a mad Vietnamese killer. They would take him into protective custody. Rubbish. They would have never listened to me. Could get my policeman friend in Hong Kong to do it, but as I sat there at Tito's cabaret I did not know how I'd ever find time alone to do all that. Ming Ho was always there. He always suspected something. I had to act like nothing had changed, continue bitching about his treatment of me.

I would have to get to the American first, or make sure we never found them. As long as they were at large, he wouldn't get to me. And that would buy me time. The night-club was cool and dark. Every time I looked at his face, my hate for him raged. What if Ming Ho was not working alone? It could be, I thought. He had the habit of disappearing and making mysterious telephone calls. If I killed him tonight, I would never know who the enemy was.

I had to find them first. Alone. I would not need any help from the Colonel. I would avenge Mr Patel all by myself. I had the right – more than the right – I had the obligation to execute Ming Ho. I knew I would only get one shot at it. I'd have to choose the moment very carefully. The thought of planning for it filled me with pleasure. Was I becoming a killer? For now Ming Ho did not suspect a thing.

Or did he? There was a man you could never be sure of. It was possible Ming Ho knew everything about my telephone call. Maybe he was playing with me like a cat would with a mouse. He was certainly clever enough for that. And cruel enough. I needed time. Plenty of it.

I sipped my gin and tonic and I looked at the stage. The gods were smiling on me. I was worried about nothing. Even if we found them together, Ming Ho would act slowly. It was part of his make up. Until we found them, and until the snake had decided where and how to bite, we were all safe.

In the days that followed, I relaxed. I did nothing to help Ming Ho. I suggested nothing and said no more than was expected of me. Sometimes I pointed at imaginary leads. We combed the island again and again. The longer we ran around, the more time I would have for my own plans. He was angry. Very angry. Some sort of vendetta was driving him and I waited for him to tell me about it. Whenever he talked about the hunt, he talked as if it was only her he was after. He began to talk of her one day. It came out of thin air, not provoked by any questions.

'She carries a French passport,' Ming Ho said. 'Maybe we could get her to come to the French Consulate here in Palma. We could advertise in the *Mallorca Daily Bulletin*. Make her come out.'

'What reason would you give?'

'She has family in France, old friends. They could be looking for her ... she never got a penny out of her father's estate. He was not a poor man.'

'You seem to know a lot about her.'

'I told you we go back a long time.'

'Is she intelligent?'

'Very.'

'Then it's a bad idea. She won't fall for that. How is anyone supposed to know she is here? Talking of inheritance, Ming Ho, could you let me have a couple of thousand pesetas? I need a pair of shorts.'

'You bought some only the other day.'

'I've had enough. I'm going to call Hong Kong. Someone in Mr Patel's office will send me funds. I am a director of the company, you know. I've been with them for years. None of his brothers was short on expenses. They know I'm on a job.'

'Okay, okay. I'll give it to you. I'll go with you.'

He didn't want me to call anyone. Or maybe he just wanted to keep me happy. I suppose I shall never know. He was losing control of himself quite often then, as we came closer to the target. I decided to tease him.

'Don't bother. I'll go call the office. I'm not a schoolboy. I can do my own shopping.'

Ming Ho hesitated. He was fighting something inside

him. I am sure he did not want to lose his temper. He put his hand in his pocket and brought out three thousand pesetas. I was having fun.

'Make it five, will you?'

Ming Ho pulled more notes out. 'Here, take ten thousand. Buy the town if you like.'

I pocketed the money and got up. 'Are you coming?'

'No. I hope you find what you want. I'll see you later. I'm going to the post office.'

'Expecting a letter, are you?'

'No, Bloomfield, not a letter.'

'What then?'

'Private,' he said. In a minute, he was gone. I didn't know where he was heading and I didn't care. My mind had seldom been so clear. I would first go into a travel agency. There was one in the American Express office. The money from Hong Kong had arrived and I was going to use some of that.

I bought two first class tickets to London. I would go to the airport as soon as it was over and hope for an available seat. The first class section was seldom full and I'd get on without any difficulty. Iberia or BEA, it didn't matter. I could go back to Hong Kong from London. I would take Bernadette with me. If she was Ming Ho's target, she had to be my friend. I'd offer her a way back to Saigon, or send her to Paris, whatever she wanted. There were flights out of Heathrow every day. I also bought a small camera.

I rushed back to the hotel and asked reception for a spare key to the partition door that separated Ming Ho's room from mine. I would have to make sure it was open on the day. I raced upstairs. I was so happy I could have been singing. I went inside and bored a hole in the wall between our rooms. I hid it with the back of a chair. Then I put the airline tickets under the plastic with my pistol.

The feel of the heavy weapon was reassuring. I was itching to use it, but there was plenty to do before then. I had to find them, lure Ming Ho somewhere out of town and kill him. Then I had to get out. I had these three actions imprinted on my brain.

Ming Ho no longer frustrated me. He was going to be nice to me for as long as he needed me. I went out again. I have always been good at guessing whether anyone was following me. I was sure he wasn't, but just in case I walked back to the centre of the old town. I went into a shop and bought the clothes I had planned to buy.

I went into the post office. There was no sign of Ming Ho. He must have gone back into the hotel. They wouldn't tell him a thing at reception. They didn't like him very much. I booked a call to Switzerland and spoke to Clay's bank manager. I put on a very British voice and said I worked for the British Secret Service. Gave my name as Commander Bloomfield. I said I was looking for Colonel Clayton Wayne-Turner. People love drama. I could hear his excitement mounting as he listened. I said we knew the Colonel had been to see him. We also knew they had been in touch when the Colonel was in Genoa. He seemed to believe every word. I asked him to tell the Colonel to contact me at my hotel by telephone. I gave him the telephone number and my room number. I said the Colonel must not, under any circumstances, come in person. I said he must speak to me before doing anything. I said I was not always alone. It was a question of great importance, life or death perhaps.

CHAPTER FORTY-FOUR

Clay avoided thinking about it too much and there was no one he could tell. He might have been afraid to face it, but something about Bernadette began to disturb him. He had tried to dismiss it. It could have been a side effect brought about by lack of occupation. He found himself lingering on the terrace café for hours on end. He talked to strangers and drank more than ever. She was always there with him and had a permanently bored expression on her face. She was alienating people by refusing to talk to them. Underneath her placid acceptance of his socializing, Clay detected resentment. She did not save her scolding when they were alone. She told him off, but then he was usually too intoxicated to care. She said Cala d'Or was small and boring. She said the people were insincere and transient. She was becoming quite restless, he thought. Perhaps she was bored. How long could they play at being tourists?

Perhaps he needed to pay more attention to her. No, she didn't like him to make a fuss of her in public. She still did not talk of herself at all. He never knew what she was thinking. Her past was still a mystery to him. Maybe her past did not matter to her, but he was responsible for her present. Had he not convinced her to come with him, she'd still be in Vietnam, where she had chosen to be. None of her comrades would be chasing her. He had to protect her because he had put her where she now was.

He did save her life, though, back in that village. The Captain had said they were going to kill her. She seemed much more frightened of her own friends. Her reaction had told him she couldn't expect much forgiveness from them. Perhaps they were only good together when there was danger. When she was angry, she was different. She was independent. Perhaps she was growing away from her need of him? He wasn't sure whether that was good or bad and tried not to think of it.

One afternoon, at the terrace café, someone suggested they go see a bullfight.

'Great idea,' Clay said. 'We'll go into Palma in the morning, look at the boats, shop around and have lunch. It'll be a change.'

'I'd like to do my hair,' she said.

'The salons are closed on Sunday.'

'Not all, surely. I could find a salon in one of the hotels. What do people wear for a bullfight?'

'Oh, a pair of jeans.'

'Don't they dress up?'

'Sometimes.'

She could be forgiven, he told himself. In many ways she was still in the convent. She hadn't seen much of life.

Clay liked Palma. If he could find something to do, he would gladly stay there. It didn't matter to him where he lived these days. He hadn't thought of his search for his identity in weeks. Perhaps he would one day wake up and never think of it at all. Nevertheless, it was time for him to do something, to act. Perhaps he would go to the American Consulate and give himself up. Bernadette would not starve. He would see to that. She didn't have to suffer the consequences of his mistakes. He would do something soon, maybe wait until the end of summer. He could go to Paris and see Marge. She would know what was best because she was good at things like that. She was a practical woman. She understood his moods and had lived with them for a long time. She was part of his past. Above all, she was still his wife, his daughter's mother. She deserved to be informed of his plans to surrender. This would affect her and she was entitled to some warning.

What was Marge doing in his thoughts now? Perhaps it was because he was going back to Palma and they had been happy there. Was he thinking of her because of the doubts he had about Bernadette? They had not made love for a long time now. She was becoming a friend, a close friend, someone who was always there. Someone he could depend on. Did he object to the strength that was emerging from her? Did he want her to be a little girl forever? No, he wanted a woman. Marge was a woman. She had always turned him on. He often caught himself fantasizing about her that way.

It was Thursday, but Bernadette had already packed for the trip. They would stay in Palma a few days, he had told her. She was pleased to be going somewhere else, even for a little. The man in whose shadow she now lived was always in agreement. He was at her beck and call. With all his worldliness, he knew nothing of books and art and history and the theatre. She could teach him about all these things, maybe go and live in Paris with him. She could show him what this old continent had to offer.

Clay had changed, Bernadette thought. The energy that used to buzz out of him when they first travelled together was gone. He didn't mind who he was with, he had no plans or ideas. He talked to anyone and everyone and listened to their life story. He didn't worry about the way he looked these days and but for her insistence, he wouldn't have bothered to shave. She did try to awake some of that old curiosity in him, but he had become too lethargic. He accepted the most ridiculous errands she tried on him and agreed with what everyone was saying. Perhaps he had always been that way and she had never noticed. He had become smug and safe and that made him boring.

Once they were back in the city, living among normal

people, she would try one more time to do something with him. He was naïve enough, she remembered, to be moulded and she would know how to do that. If he refused to take advantage of living in Europe, she would have to find her own way. A human being needs occupation, for self-respect more than anything. She would not remain a lady of leisure.

The idea of the bullfight had excited her. Years ago, in Paris, she had read *Death in the Afternoon*. It had left a thrilling impression on her and she remembered the colours and the face of courage and blood in the arena. She could hear the music and touch the elegant cruelty of it. She had tried to talk to Clay about that, but he had not read Hemingway. They never talked about books. As soon as they were back in the city she would get him to join a library, teach him how and what to read. All he said about the *corrida* was that it was informal. What was he talking about? Not dress up? All those beautiful ladies watching Hemingway's bullfight wore the most elegant dresses in town. And she would pack her best gowns and when she came out of the beauty salon she would surprise him.

There was a future for her after all. She was an educated woman and could go it alone if he didn't want her. Maybe she should, maybe she wanted to. Maybe she had stayed with him because she was grateful, but how long does one stay grateful for? Did he stay because he felt guilty about her? No, he was her family now and had been ever since they had left the village. She must not forget that.

It was late Thursday night. Clay was asleep and Bernadette sat and looked at him. She'd try, but to bring this man out of himself would take a lifetime. If only he'd want her to, she would.

Mike Carter read Marge's letter for the third time. She had enjoyed the cruise, but she had already had enough of life on board. She was going to get off the ship when it docked in Palma de Mallorca. It was not a sentimental journey. It was just to face something in her past and forget it, she wrote. He wasn't sure what she had meant. She said she would stay there for a day or two and then catch a flight to Paris. She would call him and let him know. She wrote about some of what had happened on board and about the people she had met. She did not say she had missed him, but she did say she hoped she'd see him at the airport. Could it be all was well again? Was her wanderlust now spent?

There was no further news of Clay. The American Embassy in Berne had tried to get information for him, but none of the banks they had contacted came up with anything. They would go on trying, they had said. They were sure Clay did have an account with some bank in Lucerne. They were working on it. There would be news soon.

Mike had been sleeping in his office for the last few days and was going to stay there until the search was over. If he couldn't find Clay, it didn't matter. Now that Marge had written to him he didn't care. They would find a way to sack him. They could go and do their dirty work themselves. He stretched and lifted his feet and rested them on the desk. Perhaps the letter was a good omen. Maybe things would look up from now on. Someone might come up with something, but the calendar on the wall told him there wasn't much time left.

Funny how one can lose a sense of time, Marge thought. The Captain had said they were going to reach Palma in two days. The weather was perfect, he said, looking like a well-dressed pirate behind his black beard, the bad guy from Popeye. She did not tell him she was leaving. She said she had never been in Mallorca before and let him tell her about the island all through lunch.

The passage of time and the change in her fortunes had added a touch of magic to her memory of Mallorca. She and Clay had spent no more than a week together there, yet it seemed as if they had been there on a second honeymoon. She did not write to Mike about that. That visit, which seemed more profound as they drew closer to Mallorca, belonged to her and Clay alone.

Lately, she had caught herself talking to Clay, mostly at night when she was in bed, or sometimes when she sat on deck by herself. She had learned of the extent of his travels from Mike and was eager to find out how the journey had changed him. Perhaps he had finally grown up. She could not possibly equate what Mike and the air force were saying about him with the man who had fathered her daughter. Perhaps he had come down to earth at last. Perhaps she had never seen him for what he was. Maybe there was something troubling him all the time. There might have been a little child crying out behind the cold, confident mask she had seen. Perhaps she had been too selfish and content with herself to notice.

The imaginary conversations they had were not like those short bursts of anger she had grown used to. They were light, non-committal chats about people and places. There were no surprises or traps or shocks born of bitterness. And, in her imagination, they were laughing a lot.

If they were ever to meet again, Marge would fight for him. She would fight to regain his confidence and to show him how much she had changed, how much she could see and how much she wanted to listen to him. She would avoid anything touchy, anything that could bring unhappy memories. She would forgive him any crime his situation might have forced him to commit. God, all this was exciting, but the chances of them meeting again soon were so remote.

Dreams. How could she be so naïve? It was just wishful

thinking. There might be news for her at the hotel in Paris. She would call them as soon as she landed. Perhaps Clay was trying to get in touch with her. That was what Mike had said all along. She could stay in Palma for a while, maybe get Mike to come out. What on earth for? She knew the answer. She was tired of being on her own and of being starved of decent conversation. She was eager to start life where she had left it, but she had to wait two days more.

'They are serving coffee in the lounge, Marge,' the Japanese lady touched her shoulder, giving a hesitant smile. 'Would you like to join me?'

'Why not?' Marge said and wondered where the Major had disappeared to. There was an unmistakable expression of fulfilled joy on the Japanese lady's face and Marge concluded that he couldn't be too far.

Bernadette searched Clay's face as they sat on the terrace at Fernando's. He looked happy and was buying drinks all round. This was going to take hours, she thought in dismay. They would talk about boats and football and tennis. It was by way of a little farewell party for him. They were talking about the bullfight they had booked to see. He had promised they would stay in Palma for a few days, perhaps look for a flat to live in after the summer.

Bernadette thought the others were ignoring her. Oh, they smiled and offered her drinks, but their eyes were on him all the while, searching for his approval. They talked more of boats and food and the beers of the world and where they were going to spend the winter. They had agreed to go into Palma early on Sunday morning. They would book into a small hotel somewhere and go their separate ways. Later, they would meet for lunch once she had been to the beauty parlour. She would wait for him at the Café Oriental on the Plaza.

Clay announced they would all go to the beach to celebrate on Saturday. That was tomorrow and they could drink champagne on the sand. Palma was not that far away and he promised he would be back soon. No one had said they would miss her. It was just like the convent all over again, like the time after her father had died. She felt tired. She could not possibly bring herself to prove her worth one more time. She had tried it too often before. She had to leave this place before the black horse took her. All she needed was a few hours on her own.

Bernadette excused herself and got up. Clay nodded and the others touched their hats. As she walked away, she could hear their conversation grow louder.

CHAPTER FORTY-FIVE

———◾———

Marge saw him as soon as she walked in. She could not have missed him for he had been on her mind for many days. Somehow, after the rest she had on the cruise and the drive along the palm-lined Paseo Maritimo in a city they had first seen together, there was no surprise. It was as if it was the most natural thing in the world. He had been on her mind and now he had materialized. She had expected to see him there and she thought he looked well as she crossed the lobby towards him.

People were checking in and out and with the commotion her curiosity had drained away. She did not ask herself what he was doing there or where that woman was. Clay sat down on the dark green chesterfield and the seconds it took her to walk to him extended to infinity. Everyone else was gone from the world for now and the chattering crowd did not intrude. She was coming out of a long tunnel into the light while he sat there calmly, reading a newspaper.

Marge stood over him while a myriad of memories flashed through her mind. He had wanted a separation and she was told he was dead. She had been on a cruise, had gained some weight and had fretted over her daughter. She had slept with Mike. It was all there, but now she only had eyes for him. She wanted to hold him close and be alone with him. Marge Wayne-Turner was a young bride again and full of expectations. She wanted to be touched by him and to be explored. What had taken place between them and other people had been erased, he was hers alone now. That was the only reality. Now she stood and looked at him.

Clay seemed a little lost and sad. He looked weather-beaten and drawn. She longed to take his big, tall body in her arms. Instead, she stood and watched him. The excitement of anticipation ran through her as the minutes ticked away. Her heart went out to him.

Just before she spoke, Clay's eyes left the print and he saw her. He thought he was dreaming. The soul in his body was surely not his. This was another man looking at Marge. And yet he betrayed no shock and shut his eyes and opened them again, but she was still there, in the flesh.

Clay had been curious about what they would say to each other if they ever met again and now it was going to happen. His thoughts had been a dream and here was reality. He was about to say something when Marge spoke.

'How are you, Clay?' she said, as though this was no chance meeting at all but a planned rendezvous with a man she had seen at breakfast. A man for whom she was going to cook dinner. 'What's in the papers today?'

'Fine, Marge, just fine. You look gorgeous. You still tan easy, don't you? Oh, nothing in the paper. The war's still on somewhere out east.'

He did not ask about his daughter or the house or her

studies. He had at least an hour before going down to the Café Oriental to meet Bernadette. He knew a man can travel a thousand miles in sixty minutes in a fighter plane. A man can be born and die in an hour. There was time to sort things out with Marge, but nothing needed sorting. It was all calm.

'Why don't you sit down, Marge? Have yourself a coffee or an orange juice. I'm just about to go to the terrace for a croissant. A sort of late breakfast.'

'I'll take a bite of yours.'

'Okay, darling.' Darling, he had said as if he'd always said that. She didn't care if the term was meant for her or that other woman or just came by force of habit.

Suddenly Clay's blood ran faster. The fresh fragrance of her perfume, her Halston dress and shapely legs brought back that old desire. The forgotten evenings back in Georgia, sitting with her on her porch, wanting her. It was all back as if for the first time. He could extend that free hour he had and find an excuse for Bernadette later. She'd be angry, but he had learned to deal with her anger.

'Would you like some lunch? It's early, but what the hell, it's Sunday.'

'Let us just be like we are now.'

He realized she was on her feet and he got up. 'Take the weight off those fabulous legs, Marge,' he heard himself say.

Marge sat down. The waiter came and said Clay's order was on the table outside. Where was the earth-shattering, surprising bang this meeting should produce? They followed the waiter outside. Clay held the garden door open for her.

'Sign the bill?' the waiter asked as they sat down.

'No, I'll pay.'

'You're not staying in the hotel?' Marge asked.

'I've just come to enjoy the view.'

'You've actually noticed it?'

'That's all I can afford, the view. All that gilt and marble and leather costs money. Shall I butter a croissant for you?'

Marge's mind was racing. He was not staying here. Where was he staying? The plane to Paris was leaving late that afternoon, but did she have to be on it? She could always call Mike and tell him the plan had changed. Spend a few delicious hours with Clay, or stay forever. Whatever he wanted.

'Why not?' she said softly, watching him splitting the croissant. The butter sank into the soft crust instantly. 'I've got plenty of money,' she said. 'I'll treat you.'

The image of Bernadette came to him then for the first time. It came and she was carrying a gun. 'Only if you let me buy you lunch,' he answered.

He had no cares. He was doing exactly what he wanted, yet nothing beyond lunch was possible. But why? She was his wife and she was smiling and he wanted to be with her. Bernadette would not miss him before mid-afternoon. The *corrida* didn't start until six.

Marge looked at her husband. The face she saw and the voice she heard left no room for bad memories. She was light-hearted and mischievous as if she had been drinking. She thought she should tell the hotel discreetly she would keep her room and lure Clay up there. She felt relaxed. She knew the look in his eyes. She had seen it before in their youth. His eyes said he wanted her. He had called her darling more than once. He did not mention the other woman. Perhaps it was all over. No matter, they were a man and a woman and there was mutual attraction. He had been running and she was liberated and could take him because she was strong. The croissants tasted better than ever and she took a sip of his coffee. Beneath the calm of their world, she wanted him and ached for his touch. The gods were smiling on her and where he and she had come from didn't matter to anyone.

The oppressive heat surrounded Bernadette. She came out of the shaded boulevard and walked towards the Café Oriental. The aluminium chairs outside were mostly empty. There was no sign of Clay. Bernadette was a little edgy. She had been sitting under the dryer for hours, it seemed. She looked inside. Other than a few locals, there was no one there. She found a table under a tree and sat down, fuming. She would give him a piece of her mind. He was probably staring at some stupid boat in the port somewhere, or chatting nonsense to some passer-by. She would tell him off. She would threaten to leave him. Forget all about the *corrida*. How could he leave her to sit on her own like a loose woman? Who did he think he was?

Her anger knew no bounds. The waiter came and she ordered a cold drink and just sat there. It could not have been only Clay. She was angry with herself. How weak she had been. How dependent on others, forever trying to prove herself as if she had been a little girl still, in that long gone convent, waiting for someone to like her. How could she have been so submissive? They had all disappointed her because she had expected too much of them. Oh God, she could be better than any of them. If only she could grab hold of that strength she knew was there, inside of her somewhere.

She was angry and yet she felt free. It was a Sunday and she was thirsty and soon the waiter would be there with her drink. She'd ask for another immediately. Passers-by looked happy. No one could possibly be after her today. It all could have been a bad dream. She could do better on her own, without him. She didn't need to wait for him for hours.

She could go to Paris and pick things up where she had left them. It occurred to her she might just do that, not only because of her anger. She was intelligent. She was not ugly. Perhaps she was even pretty. She did not dare suggest more than that to herself. She did not have to end her days being someone's mistress. She was important, otherwise they wouldn't have been looking for her all that time. No one would have come that far for a nobody. She could survive on her own. She had survived before. She had it in her to do things. She could be strong, she knew, and she would assert herself and find her way. But she had to arrive at her independence without anger or bitterness. She needed to stop blaming other people for her weaknesses. Time would help her.

The men in her life had failed her. Her father had died before she really got to know him. The professor had used her. Ming Ho could have helped her along, but he was too obsessive. And Clay? Not Clay, he was kind and had recognized her strength, but he was too preoccupied with his past. He knew too little of himself and what he wanted. That was why he needed other people all the time. Her presence made him feel guilty. He needed her and he would end up using her or leaving her behind somewhere. Or else he thought of her as a replacement for his daughter. She did not want a father. She would have to think of her feelings for him when she was calm. It wouldn't be fair otherwise.

The old Chinese herbalist had told her she was a good nurse. Perhaps she should study the power of wild flowers or become a nurse. Oh yes, she could get somewhere on her own. All she would need was more time. She was on her way. She'd order enough cool drinks to swim in and think things out. Think her anger out of her soul instead of burying it there like she always did. Coax it out before it sank into her heart. Get it out before it turned into the black horse of depression. She might have woken to it all too late, but now she knew there was light for her somewhere. Her time had come.

Across the road at the newspaper kiosk, Ming Ho looked at a French paper. He saw Bernadette arrive and sit down and he was amazed at her expression. She looked proud and determined and she was angry. He had never seen her that way.

He did not expect to see her that morning and he fought to suppress his emotions. His training jumped to his aid in seconds. He had to cross the road unseen and get to her from behind. He paid for the paper and calmly watched the road. With a hiss of brakes, a large shiny bus stopped for the lights. Bernadette was looking at her watch. He knew she was waiting for the American, but the man did not matter now. This was between the two of them. It was better that way. He could take them one by one. The bus started to crawl away and Ming Ho sprinted behind it. Diesel fumes hit him and he coughed.

In seconds he was behind a tree, looking at her back. Her hair fell straight on her bare shoulders. She was expensively dressed. The waiter came up to the table and she shook her head. She held it high, but she seemed nervous.

Ming Ho walked quietly towards the table and touched her shoulder. Bernadette did not turn to face him. Her expensive perfume reached him.

'If you think you can just apologize for turning up now, don't bother.' She spoke in English and her voice was confident. He had never heard her like that. She was angry.

'I have nothing to apologize for, Bernadette,' he replied in French. 'Don't turn your head and don't make a sound.

I've got a gun in my pocket.'

She froze. Whatever it was she was going to say died within her mind. Everything died. A cold snake climbed up her spine. A throbbing terror struck at her and refused to leave. Everything else was wiped away. It was all over. Her dreams shattered at the sound of his voice.

'We are all alone here, you and I. No one can help you. You understand?' he whispered. She nodded. 'Good,' he said. 'Now get up and walk down there, towards the palms.'

Quietly she rose and did not turn to see his face. Her anger was spent and with it all her determination. Her months of independence were blown away along with her willpower. She was a little girl again, but she was not afraid any more. Someone's hand was there for her. Telling her what to do, where to go. They walked. He was so close behind her and she could hear his breathing. She felt the cold metal of the weapon that was there, somewhere, pressing against her side. As they got into the pedestrian walkway, he came to her side and took her arm. Her head was low. She didn't dare look at him.

'We can't talk here,' he said softly. 'You'll have to come to my hotel.' She did not answer, but just inclined her head. Ming Ho sensed the mounting fear in her movements. She walked loosely, slowly, as if she had accepted her fate. She was an obedient little girl again. Someone else was leading her somewhere. It didn't matter where. He knew he was her guide again. They could have been walking along some boulevard in Paris. She must have known this was going to come to pass. Sinners never get away. That was what she had always told him. Her body and her soul were asking for orders, not redemption.

CHAPTER FORTY-SIX

Half a mile up the hill, across the city, Clay stood on the verandah and looked at the miracle of the bay. His gaze sailed along the palms to the cathedral and followed the boats as they glided out to sea. He felt Marge behind him, her breasts against his back, her arms around his waist. She was on fire. Her lips bit his neck. His sweaty skin tasted sweet, like the water that cascaded out of the fountain below them in the garden. She pressed closer and her fingers searched for him.

'Let's go inside,' she suggested.

'Take it easy on me darling,' he said. 'I'm burning.'

She didn't move and they stood there while the afternoon heat smothered them. He wasn't sure of anything then and she took him by the hand.

'It's cooler inside,' she whispered.

Clay didn't answer. He let her lead him into the room. Old Spanish oak furniture and prints of old warships were reflected on the marble floor. An old copper lamp hung from the ceiling and at the back, from an elevated alcove, a large bed beckoned to them.

Marge lay down and opened her arms to him. He came closer and sat by her side and kissed her hand. Her skin was hot. He had to warn her he was in serious trouble, but the moment was too sweet for that. He had waited for this all his life. She had a smile for him. He kissed her lips. Later, later, his mind cried out as all thoughts of his predicament vanished. He bit her bare arm and luxuriated in her touch.

No words passed between them. A mist of excitement floated through the cool room, hovering over their bodies, teasing, waiting. His hands stroked her long limbs and he was kissing her knees, her stomach and her neck as he peeled her dress off. Time stood still.

She basked in a slow glow of pleasure. Her man was doing things to her. His hands and his lips spread magic as she was lifted, her limbs entangled around his waist. Slowly, bit by bit, she undressed him and she felt his growing excitement hard against the softness of her body. She was losing control. She gasped for air. Clay stopped and smiled and kissed her eyes. He was in no hurry and his fingers played heavenly havoc with her skin. She was intoxicated and did not remember how fumbling and quick he used to be. This was him, but he was a changed man.

Her patience was coming to an unbearable end. Marge wriggled and heaved and waited for him to put his weight on her. Every inch of her body was aching for him, itching for his touch, screaming for him to come and thrust and rip and grind and take her. Nothing on earth seemed to make him rush now. The room had shrunk as Clay bit her nipples. She locked his body in with her knees and he slipped free and laughed and kissed her navel and bit at her there.

Marge wanted to scream obscenities, to tell him to get on with it. She caressed and squeezed his growing manhood. She lay back to enjoy his touch and he kissed her gently on the lips as if they had just started. His mouth travelled all over her. It sucked and bit and she moaned. Again he sat up and stroked her eyebrows and massaged the back of her neck.

And then he plunged into her and she arched to meet him. There was a throbbing, painful pleasure inside of her and she knew a new soul had entered his body. He was forceful but gentle and slow and he anticipated her rhythm and held her. Their bodies repeatedly scorched each other. She could think no more and she moved and her breathing became louder and her whispers turned into screams. One after another, small explosions went off within her, then a final thunder heaved through her and her head fell back.

Clay was going on as if there was no end. He moved faster and faster and she groaned with the beauty of it and then he too fell out of the sky and into her and there he rested, hugging her exhausted body with his fading strength. They were quiet now and she rolled him gently to her side and eased his head onto the pillow. She whispered sleep a little and his eyes responded with a gleam of trust she had not seen before. Whatever blemish there had been in their past life was wiped away clean and was gone in a second. She was his bride again.

He lay there and Marge pulled the sheets over his cooling body. The world, devoid of all anxiety, formed a peaceful alcove above their bed. It did not matter now who he had been and who was after him or what for.

A man's name is only a description and a label given by society, not God. His name had been given to him once, a long time ago, by people who had since passed on. Who he was really, Clay thought, didn't change the facts. In body and soul, he was her husband and all the rest could wait until tomorrow. As tiredness came closer, he thought of how he would explain it all to Bernadette and the air force and anybody else who needed to know. Especially Bernadette, who had been kind and good and he would never forget. He would show her the world could be hers too. But later. Now he was tired and there was time still. His mind's eye took him back to Howard's boat, roaming the South China Sea. It was gently pitching with the swell. He would soon get up and take Marge with him and go to Bernadette, but his eyes were forced down. He slept.

Outside, the afternoon sun set a blaze across the water. Marge woke and watched her sleeping husband. There was an innocent, childlike expression across his handsome face. There was no time to be lost. She would protect him from now on. She knew what she had to do. She dressed quietly and slipped out of the room. She took the ornamented lift into the lobby. Her luggage was being kept for her at reception and she told them she would call for it later. In the meantime, she said, she was staying on. She did not wish to be disturbed now. There were flowers from the ship's captain and champagne from the management, the porter said. She'd let them know when to send those up. She knew Mike would be waiting for her call and she wanted to tell him all was well at last. He was her friend, he had connections. She knew he would help her now.

Upstairs, Clay woke up and noticed Marge was gone. He jumped out of the bed and into his clothes. It was nearly three-thirty. Christ, Bernadette was waiting for him, he thought in a panic. He needed to go down there immediately, but didn't know what he'd say to her. He would think of something when he got there. If Marge was somewhere in the hotel, he would ask her to come with him.

CHAPTER FORTY-SEVEN

I saw it all. I stood there and watched him sneak behind her. I felt the fear in her bones and yet I was nailed to my place behind the palm. I had followed him that Sunday morning. It was I who saw her first, but I had to let Ming Ho act. I saw her while he still read his French paper. I saw her first, but there was nothing I could do. I had to wait for him to take charge. I knew where he would take her and I had made my mind up to pounce on him in my time, when he least expected it. I was going to save her, but not there, not yet.

That morning he had come into my room unannounced, through the partition door. He said he was going out and wouldn't be back until later. I could do what I wanted. I heard him lock the separating door as usual. Then he was gone.

That Sunday, as I stood there and watched her, I exhausted every ounce of self-discipline I ever had. The emotions that ploughed through me then will stay with me forever. They keep haunting me each time I live through that scene again. I saw her arrive and sit down. I saw the way she sat there, her proud posture and her anger. There was energy and resolution in her movements. There was power. She was beautiful when she was angry. She looked like an eager goddess of revenge. She could have stood up to anyone.

And then he sneaked up behind her. I was certain she would resist. I thought she would turn on him and hit his face, show him who she could be, who she really was. Instead, her demeanour collapsed. Quickly, like a poison that spreads in no time, she was transformed in front of my very eyes. The little girl she so desperately tried to leave behind was back in a matter of seconds. I was trying to force my sentiments on her to encourage her. I would have come to her aid had she resisted him then.

I saw her get up and I saw him pay the waiter. They crossed the road towards me. I was sure he had no eyes for me as they came across. He took his time, as if he wanted their stroll to last forever. He held her as she walked and I saw her change yet again. An apathy spread through her limbs, as if she was a rabbit facing a python, waiting for it to strike. That cursed acceptance came over her as he took her arm. And yet he did not look like a hunter any more. There was gentle contentment on his face. His walk was soft and slow. A young man on a carefree afternoon stroll. He said things to her and she nodded. I remember thinking how strange it was. There were many people about, but no one noticed. She did not once try to call out to anyone. She accepted it all. As if what was happening to her was ordained by the Almighty himself.

I could have watched her for hours. With all the fear, all the nervousness the darkness of her fate had printed on her face, she was the most beautiful woman I have ever seen. She could have had him eat out of her hand, yet she remained terrifyingly aloof. I had to tear my eyes away from them to get on with my plan. I was going to save her from Ming Ho and come back for the American later.

I raced along the avenue and the Paseo Maritimo to the hotel. I knew they were behind me. I didn't need to check. I sprinted past reception and crossed the lobby unseen. I flew up one floor then took the lift to my room. I unlocked the partition door and looked into his room. I had never been in there before and I didn't go inside. Perhaps I feared he would notice my scent when he returned. On the floor, by his bed, was his case. I hadn't noticed he didn't have it with him earlier. I suppose I was too mesmerized by her. I stood there for a long while and looked at the case. My desire to pick it up and have a look was painful, but time was running out. I shut the door and checked the hole I had bored in the thin wall. I was going to listen to every word they said so that I would be ready when the time came. I moved the chair away and stuck a wad of paper into the hole to keep the light from coming in to his side. I rushed to the bathroom, took my pistol out of the cistern and dried my hands. I checked the weapon. I had forgotten how heavy these automatics were. I wiped it clean and fitted the silencer onto the barrel and then I sat there and waited. Not once was I short of breath. It was as if I had trained for that moment all my life.

They took forever to arrive. Pictures of my rescue plan

were flying through my mind. I searched for any possible mistakes. I needed to calm myself with a drink, but I held on. I would need a clear head. I called reception and asked them to prepare my bill. No one would have thought it unusual. My friend was staying on, I said. I would be back in a couple of hours. My flight to London was leaving at five-thirty. Would they make sure there was a cab waiting for me at four? I knew they wouldn't say a thing to Ming Ho at reception.

And then their footsteps came alive along the corridor. I heard him open his door. They did not speak. I pulled the paper stopper away from the hole in the wall and listened. Ming Ho was speaking, but his voice was not familiar. He was speaking in French and I did not understand much, but I knew what he was talking about. His arrogant, metallic voice had gone to velvet. He was pleading with her. I bent forward and looked. Bernadette was sitting on the bed. She looked frozen. He knelt before her and spoke. His head was inclined. He sounded sad, subdued and lost. It was a lover's monologue and it sounded like a lament. I knew the words for moon and winter and sky and love and he was reciting them over and over as if he was declaiming a poem. Where is yesterday's sky, Ming Ho said, or something. I looked again. Bernadette was still sitting there. The blood had drained from her face as if he was threatening her, but he never raised his voice at all. He loved her. That was what had driven him. Perhaps there was no danger for her at all.

I heard the bedsprings creak and I looked again. Ming Ho was now sitting by her side. His hand touched her knee. She yawned. He must have seen it because his voice became harsher for a minute. I saw his hand slip under her dress. He lifted it and I saw his head there, kissing the flesh. Was the man trying to make love to her? That was even better. He wouldn't think of danger now. He wouldn't think at all. I saw him pull at his trousers as his head was lost between her knees. Bernadette did not respond.

Ming Ho was becoming aggressive. He said nothing as his fondling became frantic and rough. He tore her dress and forced her backwards onto the bed. I heard him moan and groan and saw him mount her. She did not move. She seemed to have turned into stone. He forced her legs apart. Then she spoke. *Pourquoi*, she said. Why. That was all she said and he shouted. Move, he said. Move for me, or something. I was waiting for him to do it. He would be dead to the world then. But nothing like that seemed to happen. I got up, I didn't want to see it. I knew I would hear him when the time came. The bedsprings were shaking violently and Ming Ho was sobbing. Then he stopped and said something. He spoke distinctly as if to make sure she understood. It had the French word for fire in it. Fire and death. He spoke of some great fire. It could have been something to do with religion. I only found out later what he had said, but it did shake her because when she talked her voice cracked in disbelief. She answered him, but her answer was a question. I did not understand what it was and I was by the door, waiting. Burning for the action to start. The creaking intensified. I heard him scream with relief and then there was silence.

I'd give him another two minutes, I thought. I bent down to look and I saw his hand by her neck. He held something, but I didn't know what it was. I jumped up, pushed the door and went inside.

I surveyed the room. Ming Ho lay where he had been. Bernadette's body was under his. His hand was near her neck still and then I saw the blood. It seeped slowly on to the bedcover. Ming Ho turned round and looked at me. His movements were slow and his face assumed an expression of total contentment. He looked like a man who had reached the end of the road without regrets, as if he had done all he was meant to do on this earth and was now ready to go. A man with nothing worthwhile left to achieve. It was as if he had made his peace with himself and his God, whoever and wherever he was. He spoke to me. His voice was soft yet deliberate. It sounded like a confession.

'The fire. I told her about the fire. Many died. There was nothing left of the place where I sent her to whore. I told her I had started it. I have wiped the memory of her shame clean away.'

I did not know what he was talking about. Maybe he thought I was someone else. 'You bastard,' I said. 'You fucking murderer.'

He did not react at all. Something seemed dead in him. Any shred of decency and tradition I might have had was gone from me. I went berserk. I pulled him up and hit him hard across his face with the butt of my pistol. He was as limp as a piece of cloth. I could have killed him with my bare hands. He looked at me and laughed. There was no hysteria in his laughter. He was a happy man. He was a bridegroom on the morning of his wedding.

'Do it, Bloomfield,' he said with a brilliant smile. 'You'll get a place in heaven for that.'

I stood there. For a moment, I did not know what to do. Bernadette was dead, but she looked alive. I took her arm and felt for a pulse and I knew she had crossed the barrier. All the while, Ming Ho just lay there, half-naked. His face beamed. Not once did he try to go for me. I came close and pointed the gun at him. He mumbled something. He did not look afraid or lost. There was no hate in him nor mockery. Just nothing. His skin was parched and old. He had become someone else. He looked as contented as a child on his birthday. His lips parted into a smile. I bent forward and fired into his mouth.

I had little time. I couldn't turn the clock back. I wish I could have saved her, but that was all over. I wiped the gun and pressed it into his dead fingers. His contented face seemed to commend me. I took a photograph of Ming Ho's body and made sure Bernadette was not in the frame. I searched the room for money and documents. I took all the money. There was plenty of it, but I left some in his pockets. I took the gold bars from under his pillow. This would appear to be an open and shut case of murder and suicide. The police love simple cases. I looked around the room once more. His case was still on the floor, where I had seen it that morning. I picked it up. I'd have plenty of time to look at it later.

Before leaving the room, I took a last look at Bernadette. She seemed at peace. There was a strange look of total release on her incredible face. She looked like a madonna. Perhaps she was looking at God. I crossed into my room and locked the door.

CHAPTER FORTY-EIGHT

Marge asked the operator to get her a number in Paris. It was Sunday. It wouldn't take long. Clay would not even notice she was gone, she thought, as she waited in the velvet-lined cabin. This was going to be her one last secret. A secret that would only help her husband.

Mike came on the line. Her voice was clear and fresh when she spoke. 'Thank you for waiting,' she said.

'No problem,' he said. 'What time's the flight?'

'That's just it. I'm not coming.'

'What?'

'I'm staying here for now. There's a lot going on. I

can't talk too long. I'll write.'

'What's in Mallorca?'

'Clay's in Mallorca. That's what. I've found him again.'

'You've seen Clay?' Mike spoke quietly, but she detected the surprise in his voice.

'Yes, he's with me. Not here. He doesn't know I'm calling you. He's upstairs in my room asleep. I wanted you to know. You have done so much for me. For us. I'll never forget it. None of it. I will always remember your understanding and your kindness and your caring. I'm a big girl now, Mike. With the strength you have helped me find in myself I'm able to face this new life. I'm not alone now. My story has a happy ending, Mike.'

'Yes,' he said. He knew she wanted to talk so he said no more.

'I know I was right about Clay all the time...'

'Did he talk to you about things?'

'Not yet, Mike, but I know. In time, you'll understand me and Clay and my decision to stay with him here. I must give him time. Give myself time to get used to the new man he has become. I hope we'll meet together one day and you'll see I was right all the time. Still, without having known you, I could have never done it.'

Mike still said nothing and Marge looked at her watch. She had been gone too long now.

'Thank you for your friendship and trust, Mike,' she said.

She could have been drinking, Mike thought. He was going to ask her never to tell Clay about their affair. A man never understands. We're all really children, he wanted to say, but he said nothing. Marge did not wait for his reply. She thanked him one more time and hung up.

Clay raced down the stairs. The reception was full of people, but he saw no sign of Marge. He would come back or call her later. Outside, there were two cabs and he jumped into one. 'Café Oriental, el Borne, por favor,' Clay said.

At the café, he got out and looked for Bernadette, but the place was empty. It was nearly four. He did not know where the beauty salon was. He'd better wait right there. He could buy a paper and read. Bernadette had the tickets for the bullfight. He could go meet her there. Marge was probably somewhere out on the town, maybe buying him some clothes. He must have looked like a wreck. He would call her later and tell her to come join him, but first he would sit and wait for Bernadette. She had money with her and she must have left her luggage at the little hotel they had booked into. No sense in going there yet. When she came, he would explain it all, tell her he had to go back where he belonged. Face the music on his own. She would remain his best friend forever. She could count on him for anything she would ever need.

At a quarter past four, Clay saw a cab stop by the kerb. A heavy set man sat in the back. He was dressed in tweeds and was looking at him. He must have told the driver to park there because the cab did not move. The man seemed to be deciding something. Clay thought he was going to come out to the café. The large, red face was vaguely familiar. There were two labelled suitcases on the roof-rack.

The man just sat there staring at him. He seemed in a hurry as he glanced at his watch. Then he tapped the driver on the shoulder and with squealing tires the taxi turned about and took off towards the airport.

The world is full of weirdos, Clay thought to himself. He'd order another coffee before calling Marge. Then he heard the screeching of brakes. The taxi came back. The same taxi, and in it sat the same man. Again the man sat in the back, seemingly undecided. And then Clay remembered.

He got up and sat down again. It was the man who had followed them in Switzerland, the man Bernadette saw at the restaurant in Küssnacht. And now he was clearly going away. There was luggage on the roof-rack. Clay was relieved. Bernadette was safe. They were no longer interested in her. Maybe someone had decided they were both dead. God it was great to be alive, and his friend Bernadette, who was always guided by fear, would be free of it at last. She would find a place for herself somewhere and he would help. So would Marge. He had a future after all. And a family. She'd understand.

Nothing mattered now. He had all the time in the world. On the way back to Marge, he would call at the hotel and leave Bernadette a note. He'd tell her all was clear. If the Englishman was leaving, the hunt for her was over. His own troubles did not matter. They weren't serious. They couldn't be. He would tell them he had gone crazy. But that was all over now. He would face them and above all, he would face himself. Bernadette was right. He was what his upbringing and education and career had made him. He was Clayton Wayne-Turner, in the air force or out. Optimism cleansed his system as he ordered himself another coffee. Bernadette's safety meant everything to him and now at last it was there. How great life can be when you're happy. She might have been angry at him for being late, but she'd understand. She always understood in the end. He'd wait a little longer just in case she showed up.

All the while, the man sat in the taxi and looked at him. Then he said something to the driver and opened the door. He pulled his bulky body out and came towards Clay.

'My name is Bloomfield,' the man said as he reached the table. Clay smiled.

'Would you like to sit down?' Clay asked.

'No. You come with me,' the man said.

In Paris, Mike Carter was not stung by the call nor shaken by what Marge had told him. He looked about his office. The uniform on the door and his yellowing graduation certificate on the wall sounded the bugle of obligation. He heard the staccato mention of his name and serial number on some distant, forgotten parade ground. The sound of the drums was loud and clear.

He got up and walked about the room. Outside his window, hordes of nervous weekend drivers filled the streets. Short-tempered horns blasted through the air. He went back to his desk and sat down. His confusion was now all over, for he knew that Mike Carter the man and Colonel Carter the soldier were one and the same. He was not proud nor ashamed of himself. He knew his place and his duty.

He lifted the phone to dial London. Through the window came long shadows that stretched across his room. He was going home tonight, now that his vigil was over. He would take tomorrow off, maybe go shopping. Maybe take a long holiday.

He now knew that some were born to command and some to obey. A

great emotion of relief came over him as he waited for London to come on the line. Everybody was slow on Sundays. All he now needed to do was to point his finger and wait for justice to be discharged.

Then the familiar austere voice came on the line and it occurred to him he was not a failure after all. He belonged to those who made things happen.

CHAPTER FORTY-NINE

Darkness seems to fall so very quickly at summer's end. It races just as time does at the end of a man's life. I am not being morose, just practical. It gets cold here almost as soon as the sun goes down. The young set and others who cling to it will soon begin to arrive. The coffee houses will serve more alcohol than coffee and the skirts will be shorter. Some will don evening tops and bow ties above a pair of jeans. I cannot keep up with the fashion, but I like it. In my time, it was all too formal.

People are always at their best when they come down here. I have been living here for many years. This is a paradise for people-watchers. I've seen the same faces come, year after year. Strange how perfectly normal people let vulgarity rule when they're out here. They dress like they would never dare to back home. They get richer or poorer, but everyone gets older. And then they stop coming and others come instead.

Port Banus seems to go on forever without devouring itself or losing its attraction. I have become a bit of a fixture here. My old nickname, Bulldog, is back with me. I must have told someone here about it and it stuck. I can't remember who or when. My man Pepe was here just now. He brought my old tweed jacket and helped me put it on. It is much too big for me now, but I've kept it because I wore it that day when I first saw Bernadette. I asked him to come back later. I'm not finished, I said. Pepe looked at me like I was going soft in the head. Finished what, he asked and I said it was private. Like Ming Ho used to say.

They have all crossed over to the other side, Bernadette and Ming Ho and Patel. Only I am still here and I've told it all. Almost all. My man Pepe left, saying he might not find a place to park. We'll have to wheel it to the car. Pepe does not mind pushing me along. People know me and they wave and ask how I am and some of it rubs off on him. Spaniards are very social people. You don't need to be rich or clever or handsome. All you need is to be liked. Be *simpatico*, as they say here. He said he'll have to wheel me, but I feel strangely relieved today. I feel stronger. I think I shall walk.

When I came to the reception that day with my luggage and Ming Ho's case, no one asked a thing. I had decided to arrange everything with the police on my way. The cab I had asked for was waiting for me. Everyone came to the main door to say *adios*.

The road to Palma airport was the other way, but the Café Oriental beckoned me like a magnet. I asked the driver to take me there. Maybe I thought nothing had happened. Maybe I hoped Bernadette was still there, sitting at her table like a queen. I went back there because of the American, Clay. I wasn't certain he'd be there, but I had a hunch he would. They must have had a date there and he was late or something. I recognized him instantly. He sat, I think, at the very same table as Bernadette when Ming Ho took her.

Clay was just like I had remembered him. Imagined him, rather. That first time in Switzerland, my eyes only worked for her. He was larger than life and had those film star looks. I felt a close affinity for him, like he was an old friend. We had both lost someone close, but he did not know that yet. I thought of going up to him to tell him I had just witnessed her death, but I just sat in the cab for oh, five whole minutes. They felt like hours. I was arguing with myself all the while. Should I or shouldn't I. He looked worried. I decided I didn't have the time to be the bearer of such news. I had to make the flight. I tapped the driver and told him to go. We turned around and as the tree-lined avenue came to an end, I tapped the driver again.

'Café Oriental,' I said. I knew what I had to do. The driver looked at me and touched his watch, but I repeated, 'Café Oriental' decisively and sat back. Then he stopped, turned the car about and drove back. When we got there, I climbed out of the car. I told the driver to wait and walked straight up to him.

'Colonel,' I said, 'my name is Bloomfield.'

'Hi,' he said, and offered me a seat. I was acting a part. I wasn't myself. I couldn't be anyone just then. The scene I had just witnessed had devastated me and I shall never know why I stopped. He looked at me. He must have seen there was something wrong. He was certainly not afraid of me.

'You look like you've seen a ghost, whoever you are.'

'Come on, Colonel. Come with me.'

'Where?' he asked. He was relaxed and the friendly smile that had spread over his face did not leave.

'We're going to see Bernadette,' I said.

He jumped up as if he'd been stung by something. 'You know where Bernadette is?'

'Yes.'

'Is she okay?'

'Never better,' I said. I was almost hallucinating. My heart was working overtime. 'Do you love her?' I don't know why and how, but the words were out.

'Of course I love her. She's my best friend. My only friend ... is she okay?'

'You'll see,' I said.

His handsome face was perplexed. He bit his nails. He tried to say something, but I put my finger across my mouth and he fell silent. We got to the hotel and I walked out in front. I asked reception for the key, said I had left something behind. They were all listening to something on the radio. Could have been a football game or something. I didn't wait to find out. We took the lift and still there was silence. I could feel his eagerness. He followed me like a child.

When we got to my room, I opened the door and walked across to the partition. The door was unlocked. Clay was close behind me, as if we were one. I pushed it open and pointed my hand at the bed. Clay gasped. He stood there and looked at the scene. He was pale and motionless, like a marble statue of a tired warrior. Nothing had changed in there. Bernadette lay on her back and Ming Ho, pistol in his frozen fingers, still smiled. His eyes were fixed on us.

'What happened here?' Clay asked. All the pain in the world had come to his face.

'I'll tell you soon,' I said. 'I wanted you to see...' I couldn't talk. I tried to hold him back, but he was stronger than me. He jerked himself free and flew over to the bed. He sat down by her side. His eyes appeared helpless. They seemed to hesitate and refused to look at her. They hovered around the room, they gazed at me and Ming Ho and the ceiling, as if he was scared to face her. As if he was hoping it was all a nightmare. I have seen that look before in the hopeful eyes of someone brought to identify the body of a loved one. It is the expression that prays please God make it a mistake. And then his courage returned. I could almost feel the strength that emanated from him as he forced himself to see the unbelievable. He bent over her and held her face. He looked at her with unfathomable sorrow. He was fighting something inside himself and then he whispered something to her and burst into tears. I have never seen a grown man cry before. His whole body shivered and his large hand stroked her hair tenderly, like touching a child.

'Ming Ho?' he asked quietly. His skin was grey. His moist eyes looked distant and old.

'Yes,' I said, 'Ming Ho.'

'She was so frightened of him. It's cold in here. So cold.' He covered Bernadette's body with a rug. I removed it.

'Leave it there,' he said. 'Bernadette is cold.'

'Don't touch anything. They must be found just as I had left them,' I said. 'We've got to get out of here. You are in enough trouble as it is.'

'I'm not going anywhere. Let them come. Let them all come.' His eyes seemed dead.

'No one will come now. You better pull yourself together. We must get out of here.'

He sat there for a few more minutes and then he got up. He could hardly walk. His body shook like a leaf. We walked down the stairs and I gave the key back to reception.

'When my friend comes back, tell him I've gone,' I said and they nodded. No one came out with me. They were still glued to the radio. We got to the car and I helped him in.

'Where do you want to go?'

'I don't know,' he said. 'I feel like a stray dog.' He looked completely bewildered.

I told the driver to head to the airport. All the way there, Clay sobbed.

'I am leaving the country. Maybe you should, too.' I had doubts about the whole thing. 'Perhaps I shouldn't have done this. I thought you had to know. I thought I wouldn't forgive myself if I hadn't, but I'm not sure now.'

Clay wiped his eyes and looked at me. 'I'm glad you brought me there,' he said. 'She never believed she could get away. That Ming Ho had something ... a sort of bond. She was his ... he was her ... mentor. Her Svengali. He had some sort of an irresistible influence on her ... a curse ... I don't know.'

'What will you do now? Where will you go?'

'I'm going to tell Marge,' he said quietly. 'She'll understand me better. She'll know what to do.' He looked like a lost child.

'Did you love Bernadette?'

'Yes,' he said. He looked confused. Words came from him slowly.

'Yes, I loved her. More than loved her. She was the daughter I hardly know. The sister I don't have. The mother I never met. We were lovers once, too. But that was only a transient stage for both of us. She brought me back to myself, gave me my confidence back. Showed me I could be a man ... showed me there was a life out there. I could never tell you everything. Years will pass before I understand it myself. We were together ... she was good ... she was unselfish ... she let me talk and get things out of myself. She taught me there was good in the world. She was strong, you know. Much stronger than me. But Ming Ho got to her in the end. It was as if what she had feared, what she had prophesied came true. As if she had willed it. How did she get to that room?'

'She walked there with him.'

'Why didn't she ... Christ, she could ... she was ... why didn't she run?'

'You just said it yourself. Perhaps you are right. Perhaps she wanted it to end that way. I tried to save her, but I failed. I'm not sure she wanted to be saved. I was angry before. I was angry with you. You didn't come ...'

'That's right, I didn't. I should have been there, waiting for her. It's my fault.'

'No it isn't. I was there too, before he got to her. I could have saved her, but I didn't. Don't blame yourself. Even if you had tried, it would have made no difference. I watched her with him and I saw it all. She did not resist.

289

She would have gone with him. It was her choice. I'm sure of it. She wanted it to end this way.'

'You are trying to make me feel better. Tell me the truth.'

'I can't do that. I don't know the truth. I am telling you what I believe.'

I looked at him. He was so confused and vulnerable. He tried to keep a brave face. I almost wanted to hold him, but I had to leave him. I couldn't hold his hand for the rest of his days. He was a man and he would have to wrestle with it himself, work it out for himself, just like me.

They were calling my flight and I pumped his hand. 'I have to go now,' I said. 'Look after yourself.' I wanted to hug him. I didn't know what had come over me. Tears were crowding my eyes and I turned away and walked to the desk. When I looked back a few minutes later, he had gone.

The flight to London was uneventful and four hours later I was on a plane to Hong Kong. There was nothing to keep me in England. When I arrived in Hong Kong, I went to see my friend at the police. I told him they could close the file. Ming Ho was dead. I told him most of what had happened and gave him the photograph I had taken of the body. I gave him Ming Ho's passport and asked him to concoct something for the Spanish police. He said he didn't have to. He would leave things as they were. The way I had arranged things was good enough. No one else was involved. Just Ming Ho and the woman he was found with. I don't have the details, but I know there were no problems later. The case never made the papers. They are very careful about things like that in Mallorca. Bad for the tourists, murder. I didn't tell my friend a thing about Bernadette. I hardly knew her then. Everything I know now I found out after. Finding out was the best detective work I have ever done.

I have taken to watching a lot of television, especially in winter. Producers are funny people. They make a film and then they make another film telling you all about how they made the first one. I hate them. I have said that I spent years unearthing what had happened, how all the players were led to the Café Oriental that last Sunday in Mallorca. How I went about it does not matter.

I kept four things: Bernadette's passport, the gold bars, Ming Ho's money and his case. I lived in Hong Kong three more years. That was the time of the big boom and my investments made me modestly wealthy. I had found a job with a British construction company which relocated me to the south of Spain. I saw orange groves and wheat fields disappear. The farmers have become waiters. It seems they will never run out of places to put buildings up. I retired fifteen years ago and for ten of those I travelled the world. It was during that time that she started haunting me. She did that for quite some time before I first realized I had fallen in love with her.

CHAPTER FIFTY

———◼———

I have never seen Clay again. I do not know what the end was. Maybe someone made a deal. Maybe he was allowed to live provided he'd disappear. I don't know. I met Marge at the Marbella Club. It was at one of their lavish New Year's Eve parties, where the rich and the famous meet. The theme of the party was pirates and the navy. I dressed up as a Berber boatman using some Arab head gear I once bought in Gibraltar. I had been curious about Marge. She was the woman Clay had gone back to.

She wore a magnificent costume of some kidnapped old-time princess. I introduced myself as Group Captain Bloomfield. She said her husband had been a pilot too. I said I had heard of her husband, but she didn't give anything away. Oh, she told me about the saga of Clay's sail across the South China Sea and the pirates he had encountered. Of course I knew about that. I had been to Pattaya and had met a chap who used to buy stolen goods. He knew them all and he revelled in telling me about them. How their burnt boat was found floating. How they died. Piracy is a drug, he said, but he was getting too old for that. He rents motorbikes out to tourists now. The man had told me everything and yet I listened to Marge as she spoke about the boat trip and expressed amazement. I said he seemed to have been a hero. She said all the fallen are heroes. We talked about Vietnam and other wars. I thought we got on well. I suppose I could have prodded her, found out more, but mystery always holds hope and I did not try. We chatted of this and that most of the evening and then we parted.

She was a most attractive woman. She had that special, self-assured, secret smile of rare happiness some people are blessed with. Like the Mona Lisa. I still see her in the local magazines sometimes. Her daughter married some French painter, who did quite well for himself. They live in Paris. Marge travels a lot, but she is always alone and the gossip columns never mention a man. Not long ago, I remember reading in *Hola* that their daughter had a son. Among the many names they gave him was Clayton. He was a French baby with an American heritage. The caption under the photograph said he would be an heir to a very old name and a substantial fortune.

It could be Clay is still around. Sometimes I hope he

is. Sometimes I am not sure. It depends on the mood I'm in. That other colonel, Mike Carter, was promoted. He made general, I think, and lived in retirement on a dairy farm in Wisconsin. I figure he could have told me something about Clay's fate, but I never went to see him. I almost did on a number of occasions while I was visiting America, but it never happened. I got cold feet at the last moment. I suppose I didn't really want to know. Anyway, Carter died last month so that's that. After all, in a few years, we will all be gone from here and what we did while we lived or how we end our days will be of no interest to anyone. Not unless you are a king or an actor or something.

One thing I did do. I went back to school to learn French. I did that because of Ming Ho's case, the case that never left his sight. I have taken private lessons and went to many courses and at one time I was quite proficient at it. A beautiful language. You can be the most stupid man in the world, but the language is so clever and descriptive and alive it makes you sound like a professor.

The case was packed with yellowing scraps of paper. In his orderly, childlike handwriting, Ming Ho committed all his emotions to paper. This was his life's work, his poetry. They were not dated. He must have written most of them in France, when he was a student. If anyone had seen them then, Ming Ho would have become immortal. The French adore love songs. Even their national anthem is a love song.

I read every one of Ming Ho's poems. The man was a genius. His verses were tender and his command of French was phenomenal. Ming Ho wrote of Bernadette, of what I have always suspected – of his desperate love for her. He dreamt of her on paper, of possessing her, of holding that impossibly beautiful body in his arms. His dreams of her had become exquisite poems in which appeared a vision of himself and Bernadette in soft, gentle language but with details that would have made Henry Miller blush. He managed to convey man's lowest, most basic desire and passion for a woman in a few lines of infinite beauty. He wanted to help her, but could never bring himself to climb down from his high intellectual horse.

He never opened up to her, except perhaps on that last day, but it was too late. His cruelty, too, could have come because of the insecurity his love for her had created. He could be, and sometimes was, the incarnation of the devil, but he was a great poet. He painted desolation with words, made music of hopelessness with his verses. He moulded words like a sculptor. He knew how to create the right atmosphere each poem needed. I cried. I wondered what would have happened to him if he'd stayed in France. Someone would have recognized his talent. He would have won the Nobel prize. And more important, she would have still been here.

There is one poem in particular which stayed in my mind. It is called 'The Red Pagoda'. Ming Ho poured his heart out in it. It is a stirring story of a Buddhist monk and a beautiful flower he finds in some barren field. Everything is dry and deserted there except for the flower. It is alive and its scent is maddeningly sensual, like that of a forbidden woman. The monk picks it up and brings it back to his pagoda-shaped temple. In the sunset, the wooden structure assumes the colour red. It almost looks like it's burning. The monk's heart is singing with the joy of having found the flower. He carries it carefully, holding it close to his heart. He tries to bring it into his pagoda to put it on a pedestal there forever, to possess it forever. But some mysterious power prevents him from entering. He must decide. He must either leave the flower outside or stay out of the temple himself, banished for all eternity. He chooses to stay with the flower.

Of course, I know the monk is Ming Ho and the flower is Bernadette. I think the red pagoda must be his dream of Vietnam being saved by communism. Or a place he was trying to build for himself and Bernadette where they could worship together. It was almost prophetic the way Ming Ho had tried to chain Bernadette to himself. While they were alive he had failed.

I do not know why everything always goes back to her. What was it Bernadette had that inspired Ming Ho to write his poetry, race through half the world to look for her, then kill her? It couldn't have been her extraordinary beauty alone. Was it because of the way she affected everyone who ever met her? Sure, at school the girls disliked her, but they never forgot her. Everybody who saw her remembered her. Was it her vulnerability? Was it the fact that everybody wanted to own her? Protect her? Guide her?

When I think of Clay, I feel anger. Anger at the system that had brought him into the world and created the doubts that caused his fall. When I think of Ming Ho, I feel hate and regret. Some remorse, too. Strange, but true. I now know he had loved her more than life. He must have bled while we chased them, thinking of the fear he was forcing her to live with. He had been betrayed by her for the second time. He had sent her to work in the whorehouse to cleanse her soul, but it must have crushed his heart. And then, when he knew how she had given herself to the American of her own free will, he was dying a thousand deaths each day. The fire he had started at the whorehouse in Saigon had devastated it. He did not know the place remained alive in her memory. Every time he got close to her, she slipped away, the last time by his own hand.

I weep for what Ming Ho could have been and I curse what he was. I understand him, but I shall never forgive him. He was a fake, a weakling who punished others for his own mistakes. A man who would cripple another, then kill him because he couldn't take the guilt. I regret he was so happy when he died. I suppose I begrudge him that.

And then there is Bernadette. She affected us all. I have spent forever looking for the roots of this story, and all because of her. While doing that I have become the doting, romantic, protective lover she should have had. I was a simple man raised on facts, but I learned to read between the lines of life. I have learned about music and books and places. And I have learned to feel.

She altered the course of all our lives, determined how and where we would end. This is why I had to learn all I could about her. I am no closer to solving the puzzle beyond admitting that I, too, have gone the way of the others. I have accepted her domination of my very existence. I think of her every hour, every day. Always. I talk to her and I listen. I open a bottle of champagne for her birthday. Her passport is a temple and I carry it with me. It is in a small leather pouch which hangs on a chain around my neck. At the end of the day that is all I want. I am happy just being allowed to love her.

Perhaps she would have been happy with a combination of us all. Someone who had Clay's courage and possessed Ming Ho's poetic sensitivity and my patience and persistence. Would she have stayed in that red pagoda Ming Ho built for her? I don't know. This and all the other questions will remain unanswered. I won't search for them any more. She is the sun and the moon and all the stars combined. Of course it's love, and more. She is my world, but she never had a chance.

I get despondent at the injustice of it all. Here was a woman who wanted so little, just to live and contribute and be accepted and loved by someone. A woman who could have achieved things, but we were in the way. We told her she should have never been born. She had been told that so often she believed it. And that brought fear and insecurity and self-hate. And then the guilt she carried after working in that place. She craved punishment for it. She believed fate had sent her there to follow her mother. She believed her mother had died for having been a whore. These were the emotions that suffocated her. They killed everything she might have become. And we are to blame for that. All of us. Not her mixed blood, but society. Suspicion and jealousy and greed. The way people feel when they see someone who is different. One day whites and blacks and yellows and reds will marry each other and mix and create a race of humans who would feel at home anywhere on earth. If that happens, I might start to believe in God.

Of all the people involved in this tale, Ming Ho alone got what he wanted. He is buried in a small cemetery outside Palma, in the hills. They are buried together. Tragic lovers, known only to God, the stone reads. You'd have expected me to visit the place often to lay flowers and make a monthly pilgrimage of it. But I do not believe they are really there. The bones drying under the stone are just bones. Where Ming Ho is I do not care. I know where Bernadette is. She's with me.

I have only been up there twice. The first was in daytime, the second at night. I spent many hours there, digging under the headstone. I dug deep. I carved a place there for Ming Ho's case and his poems. Someone might find them one day.